THE LAND STEWARD'S DAUGHTER

BECKY MICHAELS

Mildred Press

THE LAND STEWARD'S DAUGHTER

Edited by Melinda Utendorf of M.Ute Editing

Cover Design by Agata Broncel of Studio Bukovero

E-Book: 978-1-7351401-0-0

Paperback: 978-1-7351401-1-7

www.MildredPress.com

For Chris

PART ONE

CHAPTER ONE

Your brother is not terrible company, but he doesn't quite understand me like you do. I often find myself reflecting on the unfairness of it all, for him to be the heir to a duke and you to be fighting for crown and country in some foreign place, just because he was born four years before you. Speaking of which, I had never heard of this place you call Gibraltar before, so he graciously showed me where it is on your father's globe in his London study. I traced a line between you there and me in London with my finger, and I decided that yes, we are much too far apart... so when are you coming home?

—an excerpt of a letter from Elaina Walker, written in May 1809, the end of her first Season, to her friend Will Winter, the second son of the Duke of Blackmore, a captain in the 30th Regiment of Foot

Hampshire, England
August 1815

ALL OF BLACKMORE Park was abuzz with the impending arrival of one Clara Haywood. All of Blackmore Park, that is, except for Elaina Walker.

Elaina sat across from Helena Winter, the Duchess of Blackmore and the lady of the house, as the woman reviewed guest lists, seating arrangements, and dinner menus for what felt like the hundredth time.

The duchess was a meticulous woman with a keen eye for detail and an incessant desire to please her guests, well known for her lavish events all across England. The duchess took her reputation as "expert party planner" seriously, and she would not let that year's annual house party be anything less than a success.

After an hour together in her private sitting room, Elaina was only half listening to the woman's ramblings, doing her best to pretend to be interested in what was for dinner each night of the party but finding it increasingly difficult to maintain her focus, despite the fact she should've been used to planning a house party with the duchess by then.

At five-and-twenty, Elaina had been through this at least six times now since she completed finishing school and had her debut. The Winters held a house party every August at their sprawling, three-thousand-acre estate in Hampshire. It was the largest in the county, the crown jewel of the prolific Winter family, who had held the Blackmore title for some two hundred years.

Each summer, the duke and duchess's closest friends and family would come and visit for a few days, eager to partici-pate in various country activities—shooting, lawn games, long walks through the family's prolific gardens—with the entire affair eventually culminating in a great ball that attracted important members of London society as well as Hampshire's most influential country folk.

The ball was one of the most talked about events of the

year. If someone wasn't invited to the house party, they prayed they might be invited, at least, to the ball.

This was all something that the duchess took great pride in. On her part, Elaina didn't mind playing games of charades or lawn bowls with the guests in the afternoons after her daily morning ride to visit the Winters' tenants, but she could have done without the ball at the end of it all, especially after she'd spent all spring dancing with the same exact people in London.

It wasn't that Elaina didn't like the *ton*. She only felt that she had nothing in common with them, being the daughter of a land steward.

But this year's house party was slated to be especially grand, and the duchess and Elaina needed to be especially prepared, as Lady Clara, the Duke of Edgerton's only daughter, would be the Winters' guest of honor. Eighteen years after the two dukes made their first agreement that their eldest children should wed, Blackmore's heir, Graham Winter, the Marquess of Montgomery, would finally meet his betrothed.

Despite the ten-year difference in age—Lord Montgomery was eight-and-twenty, and Clara had only just turned eighteen—and the fact that they had never met before, Clara would be expected to marry him as long as Montgomery proposed. And he would propose, for that was his duty as Blackmore's eldest son and heir, and there was nothing more important to Montgomery than duty.

Elaina had known Montgomery most of her life, and she had never known him to do anything to shirk his responsibility at home, and he was rather well-behaved for a young man in his position. There was no extreme philandering or gambling on his part, and Elaina didn't think there was ever a moment when the duke was disappointed in his heir, something she gathered was not usual for people in their position.

"You must take extra care to make Lady Clara feel at home," the duchess said. "You are as much a lady of the house as I am."

Elaina supposed she should've been excited over such a proposition. She'd have a new companion—and not just any companion, the daughter of a duke—and there'd be a grand wedding to plan once the party was through. But Elaina doubted her words. No amount of finery or favoritism could make her a lady of the house.

The duke and duchess cared about her well-being to be sure, but Elaina knew she was nothing more than the land steward's daughter, and the kindness they showed her was only due to the closeness between the duchess and her mother, the late Lady Eleanor Crawford. She often wondered if her mother had despised these sorts of events. House parties and balls, that is. She must have to some extent, if she threw it all way just to be with Elaina's father.

Aside from that, she also couldn't quite bring herself to care about Montgomery's future fiancée. Elaina and Montgomery maintained a lukewarm friendship now that they were older, but before that, the two of them tended to keep their distance from each other. They weren't the type of friends to share confidences or secrets with each other, though she supposed they got on well enough, if only because they were forced to, being the duchess's sole companions on her trips to London every Season.

Elaina only came to live at Blackmore when she was five, shortly after her mother's untimely death. Despite the duchess's pleas, eight-year-old Montgomery did very little to make Elaina feel at home. Instead, he had always made her well aware of her lowly place in the world with sly comments about her hair and clothes until the duchess resolved to buy her new ones and take her to a hairdresser.

Still, Elaina knew she was different from him. She was

the daughter of Blackmore's land steward, and Montgomery was the son of a duke. Yes, she was also the daughter of Lady Eleanor, the daughter of an earl and the duchess's closest companion before she passed, but Eleanor had given up everything besides the duchess's friendship to marry Mr. Walker. Her family, her dowry, her standing in society—everything.

The stigma placed on Eleanor due to her so-called poor decision would be passed down to her daughter when she came out in society, even though the duchess was determined to turn her friend's daughter into a gentlewoman after her mother's death. Elaina's father was given a suite of rooms in the house, despite already working for the duke, while Elaina was deposited in the nursery with Montgomery and four-year-old Will, the duke and duchess's second son.

Being closer in age and temperament, Elaina and Will were fast friends, often participating in mischief together in the nursery and throughout the grounds of the estate. They also enjoyed playing baseball or fishing down at the river with the children of the tenant farmers. Montgomery would only watch their behavior with disdain, preferring to practice his letters and arithmetic instead of gallivanting across the countryside like Elaina and Will, who he called "two little ruffians."

"One day I'll be duke," he explained to them once. "When the estate comes to me and I'm forced to take care of the both of you, you'll be thankful that I studied so hard."

Elaina and Will only looked at each other and giggled in response, happy to let Montgomery study enough for all three of them, for they were too busy becoming thick as thieves. The nursemaid always commented to their parents that wherever Elaina went, Will closely followed. She was often the leader on their adventures, and thinking back on it, Elaina was amazed just how many of her harebrained plans that Will ended up agreeing to, especially as they got older and both should've known better. For instance, the time she challenged him to a tree-climbing contest, which led to him falling and breaking his arm, or the time she nearly blinded him during a particularly enthusiastic volley during a game of battledore and shuttlecock.

Perhaps one of the hardest days in Elaina's life was when Will went to Eton at thirteen, leaving Elaina behind at Blackmore with no companion except her governess, as Montgomery had already been at the boarding school for the past four years. They both begged the duchess to send them together, who had to explain to them that Eton was a boys-only boarding school. Elaina thought the whole idea of a boys-only boarding school was preposterous, and the duchess promptly explained that little boys did better in school without little girls there to distract them.

She insisted on distracting him anyway.

"I'll write to you every single day," Elaina swore the day before Will left, sitting together on top of St. Catherine's Hill, a six-mile hike from Blackmore Park. They shared the contents of a small picnic basket one of the maids, Gracie, had packed for them. Inside were a collection of finger sandwiches, biscuits, and small pies.

"And I you," he promised.

They shared their first kiss that day, chaste and sweet and something that Elaina remembered all the while her best friend was away at school. They never mentioned it for as long as they corresponded, and Elaina wondered if it meant the same to him as it did to her. Even if it didn't, they still wrote each other frequently.

Elaina kept Will abreast of the comings and goings at the estate, while he told her all about boarding school. His dislike for his brother only grew while he was away, as Montgomery enjoyed tormenting his younger brother as much as any of the older boys who would pick on the younger ones. Montgomery only seemed to give it to his little brother worse.

Eventually the duchess sent Elaina to school as well, though it was a very different sort of school from the one that Will attended. It was a finishing school just outside of London, one that the duchess said would turn her into a lady before she had her official debut in society when she turned nineteen.

At first, Elaina wondered why she needed a come-out at all, seeing as how she always thought she would marry Will. Other than that one kiss, he'd never explicitly expressed his intentions toward her, but Elaina had a certain intuition about their future, though she knew his parents wouldn't approve. If Montgomery was being made to marry a lady, surely Will would be as well.

Elaina took finishing school very seriously as a result, giving up her tomboy ways for etiquette lessons. Elaina flourished at school despite her parentage, making plenty of friends, impressing her teachers, and proving that perhaps refined tomboys made the best ladies. Even Montgomery seemed impressed by her transformation when he beheld her for this first time when she returned to Blackmore. He had just finished Oxford himself when they met again at the Winters' country house, only a week before her come-out ball in London.

Elaina had been given a lady's maid by the duchess and was all done up in the latest fashion, wearing a sheer white muslin gown with ruffles at the neckline. A matching jade-colored chemise and petticoat peeked through underneath. Gold jewelry gifted to her by the duchess had adorned her neck, right wrist, and one of her ring fingers. Her dark brown hair had been done up in curls rather than left down and unruly like it had been in childhood, and she stood up straight as she descended the stairs, chin pointed high and shoulders thrown back.

She still remembered the little thrill she felt when Montgomery hadn't even recognized her, believing if he was impressed, surely Will would be as well.

But Will would never see Elaina with her final "polish." He had already left Eton two years prior, determined to take a commission in the army, and he had not returned home before being sent to fight in the Peninsular War.

Before he left, he wrote and explained that he took a commission because he wanted to make a name for himself, one unrelated to the duke or his brother the marquess. She could still remember what his letter said: *I should like to make someone of myself, someone that Father or Mother or even Graham could be proud of, though that feels quite impossible now. At least I know* you *will be proud of me for whatever I accomplish in the army, even if my parents are not.*"

Elaina cried when she read it. She already *was* proud of him, with or without the army. She wanted to write back, though she couldn't exactly put her finger on why. Perhaps it was because of the fact that he was best friends with her—a *girl*—regardless of what his schoolmates said.

As for his family, who cared what they thought? *She* was proud of him, and that was all that should've mattered—right? Will didn't agree, deciding to put his life in perpetual danger abroad regardless of her feelings.

She did her best to support him anyway, writing him often, even when his letters became intermittent due to the nature of his work, all the while secretly longing for him to return home. Her devotion to him made it near impossible to consider any of the men who courted her during her various Seasons.

When they were in London, the duchess always asked Montgomery to keep an eye on Elaina. Elaina half expected him to bemoan her presence whenever she was near, but they began a tepid friendship instead, sharing a similar sense of humor when dealing with the likes of the ton in London. Elaina was surprised when Montgomery did not partake in the snobbery of some of his peers, which helped her feel more at ease whenever he was around her, forgetting all about who her mother and father were. Eventually, the Marquess of Montgomery and the Duchess of Blackmore's favorite, as Elaina came to be known, became quite a hit with the ton.

The only people they didn't seem to impress were Elaina's relatives, particularly her mother's cousin and his son, Earl Gillingham and Viscount Fitzroy. After the death of her grandfather shortly before her come-out, Elaina hoped she would become friends with her cousins. She even tried writing her aunt again, her mother's sister, a known country recluse who had ignored Elaina's letters ever since she knew how to write.

It was no use. Her letters still went unanswered. The earl and viscount turned their noses up at Elaina if they ever saw each other at parties. The duchess and Montgomery responded by turning their noses up even higher, fully claiming Elaina as their own. She loved them for that, though there was a decided emptiness in her heart where her mother's family ought to have been.

It was an emptiness Elaina hid well. With Will at war and her mother's family distant, Elaina decided to make the most of her life as the duchess's favorite and Montgomery's companion. The ton enjoyed talking about Elaina's closeness to the Winters, speculating over the "why" instead of accepting the fact that perhaps someone was fond of her dead mother—even if her own family was not.

People even said Elaina and Montgomery would make a well-matched couple. Both were attractive and carried themselves in social situations with ease. Comments made about them only seemed to embarrass him, though, and would cause him to be cold and distant toward her for at least a few days afterward, and she knew he must've felt some sort of shame for knowing her despite her standing in society.

She never came to depend on Montgomery for anything as a result, saving her innermost thoughts and feelings for her letters to Will, who had cared for her since she first came to the Blackmore nursery. Besides, despite what people said, Elaina knew Montgomery would never consider her. His duty was, and always would be, to Clara Haywood, despite not knowing her, not to mention the fact that Elaina would never consider him for herself. He may not have been a complete snob like she once thought, but he was still reserved, never one to join her for adventures out of doors when they were back at Blackmore Park.

Besides, Elaina was not cut out to be the Duchess of Blackmore, no matter how much time she spent with the current one. Elaina cared for the duchess as a mother figure, but she found they had very little in common, as she did not particularly enjoy planning parties for or mingling with the ton, finding most of the women vapid and shallow creatures and the men equally so, if not worse. They cared very little for the land that made them rich, preferring London and the frivolities it held there.

Truthfully, Elaina only felt at home in the country, where she was allowed to have a muddied hem and occasionally get away with not wearing a bonnet and letting her hair down without any judgment.

She took more and more interest in her father's work at Blackmore as she grew older, often joining him when he called on the tenants every morning and listening carefully as he gave advice on farming or taught them how to use newer machinery, deserting her more fashionable spencer jackets and pelisses for simple riding cloaks and bringing the wives and children of the farmers baskets of baked goods from the kitchen, as well as various sundries.

Elaina supposed she ought to be thankful that the duchess was kind enough to not protest her extracurricular activities as long as she made herself available for a trip to London each spring in search of a husband, as well as to plan the annual house party every August.

Speaking of which…

"Elaina, are you paying attention?"

For a moment, Elaina only stared back at the duchess. "Yes," she finally said. A lie, of course. "You were saying something about tonight's dinner menu, right?"

The duchess sighed. "You aren't paying attention."

Elaina half smiled. "I'm sorry, ma'am," she said.

"I was only asking if there's someone you'd like to be seated next to at dinner over the next few evenings," the duchess said. "I was thinking Mr. Hunt."

Elaina held back a groan. Mr. Giles Hunt was a friend of the family. Actually, he was more than a friend of the family. He and his father before him were the Winters' bankers, trusted with large sums of the family's money to be invested in whichever way the Hunts saw fit. Montgomery and Hunt were also the same age, making them particularly close, seeing as how they went to Eton and then Oxford together.

Hunt was one of the first people Elaina met in London, introduced to her by Montgomery at one of her first balls. Hunt was a standoffish sort of man, seemingly bored by the frivolity of the ton but still coming to all of their events anyway. Elaina couldn't be sure why. Although they shared a mild flirtation throughout the years, it was hard to tell what Hunt was really thinking most days.

Such as when he told the duke his intention to court Elaina this past spring. The duke was thrilled with Hunt's announcement. Elaina, not so much. She wasn't sure what he was thinking then, other than perhaps, *Well, if Montgomery is to be engaged this year, I might as well become engaged as well.* Elaina found it difficult to imagine Hunt as anything more than a friend, even when the Winters became convinced they were a more than fine match.

The duchess meant well, wanting to sit Hunt and Elaina next to each other, but after six years of no marriage proposals, Elaina had resigned herself to an eventual life of spinsterhood, which was why it was especially shocking when Hunt announced his intentions.

As for Will? Well, he seemed more content fighting on the Continent than having a quiet life in England, despite what his letter two months ago said. If he *did* ever return, it was doubtful he would want a wife one year older than him, especially when he could have his pick of young girls as Captain Lord William Winter—at least that was what Elaina told herself. She had decided if she prepared herself for the worst, she could never possibly be disappointed.

What she should have done was forgotten Will and encouraged Hunt, especially with her suitors dwindling every year. Her father's status as a land steward and her mother's family's lack of acknowledgment in society put her in an awkward position with the ton, no matter how much they seemed to like her. Men especially liked to look at her, and talk to her, and dance with her, but when it came to marriage… well, they all seemed to get cold feet after months of courtship, even when they were supposed to be getting down on one knee and presenting a ring. The duchess hated those men, refusing to invite them to any of her parties, which only made more and more eligible bachelors avoid Elaina.

Even if any of them had proposed, she couldn't say with any sort of certainty that she would have accepted any of their offers. Truthfully, she wouldn't have considered anyone with any amount of seriousness until Will returned—which could very well be *never*—that way she could finally determine if her tender childhood feelings had carried over to adulthood, but as of that moment, she hadn't heard from him in two months.

After the Battle of Waterloo, he wrote that he'd resolved to leave the army at the behest of his father, who she later discovered had plans in England for him. Still, it'd been two months, and she had yet to hear anything else about his return to Blackmore. Elaina longed to see him and wondered how changed he would be after eleven years apart.

The duke's plans for his second son involved overseeing an estate called Larkspur Castle in Cambridgeshire. Now, if it were Elaina, she would have taken the duke up on his offer right away, but she also found land management fascinating, a topic that many others found dreadfully boring, preferring the aforementioned society dalliances that the ton could enjoy in London and avoiding their country estates for the majority of the year. That being said, she was her father's daughter, and if she were a man, she had acknowledged in the past that she'd probably follow in his footsteps… but she wasn't a man, so her job was to marry well, and do so as soon as possible.

As for Will, she had no idea what he thought about country living. Perhaps he took so long to return because he would have preferred to remain in the army and fight whatever villain came after Napoleon, though it was hard for Elaina to imagine a greater villain than him.

"Elaina?"

"Mr. Hunt is fine," she finally replied.

When a footman appeared with that morning's post moments later, Elaina perked up in her chair. "Anything?" she asked.

The footman only shook his head, knowing exactly what she was looking for without her even elaborating, as she had been asking the same question to him for months whenever he delivered the daily post. The whole house knew she was hoping for a letter from Will at this point.

The duchess frowned at her as the footman left the room. "I wish you wouldn't fret so much over Will," she said.

"Perhaps *you* don't fret enough," Elaina countered.

She often felt like Will's family had forgotten about him, especially after he'd been away for so long. Montgomery, being the heir to the dukedom, had always been treated as the most important child of the two for as long as she could remember. Will had always been an afterthought, and his parents always made comments to her and her father that the elder Winter brother was the superior academic and athlete at Eton. The duke and duchess would have denied it, of course, but she felt there was at least some truth in her suspicions that they preferred Montgomery over Will. That was why he determined he'd be better off in the army in the first place.

"Perhaps I don't," the duchess said, "but as you know, no news is good news—or so I like to believe."

Elaina silently disagreed. No news was torture. She thought she might have preferred to receive bad news, if only to put herself out of the misery she felt from constantly wondering where Will was or *how* Will was. For all she knew, he could be dead, though she'd heard of no conflicts since Waterloo.

If he were dead, then her last memory of him alive would be that kiss on St. Catherine's Hill when she was fourteen and he was thirteen. As she sat across from the duchess in her sitting room, she vowed then and there that if he did not come back from France alive, that kiss would be her last and final one. Oh, how she hoped that wasn't the case, eager to see him again even if his mother wasn't.

Meanwhile, Elaina often wondered how Will would find her if and when he returned home. Would he be impressed by the changes in her like Montgomery had been? Or would he prefer her when she was riding with her father or passing out baskets to the tenant farmers, so unchanged from her younger self? Perhaps she should've considered how *she* would find *him*, but the idea of him being anything less than perfection, even eleven years later, was hard to imagine. The idea of him intimidated her, knowing he had seen much more of the world than her, and if he was anything like his older brother, then he'd be terribly handsome and quite the catch to anyone who saw him.

Her biggest fear, of course, was that he had fallen in love with another woman while he was away, and he had only maintained their ongoing correspondence out of friendship. Where he would find said woman, she wasn't sure, but the possibility was enough to terrify her. Of course, he hadn't mentioned anyone to his mother, but Elaina dreaded such news, for she was positive the thirteen-year-old boy she once knew would have grown to be a hit with the ladies, whether she liked it or not.

"Well," the duchess finally said, "if you're going to insist on being distracted, I have no use for you this morning."

Elaina smiled at her with relief. "Thank you, ma'am. I think I'll go for a walk before Clara and the other guests start arriving." Pausing, she asked, "Do you think she's one to enjoy things like walking? I do hope she's not excessively prim and proper if I'm meant to be her companion for the next few days."

The duchess shot a warning look at Elaina. "She's the daughter of a duke. I doubt she'll be wanting to check on the tenant farmers while she's here, if that's what you mean."

The younger girl sighed. "I suppose you're right, but a girl can dream, can't she?"

She started to get up and leave the room then, but the duchess stopped her. "You ought to spend some time with Mr. Hunt at the party as well. He'd be disappointed if you didn't, and I would hate to upset him. He's the duke's banker, after all."

Elaina swallowed nervously before slowly nodding. She left the room, walking to her bedchamber on the other side of the house in search of her pelisse, bonnet, and gloves. Now that she was older, she had moved into her father's apartments in the back corner of the house. They shared a sitting room, which split off into two separate bedchambers.

Her father was nowhere to be found, of course, most likely dealing with estate business with either the duke or Montgomery at this hour while Elaina had been forced to keep the duchess company. Mr. Walker was well respected by the two men, and his opinions on the business were given equal weight when compared to theirs.

She sat down on her bed for a moment, sighing and grabbing a stray piece of parchment on her end table. It was her last letter from Will, dated two months ago, shortly after the Battle of Waterloo.

Dearest Elaina,

By now, you must have heard about the great battle in Waterloo, and I am happy to report that I have survived. I count myself lucky, seeing as how they are saying some fifteen hundred men have perished. Napoleon has abdicated his throne for the second time—and hopefully for the last—and I myself have decided to sell my commission at the behest of my father. I will be returning home soon, my dear Elaina, and perhaps then we can discuss our future.

Yours,
    Will

She sighed. A short missive, as was typical for him, but a missive nonetheless. "Soon" no longer felt soon, though, but she could not dwell on it, not with a house party starting that day. She would put on a smile and be the epitome of a gracious "co-hostess" with the duchess. She placed the letter back on her end table and stood up.

After putting on her pelisse and bonnet, she made her way to the front entrance of the house, gloves in hand as she hummed a song to herself as she descended the main staircase and walked to the entrance hall. She opened the front door and stepped outside, head down, not noticing the man standing on the other side of the front door until she ran into him, her forehead coming into direct contact with one very firm chest. She made a sound, something like an "oomph," and then slowly looked up, mortified by her clumsiness. Her eyes widened when she saw who it was. She gasped, bringing her gloved hand to her lips, only narrowly avoiding swooning. She removed her hand, daring to speak.

"Will?"

CHAPTER TWO

I am sorry that you hate Eton so much. If it makes you feel any better, Miss Hyatt has become increasingly strict. I feel as though I'm in lessons from dawn until dusk, and I've been all but forbidden from seeing our old friends in the village. She says we have much to do before I go off to finishing school, so there's no time for playing anymore. Fourteen-year-old girls don't play, she says. Becoming a lady seems very tedious indeed, though I'll do it for you and your mother since I would never wish to embarrass either of you with my more wild ways. Still, I'd much rather be at Eton with you, where I could help you give Montgomery and his friend Giles a taste of their own medicine.

—an excerpt of a letter from Elaina, written in September 1804, to Will at Eton College in Berkshire

WILL STOOD in the driveway at Blackmore Park, staring up at the vast house that he once called home. At over two hundred years old, the country house had been built by his six (or was it seven?) times great-grandfather, the first Winter to hold the ancient dukedom of Blackmore.

Made of two stories of red brick with a roof of slate and lead, the house had a white portico at its front center with four separate columns extending from the ground to the sky. The house faced west, looking out onto a lush green lawn and seeing the sun set every evening, with acres upon acres of farm fields and meadows after that. There were expansive, well-groomed gardens off the house's north and south wings, making Blackmore the perfect picture of an English country home.

The estate was quiet except for the faint rustling of the nearby River Itchen, making it an altogether extremely different setting from Brussels, where he had been stationed with his regiment since early spring, though he supposed they were his *former* regiment now. Although Will had returned to Blackmore Park much taller and perhaps a little bit wiser—he had left when he was only thirteen, after all— he took comfort in the fact that the house had remained overall unchanged, despite the fact that he had been away for over a decade.

He wished he had known exactly how much he had grown over the past eleven years. He'd been a small boy, and at five foot ten, he wasn't exactly a large adult. Nevertheless, looking up at the house from the front was much less intimidating at four-and-twenty than thirteen. He almost wished he'd worn his captain's uniform, but since his father had forced him to give up his commission in favor of managing an estate in Cambridgeshire, it didn't quite feel appropriate, so he'd packed them away in his trunk instead.

Despite his reluctance in leaving the army for his father's selfish purposes of expanding the Winter family's reach past Hampshire and London, he couldn't help but sigh with content as he breathed in the fresh country air, a special mixture of wet grass and fresh flowers permeating from the garden. It felt good to be home in England. He had been fighting the French for his entire adult life, and he had already begun longing to return to his friends and family just as Napoleon escaped Elba. Well, he longed to return to one friend in particular, that is.

Elaina's letters carried him through his three terrible years as Eton as well as all of his military training and time abroad fighting the French and Spanish. His fellow officers had come to think of Elaina as his sweetheart, though no formal promises had ever been made between them.

If he was being honest with himself, he wasn't even sure if she thought of him like that, especially when, as far as he could tell, she was husband hunting with his mother in London every spring. They hadn't seen each other in eleven years now, making them nothing more than two childhood friends who happened to share a single chaste kiss as young teenagers, which he knew hardly meant anything.

As he stared up at the house, he heard the front door open. He looked down and froze, for it had to be her, despite her more dignified appearance. Yes, it was her. Elaina Walker had indeed appeared in front of him and was now walking his way. He felt as though he might have summoned her with his mind, for there she was, in a mustard-colored pelisse and navy-blue chapeau bonnet, pulling on a pair of white-laced gloves.

She set off, still looking down and adjusting her gloves, and he was too overawed to move out of her way, causing her to bump right into him, her forehead colliding with his chest. She made a startled noise, one that made him smile. When she looked up, her eyes widened. She seemed to recognize him right away. He wasn't sure if that was a good or a bad thing, since the last time she saw him, he was a mere boy.

"Will?"

"Elaina," he said, trying to make his voice sound as cool

and indifferent as possible, but he found it almost impossible in her presence, especially after not seeing her for so long.

Instead, he knew the warmth and excitement in his tone must've been obvious, just by only uttering her name. He couldn't hide how happy he was to see her again, his brown eyes twinkling as she looked up at him. Her eyes contained the same playful nature of her youth, but her brown hair seemed to have grown darker from what ringlets he could see peeking out from underneath her bonnet.

The woman he had been exchanging letters with for years —his so-called sweetheart—was a beauty to be sure, that he could not deny.

She grinned back at him, then threw her arms around his waist in an embrace. Something inside him stirred when he felt her body pressed against his, a feeling that only seemed to come to him in dreams about her while he was away. He had dreamt about what she would look like as an adult, even what she would feel like.

Nothing could compare to the reality of what he was doing now. He had wrapped his own arms around her as well, daring to hold her more tightly than he ever did when they were children. He was a man now, after all, and he had certain needs that he hadn't had—or maybe just didn't understand—back then. When she pulled away from him, she was still smiling from ear to ear.

"It really is you!" she exclaimed. "I can't believe it. Why didn't you say you were coming home? I haven't heard from you in two months."

"I'm sorry," he replied, frowning. "There was much to take care of in Brussels before I could return home a free man. I do hope you'll forgive me."

Luckily, she was still smiling, an expression that was beginning to cause something inside him to melt. He could still remember the longing he felt while he was away, the longing to see her smile once more.

"I suppose it's rather easy to forgive you when you're standing right in front of me, though I'll admit I was very cross with you for not knowing when you'd be returning," she replied. "I was just about to go for a walk, but I suppose you'd like to see your parents and brother."

For propriety's sake, he should've gone inside and announced himself to his family. Will, however, had never been one to care too much about propriety, especially after taking his commission and becoming a more independent man, so instead he offered her his arm, wishing to be alone with her for as long as possible before being thrown to the wolves that were his mother and father.

"May I join you instead?" he asked. "My parents will be there when we return."

"Of course!" she exclaimed, taking his arm as a slight look of surprise flashed across her face. He wondered what she was thinking. Perhaps that it was unseemly for the two of them to be alone together without a chaperone at their ages. That didn't stop her from springing a multitude of questions upon him. "Oh, you must tell me everything about the army and the places you've seen. What was Belgium like? And what about Portugal?"

He chuckled. "I think I'd rather talk about you than those places," he said as they started to make their way to the gardens at the north side of the house. "They are not as exciting as you may assume them to be, especially in times of war, and Lord knows you must've already read enough about them in my missives."

She shook her head rather emphatically. "Oh, no! I could never get enough of your letters, though I do suppose they could have been a little longer." She seemed to realize the frankness of her words, flushed, shook her head, then added, "I mean…"

Will smiled at her as she trailed off, struggling for words and biting her lip. As he watched her front teeth let go of her bottom lip, he wondered where she had picked up such an adorable habit. Did they teach classes on how to be coy in finishing school?

"The last I heard from you," he said, "my father was building a hothouse and was allowing you full rein of the place. Is that still true?"

"Oh, yes! The hothouse was finished only a month ago, and your father has been very kind to me in letting me use it. That is, he's always been very kind to me, but he brought in a whole slew of exotic flowers and citrus trees for me to tend to. I can show you, if you'd like. It's just through the north gardens."

"Lead the way."

She broke away from him then, walking more quickly to go in front of him, guiding him through the gardens, the layout of which was only just starting to come back to him, as well as memories of long-ago hide-and-seek games. There was plenty to admire now that perhaps he hadn't noticed as a child, with everything in full bloom at that time of year and colorful flowers sprouting everywhere, but most of all, there was Elaina.

As they walked past the fountains, hedges, and benches to the hothouse, he couldn't help but appreciate her form from behind. The fourteen-year-old tomboy he once knew was now a well-formed lady with an elegant neck, defined waist, and perfect posture. It had always been strange to him that she remained unmarried while he was on the Continent. It was even stranger to him now that he saw her in the flesh, though he could not make himself hope that she may have been waiting for him to return before making any matrimonial decisions—not yet, anyway.

"Here we are," she said.

Blackmore's hothouse was a relatively simple but rather large rectangular structure, made entirely of glass aside from the wrought-iron frame that made it stand upright. Even the gable roof at the top of the structure was made of glass panels, an architectural feat that would make any man stand back and admire it. Perhaps he was only a simpleminded soldier, but Will thought it was a wonder that the structure could stand at all through the various elements that Hampshire experienced through the seasons.

Elaina opened the door, and he followed her inside, happily inhaling a mixture of floral and citrus scents. "It smells heavenly in here," he observed.

She turned back at him and smiled. "Doesn't it? I'm quite taken with the place. I wish your father would have commissioned it years ago."

As they walked through the hothouse, examining the various plants and trees and flowers together, Elaina said, "I know your father has plans for you at his new estate in Cambridgeshire, but I do hope you'll stay in Hampshire for a while. You've really come just in time, if you ask me."

They stopped to look at a collection of potted red carnations. "And why's that?" he asked, genuinely curious.

"Ah," she said, clapping her two gloved hands together as if she was excited to tell him. "Well, I suppose you've been gone so long you probably don't even remember what week it is. We here at Blackmore are about to embark on your parents' annual house party. The long mentioned but never introduced Lady Clara Haywood will be this year's guest of honor, which makes the affair particularly special. I've been trapped in your mother's sitting room all morning, looking at menus and seating arrangements and the like."

Will knew the name. Lady Clara was his brother Montgomery's betrothed. They'd been pledged to marry each other by their fathers since his brother was ten. Will, only six at the time, remembered being thankful that as the second son of his father, the man would not see the need to make up any marriage contracts for him. After all, he'd been quite confident he would end up with Elaina at the time, for he was quite smitten with her even at such a young age.

Perhaps it was strange for a boy's closest companion to be a girl growing up, but Elaina enjoyed all the same things he did as a child, and unlike Montgomery, she was willing to play with him and the children in the village. Despite the duchess's misgivings, her father even encouraged it, not wanting his daughter to become too coddled.

With Elaina as his companion, why would Will need an arranged marriage like his brother? He wasn't quite as confident now that he'd returned and they were both of marriageable age, especially seeing how beautiful she had become, and he wondered if she'd have any suitors arriving at the house today for the party.

"Well, let's hope my mother will clear a space near you at dinner," he said, thinking of those potential suitors that might interfere with his own mission to reacquaint himself with her. "I will need much guidance to navigate such an illustrious event. I've spent most of the last eight years camping outside amongst soldiers, after all."

"Luckily for you, your mother insisted that I attend one of the finest finishing schools in the country, so I'm sure I will be able to offer you plenty of advice."

"Finishing school seems to have suited you," he said, watching as she blushed, hastily looking away from him. He wondered if it made him a cad for enjoying the way her cheeks went pink with embarrassment. He resolved to continue his onslaught of compliments, unable to help himself. "I must say, Elaina, I'm very surprised to return home and find you unmarried."

She laughed at that. "Oh, yes, your mother says I'm quite on the shelf now at five-and-twenty." Her voice seemed to waver, but she continued on anyway. "I doubt I'll ever marry at this point. Ask anyone—I'm a genuine spinster! At least, that's what many of the younger ladies say. My only comfort is knowing one day they'll be as ancient as me."

He tilted his head to the side, finding her words hard to believe. "But why has no one offered for you? If you don't mind me asking, that is."

She shook her head. "I don't mind," she said, clearing her throat. "You see, your mother insists on showing me off to the... well, the crème de la crème of the ton, if you will. The problem is none of them want to marry the daughter of a land steward. Your mother doesn't quite understand this, thinking the blessing of her and your father should make every dandy in London come running, but there's also the matter of my mother's family refusing to acknowledge my existence." She paused to sigh, shaking her head again. "As you can see, it's very complicated."

Will frowned. Elaina had written to him when she learned her grandfather died, filled with hope that she might be able to become better acquainted with her aunt and her two cousins, Earl Gillingham and Viscount Fitzroy. Such hopes never came to fruition, and he knew how much it hurt her, though she decided not to let it bother her.

As for the men of the ton who would not have her due to her mother's family's disinterest in her... well, something about that made him angry, though he knew their disinterest in marrying her had kept her free until he could return to England.

"None of that would matter to me," he murmured before

he even realized what he was saying. She stared at him, seemingly not with shock or abhorrence, but what appeared to be bated curiosity. Her mouth slightly open, she took a step closer, and he suddenly became distracted by her two perfectly formed lips.

Swallowing, he continued, this time more thoughtfully. "Elaina, I know I've been away an awfully long time, and we are practically strangers at this point, but—"

"We are not strangers," she cut in, shaking her head vehemently in apparent disagreement. "We know each other through our letters, don't we?"

"Yes, well," he said, slightly nodding his head as he promptly lost wherever he wanted to go with that sentence, distracted by her slightly parted lips once more. He wondered what would happen if he bent down and took the lower one between his. Would she be outraged?

Eventually, he cleared his throat and continued. "Nevertheless, one of the reasons I came home was to…" He trailed off again as he searched for the right words. He wasn't having much luck with the power of speech that day. "I suppose you could say reacquaint ourselves—or at least that's what I've been calling it in my head." He laughed then. "The soldiers in my regiment used to call you my sweetheart. Is that too bold of a revelation to share with you?"

Slowly, she shook her head, biting her lower lip again as she looked up at him through her dark eyelashes. He could have groaned. Between that look on her face, the exotic scents of the hothouse, and a wanting feeling stirring below his waist, it took all his willpower not to confess his deepest, most secret desires for her right then and there.

Instead, he daringly took one step closer to her, reaching to brush his index finger along her upper arm, tracing a line across the soft yellow cotton. How he longed to see the skin beneath that jacket. Although he shouldn't have been surprised by it, his sexual attraction to her seemed to have almost snuck up on him, for she had always been his sweet and steadfast Elaina before he walked with her through the garden to that greenhouse, his dearest childhood friend. He had dreamed of what it might be like to lay with her, of course, but nothing he imagined could ever compare to the reality of her standing in front of him as a woman of five-and-twenty, looking as tempting as she did.

"Perhaps there are even more revelations we have yet to discover," he murmured, his voice low and gravelly.

He was just bending down to kiss her when he heard the door to the hothouse open, and a familiar voice sounded from that direction. "William? Is that you?"

He withdrew his hand immediately and backed away, turning to find his brother standing there, watching them. He forced a smile after he stifled an audible groan of displeasure upon him arriving just as things were about to become really interesting. He hated for such a moment to be interrupted, but even he could admit that perhaps it was for the better.

"Yes, brother, it's me," he replied, forcing a smile and approaching him. "As you can see, I've finally returned home per father's request. How good it is to see you. Elaina has been so kind as to show me the new hothouse."

He turned back to Elaina, who looked flushed. "Montgomery," she practically squeaked. "What are you doing here?"

Will watched her shift her weight between each of her feet, clearly uncomfortable with his brother discovering them together in such a way. He knew the two had become friends in his absence at the behest of his mother. She had mentioned to him that the duchess demanded that Montgomery look out for her whenever the family traveled to

London during the Season. Elaina implied that Montgomery wasn't bad company, though there was a certain guardedness —Will would have chosen to call it snobbery instead—that she claimed she couldn't get past.

"Am I not allowed to visit the hothouse? Have I interrupted something?" he asked, his eyes narrowing as he came closer, closing the distance between all three of them until they were standing in a circle in one of the pathways of the hothouse.

"No!" she exclaimed, perhaps too quickly. In a more controlled fashion, she added, "I mean, yes, of course you're allowed to visit the hothouse. You see, I happened upon Will as I was about to leave on my morning walk. I told him he should go inside and make his arrival known to his parents, but he wanted to join me instead. We eventually came here because he wanted to see the property's latest addition. We were just admiring the carnations while I told him about the upcoming festivities planned for Blackmore Park."

Montgomery eyed Will, frowning disapprovingly. Will returned his sour look. He and his brother had never gotten along as young children, and Montgomery's never-ending bullying while they were at Eton hadn't improved matters. He didn't get the feeling that they would become friends in their twenties, either.

"I must say, William, I am surprised to see you home," he said. "One would think you would have written before just showing up. As Elaina must've been telling you before I interrupted, our annual house party starts today, and Mother has the whole place on the verge of conniption. I'm sure you can imagine. She hasn't changed much from when we were boys. Seeing you will send her over the edge."

Will smiled slightly, nodding. "Yes, Elaina's told me. She also mentioned that Clara Haywood is finally eighteen and will be the guest of honor this year."

"That's right," Montgomery said. "She should be here any minute now, and I shall finally be left to my fate."

An uncomfortable silence settled into the air as Montgomery looked back and forth between Will and Elaina. "Are you sure I haven't interrupted anything other than Elaina's report on Mother's party?" he asked.

"What else could you have been interrupting?" Elaina quickly asked, her voice tense. Will looked at her out of the corner of his eye and smiled, feeling a sense of pride that their almost kiss had frazzled her so.

"Do you mind if I steal my brother, then?" he asked, shooting a pointed look at Elaina, who regarded Montgomery with an equally leveled glare. He wondered how many times Montgomery had to warn her away from men in London. He hoped not too often. "The duke is visiting one of the farms with your father, but I'm sure Mother will be eager to see her son back from the war."

"Of course," Elaina said. "I'll come with you."

Montgomery shook his head. "Why don't you continue your morning walk, Miss Walker? I know how fond you are of your exercise."

Will's hand involuntarily clenched into a fist as his jaw tensed, not quite understanding his brother's meaning by being so insufferably rude to the poor girl. He watched as Elaina seemed to force a curtsey in response to his command.

"Yes, my lord," she murmured, her voice tense, eyes narrow. Upon turning to Will, she smiled, though not as brightly as before. "It's so good to see you again, Will."

He took her hand, bending over to kiss it, causing the sparkle in her eye to return. "You as well, Elaina." With a wink, he whispered, "I'll make sure to mention tonight's seating arrangements to my mother."

He turned back to his brother then, who seemed rather

annoyed by the whole scene as they left the hothouse. Will could probably guess as to why, but he decided to ask anyway as they walked through the gardens back to the house's entrance.

"Is something the matter, Montgomery?" he said. "You don't seem very pleased to see me. I know we didn't get along as children, but I thought perhaps we could turn over a new leaf now that we're older."

His older brother turned to look at him, his jaw hard-set as he regarded Will. "I'm pleased to see you," he muttered in an annoyed tone after a moment's pause. "Father and I have been waiting for your return for months now, what with the estate in Cambridgeshire desperately needing an overseer." With a sigh, he added, "I'm only worried about you and Miss Walker. I could have predicted it would happen—we all could—but I'd still hate to see you fall under her spell when you've only just returned home."

"Fall under her spell?" Will echoed, a perplexed look on his face.

Montgomery nodded. "I know how much you cared for her as a child—continued to care for her, judging by your long-held correspondence with each other as you became adults—but you're a decorated soldier on his way to becoming a squire now. There are plenty of more suitable women—"

"More suitable?" Will asked, coming to a stop as he squinted at his brother in the hot August sun. He wiped a bead of sweat from his brow. "Isn't Elaina considered suitable? Mother's turned her into a genuine lady, hasn't she? She says she's been shopped around to only the best of the ton."

His brother sighed again. "It's not that she's not suitable. She's only not as preferable as, say, an heiress or—"

"An heiress? What would I want with an heiress?"

Shaking his head, he suddenly felt determined to change the subject, as he was sure he didn't want to hear his brother's answer, which he knew was bound to be snobbish. "Never mind. Don't answer that. Take me to Mother, will you? We'll discuss Elaina some other day."

"There is something you should know before we drop the subject altogether," his brother said, stopping after they passed through the garden's entrance back onto the driveway leading to the house.

Will stopped as well, turning back to his brother. "What is it?"

"This past April, Giles Hunt made it known he's interested in marrying Elaina."

Will narrowed his eyes. "Giles Hunt?"

He couldn't help but say the man's name with disgust. Hunt had been Montgomery's best friend at Eton, bullying him whenever Montgomery did. To think that some vulgar son of a banker thought he was good enough to court Elaina… well, it was inconceivable.

"Surely Father told him no."

Montgomery twisted his brow, confused. "Why would he? Elaina would be lucky to marry a man like Hunt. He's well respected, handsome, and rich. His last name will lend her the credibility she has somewhat lacked since she first went to London. We all think it's a smart match, and you would do well not to interfere if you truly care for her."

Will stared at his brother for a long moment, lips pursed. "Of course," he finally said. "Whatever you all think is best."

He didn't mean it. After spending his entire adult life without her thus far, he was quite determined to change that upon finally seeing her again. He was sure of one thing and one thing alone as they walked back toward the house: Elaina Walker would be the lady of Larkspur Castle as much as he would be the lord if his father was so determined to send him there.

ELAINA WATCHED Montgomery and Will as they left the hothouse, unable to keep her brow from furrowing as she did.

She knew it was Montgomery's duty to protect her from things like ruination and bad matches, but she could have killed him for interrupting her and Will.

Before he had come into the hothouse, she was sure Will was going to kiss her for the second time in their lives, though it felt more like their very first time if she was being honest with herself. The kiss they shared as young teenagers could hardly count now, as there was something about the way he had looked at her earlier that she had never experienced before that day. His eyes had been filled with what she only could have described as need and want, and she was sure no man had ever looked at her in the same way before, even when she considered her most ardent suitors over the past six years.

There was a sense of shame as well, as she wondered what would have happened if Montgomery had walked into the hothouse only a moment later and found them in each other's arms. She had known girls where such things had happened to them. There was something about his reaction upon seeing them, even standing a mere foot apart, that told her they both would have paid dearly for any sort of indiscretion, not to mention the way he ushered his younger brother away from her so quickly.

Pushing her troubles from her mind, she decided she would forget about the scene in the greenhouse and enjoy the rest of her walk. Perhaps she would happen upon the duke and her father on their way back from the farm they were visiting so she could share the good news that Will was home.

Determined not to let Montgomery deter her from being excited about Will's return, she went on her way with a smile on her face.

CHAPTER THREE

*I've been missing England terribly as of late. No, not England—
just you, if I may be so bold as to declare. You have been my friend
and my family my whole life, more true to me than anyone else I
have ever known. You have been my North Star through all of this
—pardon my clumsy metaphor—and I can only hope this is the end
of it, for I'm not sure how much longer I can remain here on the
Continent without something terrible happening to me.*

—an excerpt of a letter from Will, written in 1812, to Elaina,
just before the Battle of Salamanca

WILL SAT with his brother and mother in the duchess's
private sitting room, watching as she poured each of them
tea from a tray that one of the servants had brought upstairs.

His brother had entered the room before Will, telling him
he would inform his mother of his arrival first.

"Seeing you without any warning might cause her to
swoon, and I haven't got any smelling salts on me," Montgomery said quietly in the corridor. "Have you?"

Will shook his head.

"Right," Montgomery replied, nodding once. He slapped his brother on the shoulder. "Then this is how we'll do it. You wait here, looking like the soldier that you are. I'll be right back."

Will watched as his brother turned the corner into his mother's room, thinking that perhaps that was the kindest Montgomery had ever been to him, helping him avoid a swooning mother. Perhaps they could turn over a new leaf once he accepted the fact that Will would marry Elaina.

Pleasant thoughts turned to alarm when he heard a muffled shriek come from his mother's sitting room. There were sounds of shuffling, then his mother appeared around the corner of the doorway, looking older—but just as lovely —as he remembered her. He smiled broadly at her, and she gasped, covering her mouth with her bare hands.

"Hello, Mother," he said simply, holding his arms out. The duchess nearly ran to him, allowing her younger son to embrace her.

"I told Elaina not to fret!" she said, her voice muffled against his chest. "I knew you would come home soon."

She backed away from him suddenly, as if she was just remembering something horrible. "Oh, but you picked the worst time to come home," she continued. "The numbers won't be even now, and I'll have to change all the seating arrangements!"

Will laughed once. The duchess was just as he remembered. "Come along, Mother. We'll ring for tea, and we can talk about seating arrangements afterward."

So there they were, sitting in his mother's room together, having tea and discussing the house party. Unlike Elaina, his mother did not ask him any questions about the war or the foreign places he had seen. His mother did not like thinking about unpleasant things, which was probably why he heard so very little from her while he was away. War was an unpleasant thing.

When they got to that night's dinner, Will bravely asked, "I was wondering if I could sit next to Elaina tonight. We haven't seen each other in so long, and there's so much to catch up on."

He glanced at his brother, who wore an expression of disappointment. His mother sighed as she placed her teacup back on its saucer on the table. "Well, I had already placed her next to Mr. Hunt…"

As his mother's voice trailed off, Will fought back a groan. Even his own mother thought his father's banker would make a more suitable husband for her beloved Elaina than him, her own son.

"Montgomery did mention that Mr. Hunt is interested in marrying Elaina," Will managed to say. He chose his next words carefully. "Surely one night away from her won't damage what rapport they have already built in London over the Season. If anything, I believe absence makes the heart grow fonder."

How true that was. If Will could survive eleven years of separation from Elaina, Hunt could survive one night. Before his mother could respond, a footman appeared in the doorway, announcing the arrival of the Duke of Edgerton and his daughter, Lady Clara Haywood. The duchess gasped excitedly, while his brother paled and fiddled with his cravat. His mother waved her hand at Montgomery.

"Oh, there's no need to be nervous, my dear," she said, rising from where she sat. Will rose with her, watching helplessly as his mother found a more pressing issue to address: Montgomery and Clara's first meeting. "Come along, now. You too, Will."

"But you did not answer my question, Mother."

The duchess and Montgomery froze, turning back to

look at him. His mother made a little sound of frustration. "Oh, very well. You can sit with Elaina tonight—but tonight only. After that, it'll be better for her to be with Mr. Hunt and you to be with one of the other eligible ladies. I'll introduce you to some of them now."

Will nodded once, smiling as he followed the duchess and the suspiciously quiet Montgomery out of the sitting room. Well, he supposed his brother had other things to think about, namely one Clara Haywood.

As for Will, he was fine with one night of dinner with Elaina, for he only needed one night to convince her they belonged together.

Elaina did not happen upon her father or the duke on her walk that morning but found Mr. Walker in his favorite armchair in their joint sitting room when she returned. Their sitting room was probably the smallest in the house, but it had everything they needed to relax or write: a settee, two armchairs, and a small writing desk and complementary chair.

"Papa!" she exclaimed as she worked to remove her gloves, bonnet, and jacket. "Did you hear the news? Will has finally returned."

Mr. Walker looked up from the newspaper he was reading, adjusting his spectacles with his finger so they were sitting further up his nose. Elaina's father was in his mid-fifties, tall and in rather good shape for his age. His thickening spectacles and increasing gray hair seemed to be the only evidence of his aging. "Montgomery mentioned it to Blackmore and I upon us returning to the house," he said. "I believe he's with his mother now, who I'm sure will be eager to show off her war hero to her guests."

Sitting beside her father, she took an inward breath,

unable to stop herself from smiling as she said, "Oh, Papa. You should see him. He's changed so much."

"I would hope so," he said, a twinkle in his eyes as he folded his newspaper and placed it on the nearest end table from his armchair. "Has it not been eleven years since he's been at Blackmore last?"

"That's right," Elaina replied.

"The last time I saw him, he was crying about you not being able to go to Eton with him," he said with a chuckle.

Elaina half smiled. "I remember that," she said. "We even hatched a plan to have me stow away in one of his trunks, but my governess discovered me at the last minute."

"It's a shame," he mused, nodding his head slightly. "You would have been their best student."

Elaina laughed before turning the subject back to the Will of the present. "I do hope he'll be allowed to stay awhile," she said, frowning. "I know the duke is eager to have him take over that estate in Cambridgeshire, but shouldn't he be allowed to visit with his family for a little while before traveling so far away?"

Mr. Walker chuckled, giving his daughter a coy look. "Do you hope he's allowed time to visit with his family, or do you hope he's allowed time to visit with you?"

She flushed under her father's discerning gaze. If anyone was aware of how Elaina felt about Will, it was her father. While the duchess and Montgomery did their best to distract her with other suitors over the years, Mr. Walker was indulgent of his daughter's growing affection for her childhood friend, always listening patiently to Elaina recite her letters from him for the second, sometimes third, time. There were certain paragraphs she did keep to herself, though, mostly the ones where he confessed to missing her company.

"I'll only admit to hoping the duchess doesn't dominate *all* of Will's attention during the party," Elaina replied slyly.

"Even if she tried, I doubt she would succeed," her father told her reassuringly, "but I fear I must ask you to proceed with caution, Elaina."

Elaina furrowed her brow. "What do you mean?"

Mr. Walker sighed. "The duke and I have spoken about this at length. The estate that Will is meant to oversee was bought from an earl who cared very little for his property's health when compared to gambling in London and outfitting his young wife in the latest fashions. Blackmore bought the property at a low cost, but it will take a large sum of money to bring it back to its former glory. I think the duke hopes his son will marry advantageously in turn."

"Oh," Elaina said, frowning as her shoulders drooped. She sighed, wondering why she was good enough for what the duke and duchess deemed the very best of the ton but not their own son. "I suppose aligning himself to me would not be the most pertinent thing to do considering I have so very little money of my own."

"I'm sorry, Elaina," his father said, reaching out to take his daughter's hand and squeezing it gently. "I wish I could provide more for you, but I'm afraid one thousand pounds is the best I can do."

Elaina shook her head. "Oh, no, Father. Please don't say it's the best you can do as if it's not nearly enough. It *is* enough. Some of the men I meet are so rich that it's a wonder they care about my dowry at all." She paused for a moment before adding, "I suppose I would understand if Will cared with such a momentous task ahead of him. Of course, he'll need a certain amount of financial backing to make himself successful." She paused again, this time sighing. "I can't help but feel the duke and duchess are a bit hypocritical, though."

"Why's that, my dear?" he asked, his brow crinkling.

"The duchess would like me to spend time with Mr. Hunt when he's here at Blackmore for the house party. How can they think I'm good enough for Mr. Hunt—independently wealthy and handsome—if they wouldn't even wish me upon their own son, who has no wealth of his own and whose title is only out of courtesy?"

"You mustn't think too badly of the duke and duchess," Mr. Walker warned his daughter with a shake of the head. "They only want what's best for both of you, which is for you to marry a wealthy man and Will to marry a wealthy heiress. Although you might like each other, neither of you are what would be the other's most advantageous match."

"We are not," she murmured softly. "Of that I am well aware, but please don't make me promise to stay away from him during the party so I can throw myself at Mr. Hunt instead. Let me enjoy these few days with him before he is forced to leave again. One day we'll both be married to other people and won't see each other at all."

Mr. Walker seemed to consider this before slowly nodding. "Of course, my dear," he said. "I only ask that you be careful. You might not have another opportunity with Mr. Hunt, and you wouldn't want to deter him by showering another with affection right in front of his eyes. Men are much more delicate creatures than you think, full of ego and hubris. Besides, you and Will are much older than you used to be. It's not right for a young man and a young woman, both unattached, to be gallivanting around the estate as you once did."

Elaina only laughed in response. "Don't worry, Father. We've already had our hands slapped by Montgomery for daring to go to the hothouse together, and you forget that I must entertain Lady Clara as well. I'm afraid there will be no time for gallivanting. A pity, really. You know how much I enjoy gallivanting."

"Indeed," her father said, shaking his head as he took up

his paper from the end table, unfolding it and returning to his reading.

WILL STOOD in his father's private study next to his brother. Blackmore sat at the desk across from them, smoking his usual pipe and already nursing his second glass of brandy, a cock-a-hoop expression on his face. It was the first time all three of them had been alone together as adults, and Will observed that his father had grown rounder in his absence, all the way from his cheeks to his stomach. He wore what looked to be an expensive wig, his hairline receding completely, and his cheeks seemed to have taken on a perpetual ruddy state.

"How nice it is to have all the Winter men in one room," he said, standing and raising a glass. "Here, here!"

Will and his brother echoed their father's sentiment, though Will's mind was hardly in the room with them. His thoughts were first and foremost filled with Elaina. He hadn't spoken to her since this morning, but he had seen her again. After his audience with his mother, he went to luncheon with her to greet her guests. She showed him off to her friends who had not seen him since he was a little boy, and she took even more time to show him off to her friends' daughters.

On his mother's part, the duchess seemed delighted with the way the younger ladies in the party looked at him, but if any of them were pretty or interesting, he hadn't noticed, as he was too busy watching Elaina out of the corner of his eye.

She was standing with Montgomery, Lady Clara, and Edgerton, helping Montgomery to introduce the newcomers to their other, more regular guests. He realized then just how much of a gentlewoman she had become, all demure smiles and making herself smaller so that Clara could be the center of attention, though it wasn't exactly a difficult task to make Clara stand out in the crowd.

The girl was uncommonly tall with at least three inches on Elaina, who was by no means petite either, with perfectly coiled blonde hair, a distinctive pair of blue eyes, and rose-colored lips. From a superficial point of view, she seemed to be the perfect match for Montgomery, who was also tall and lean with fair features.

For his part, Montgomery seemed quite taken with the girl. He could not stop looking and smiling at her throughout luncheon, though Elaina was always nearby as well, and she also received a fair amount of attention from him as well. Montgomery was just as charming as he expected him to be at eight-and-twenty, seemingly captivating both girls with his conversation easily. At one point, his mother had left him alone to see to some issue with the servants, and he was left listening to the conversation of two men around his age, if not younger, nearby.

"Why should he monopolize the attentions of the two most attractive women here?" one of them asked.

Will wondered the same thing, though he didn't dare approach the threesome and interfere. He'd leave that to Hunt, who still hadn't arrived. As for Will, any courtship of Elaina would have to be done furtively, or else his brother would work on ruining the whole thing until it was completely unsalvageable—at least that described his previous interactions with his brother, especially the ones at Eton.

Montgomery had done his best to make his life a living hell at Eton. He made making friends a near impossibility with the ruthless pranks he pulled and vicious rumors he spread. He didn't know why his brother did it, and he probably never would. He supposed the man was like any other teenaged bully, though. He didn't need reasons.

Standing in his father's study, Will glanced at his brother, knowing the marquess and his father's heir would do anything to make the duke happy, even marry a girl he hardly knew and was ten years his junior, but by the way Montgomery looked at Clara earlier that day, he surely would have no doubts about proposing if he was basing his decision on looks alone. There was no question that Clara was beautiful, and Montgomery must've at least recognized that. At least that was what Will thought at luncheon earlier. Now his brother looked more pensive.

"What did you think of Clara, brother?" Will asked him with a raised eyebrow. "Is she up to snuff for the future Duke of Blackmore?"

He took a moment to respond, but finally said, "She seems very agreeable."

Very agreeable. His brother said the words with no sense of enthusiasm. Will nearly snorted in response. Although he hadn't seen him in years, he should've remembered that his brother wasn't a man of passion unless the subject was the Winter family dynasty. He was just like their father that way, and Will often wondered if what Elaina described as guardedness was just a way to protect himself from caring about anything other than the estate and his duty. He certainly had done a good job at never caring about Will.

"Then you will propose tonight?" Will asked half-jokingly.

His brother scoffed. "Of course not. That would hardly be appropriate. I should at least court the girl first."

Turning to his father, Will smiled, eager to incite his brother like Montgomery had always done to him before. "Always the gentleman, my brother is."

"Edgerton and I have been waiting a long time for this," their father mused, seemingly to no one in particular, stroking his chin as he looked at some indeterminant object on the wall. Turning to Montgomery, he added, "You should probably propose as soon as possible. I'd hate for anyone to doubt your interest in her."

"She's having her come-out ball at our house," Will said before Montgomery could respond. "I think everyone from the nearest village to London knows we intend to make her a Winter."

"Not *we*," Blackmore said. He gestured to the ever stone-faced Montgomery. "*Him.*"

"Ah," Will said, raising his eyebrows. Although he was surprised anyone would doubt his brother's conviction to marry Clara, not everyone knew his brother like Will did. His duty was to marry the girl, and Montgomery would do his duty, whether he was truly interested in Clara or not.

"I'm interested," Montgomery said, a little bit too defensively to make his words entirely believable. "If they want a flashy show of my affections, I will give them a show."

"Now, now," Will cautioned after a low chuckle escaped his lips, "let's not get too melodramatic here."

Then again, he thought to himself, that could work in his favor. If Montgomery was focused on Clara and Clara alone, there would be ample opportunity for Will to court Elaina without his interference. As for Hunt, surely he couldn't be a threat. Will did not believe for one moment that Elaina was seriously considering the man.

"Although you might have a point with what you said earlier," Will said. His brother shot him an incredulous gaze, not understanding Will's meaning. "You should court her. Really woo her. You wouldn't want to give her a reason to say no, would you?"

"Say no to a future duke?" their father asked incredulously. "Would any gently bred lady do such a thing?"

"You never know," Will replied, shrugging, turning to look out the window of his father's first-floor study. The sun was beginning to set over Blackmore. "She may have someone back home. Someone she grew up with. Someone she always imagined herself marrying, despite the knowledge she was promised to someone else."

There was a pensive silence between the men… just before the duke nearly keeled over from laughing so hard.

"Oh, William!" he exclaimed, still laughing. "I'm so glad you're home! How I've missed your sense of humor."

Will smiled at his brother, who only looked distressed. "I should go," Montgomery said. "Mother's houseguests will have assembled in the drawing room by now. It's rude to keep them waiting."

Will's smile turned to a smirk. "Them? Or her?"

His brother glared at him, and Will decided he rather enjoyed his newfound ability to get under Montgomery's skin.

"No matter," their father said, waving his hand. "Go to them. I have things I'd like to discuss with your brother. We'll join you in a few minutes."

Will sighed, supposing his father wanted to discuss the new estate. He wasn't particularly crazy about the idea of quitting Blackmore for Cambridgeshire when he'd only just returned home that day. From what his father told him in his previous letters, it was at least a two-day journey there if one didn't want to spend all day and night in a carriage, and he wasn't eager to be that far from Elaina again after only just returning to her.

He was still determined to take him with her, of course, but he knew the opposition would be strong, with the strongest of this sitting in front of him. His father had intimidated him as a little boy, but now that they were both adults, he was beginning to see the duke was a man like any other, and there would be ways to get around him like any other. He had fought Spanish and French armies on the Continent.

He would not let the duke prevent him from getting what he desired now that he had returned home, the one thing he desired being Elaina Walker.

"And what would you like to discuss, Father?" Will asked, feigning ignorance as he sat down in one of the armchairs across from his father's desk.

The duke narrowed his eyes. "You know very well what I'd like to discuss, boy."

Will had almost forgotten his father could see right through him. Although he was less intimidating now, his ability to read his younger son had not left him. Montgomery may have been his father's favorite—in Will's mind, anyway, and anyone would have a hard time convincing him otherwise—but Will and his father did share a certain kinship as well.

The duke was the least surprised when Will decided to take a commission. After all, the duke was a second son at one point himself, before his elder brother died in a carriage accident and Blackmore Park fell to him, and he too once dreamed of glory on the battlefield before everything changed for him and he became duke.

Before he left, his father went to Eton to talk to his son before agreeing to pay for his commission. Although it had been eight years ago, Will still remembered the conversation well. His father said he was much like Will when he was his age—hated school, eager for adventure—but when the unthinkable happened, his father rose to the occasion, something which Will supposed he admired the man for, as he was not sure he'd ever be able to do the same if God forbid something happened. Will and Montgomery may not have seen eye to eye on much of anything, but Will did not envy his older brother's position, though he knew his father expected Will to rise to the occasion just as he had if anything were to happen to Montgomery.

Will, for one, wasn't sure if he could live up to his father's expectations. He wasn't even sure if he could manage the new Cambridgeshire estate. When it came to duty or passion, the younger Winter brother would most certainly choose passion, and he wasn't entirely sure how passionate he felt about farming, cattle raising, or becoming the local magistrate. Luckily, those were some of Elaina's passions—believable for a girl of five-and-twenty or not—which was another reason he had determined she'd be the perfect wife for him.

"You want to discuss the new estate in Cambridgeshire," Will said with a sigh. "I know. What's the name of it again? Lark-something-or-another?"

"Larkspur Castle is the name, and you would do well to remember it," his father said with narrowed eyes. "We acquired it with you in mind."

"We?" Will asked, raising an eyebrow.

"Your brother, Mr. Walker, and I. We think it will be good for you."

"I had no idea all three of you had such an interest in my well-being."

His father harrumphed. "Regardless of what you may think, I want to leave this earth knowing you are as well off as Montgomery."

"You act as if you plan on dying tomorrow."

"Hardly. But now that you've returned, it's time you start making good on my investment."

"Ah, there it is."

Investment. Will hated the word. His father often wrote to him about his various investments. They seemed to be his favorite subject. Investments in the land and in the village. New equipment for the tenants or improvements to the schoolhouse in the village. All decisions were made based on assumed costs and presumed profit. There were no gut feelings or rash decisions in Blackmore Park's study.

"What?" his father asked. "If the Winter family wants to survive, we must make smart investments. Do you know what that means?"

"Do tell, Father," he said, sighing.

"We are all betting that *you'll* be a smart investment."

Will nearly laughed. "Montgomery thought *I'd* be a smart investment? After the way he treated me at Eton? I find that hard to believe."

His father chuckled. "Mr. Walker can be very persuasive when he wants to be."

"Mr. Walker?" Will asked incredulously. Mr. Walker was the one who convinced Montgomery that the family should buy the land for Will?

"The very man. He is fond of you. Didn't you know? You are his only daughter's closest friend, after all."

"Surely she's made other friends while I've been away," Will said coolly, despite the feeling of rising glee in his stomach at his father's declaration.

His father sighed. "Miss Walker is a good sort of girl, and you can certainly see Lady Eleanor in her now that she's older... but certain people will never accept the fact that her late grandfather, the old Earl of Gillingham, never acknowledged her existence, nor did the new Lord Gillingham move to make up for his cousin's slight. Even that reclusive aunt of hers makes no move to acknowledge her. I have to admire the girl's resilience for not taking the rejection to heart."

Will frowned. "In other words, you're saying that all of Elaina's current acquaintances offer nothing but shallow showings of friendship due to my mother's favoritism?"

"That's exactly what I mean," the duke said before waving his hand, clearly tired of the subject. "Of course, all that will change once she's married to Hunt. Now, back to Larkspur Castle…"

"I'll go if I can take a wife," Will said without thinking, ignoring the fact that his father seemed quite determined to marry Elaina off to Hunt like the rest of his family seemed to be.

"Oh?" His father raised an eyebrow, leaning back in his chair. "Well, I suppose if you can find one quickly, her dowry would help with the improvements that the estate needs."

Will swallowed, knowing that wasn't exactly what he had in mind. "I don't think you understand my meaning, Father," he said, speaking slowly, cautiously. "I'm going to ask Miss Walker to marry me. I won't go to Larkspur without her."

Blackmore's face turned an even deeper shade of red than what it normally was. "You're going to *what?*" He shook his head. "You've only just returned. I would advise not making any rash decisions. Matrimony is a serious thing, and—"

"I've always felt a measure of affection toward her, and after maintaining such a lengthy correspondence with her, I feel like it's the right thing to do," Will said, cutting him off and trying to keep his voice level despite his father's heightening color. "Seeing her today only confirmed my desires."

"No," his father said after a moment of silence. "I will not allow it."

Will sat back in his chair. He couldn't say he was surprised, but was the man really that determined to make him marry for money? If that was the case, why didn't he arrange a marriage for him when he was a child like his older brother? Shaking his head, Will asked, "Why not?"

His father shot him an incredulous look, as if he could not believe his son was questioning his judgment. "Why, she's the daughter of our land steward!" After taking a drag of his pipe, he added, "Perhaps we were wrong not to discourage your friendship as children and your ongoing correspondence as you grew older, but surely you know you would do better with an heiress of some sort, and she would do better with a first son."

Will flinched, a heat rising in his body. His father's words hurt, though he knew they were true. Any woman would do better with the heir to a great family fortune and title. Will was only entitled to whatever scraps his father, and later, his brother, would allow him, which apparently was an estate in Cambridgeshire on the verge of failure.

"But she'll never induce a first son to marry her," he countered. "You said it yourself. She's your land steward's daughter. The ton still holds her mother's decision to marry down against her, though they pretend they do not in front of her and Mother. Perhaps we ought to consider whether or not I'm the best she can hope for."

Blackmore harrumphed. "She is still the granddaughter of an earl."

"Whose heir won't recognize her!"

"That might change one day," his father argued back. Lowering his voice and leaning over his desk, calmly folding his hands as he did, he continued before Will could respond any further. "Please, you must drop the subject. Hunt wants her, and he will have her."

"What about what she wants?"

The duke laughed. "Who cares what she wants? You, meanwhile, should prepare yourself for what is to come. Undertaking an estate is no easy task. Now…"

Will only half listened to his father's diatribe after that, disliking the duke's dismissal of Elaina's feelings and considering the other ways to get what he wanted without his father's approval. They were devious ways, yes, but if Blackmore insisted on keeping him and Elaina apart, he would be forced to act. No amount of dissuading from his father or brother would deter him.

Elaina would be his, no matter how many people he had to disappoint in the process. He was sure of it.

GILES HUNT STEPPED out of his carriage in front of Blackmore Park with a sigh, stretching his back. Why did his friend have to live so far away? He enjoyed Montgomery's company, but he hated the country, mostly because he couldn't stand the carriage rides to get there. All the jostling made him nauseous.

Still, he could not avoid this particular house party. Elaina Walker lived there, and he planned on making Miss Walker his wife. He did not love the girl, but when he started considering marriage earlier that year, she was the first woman to come to mind. He liked Elaina Walker—always had, probably always would. She was sensible and intelligent, and she would make a fine wife.

There was the issue of her parentage—her parents' marriage had caused quite a scandal some thirty years ago—but what did he care? The ton trusted him with their money. Surely they would trust his judgment on who should become Mrs. Hunt.

As for love? Well, maybe he could come to love her someday, but he was wary of the emotion altogether. Love caused people to do stupid things. Case in point, an earl's daughter marrying a land steward. His mother, who could have been a duchess, marrying a banker. Unlike them, Giles was not stupid. He was proud to have never fallen in love. What a useless emotion that was.

No, Giles was in no danger of falling in love with Miss Walker, and she was in no danger of falling in love with him. That was the beauty of their relationship, he thought as he entered the house that night, coming upon a crowded drawing room. He found her easily, standing by herself in the corner of the room, seemingly surveying the scene. He always liked how observant she was.

He was about to go to her when he was intercepted by Montgomery's cousins, Robert and Julia Winter. He had not spent much time with Robert—his idea of fun was a bit too wild for Giles—but his younger sister Julia was pretty and pleasant enough, though she always seemed to be a bit tongue tied. He decided that was only because she was young.

"Mr. Hunt!" Robert exclaimed. "You're late."

Giles nodded once. "My apologies, Mr. Winter. Business in London delayed my departure. I trust I haven't missed much."

"Oh, but you have! Lord William has returned."

Giles frowned. "Has he?"

Giles barely listened as Robert went on about his other cousin's sudden return to England, realizing then his much-planned-for engagement was in danger, for although he was in no danger of falling in love with Miss Walker, someone else very much was if that man wasn't in love with her already—and where did that leave him?

CHAPTER FOUR

Finally! We have returned to Blackmore Park after what felt like a very long first Season in London. I've already grown rather tired of balls and dinner parties and carriage rides through Hyde Park. Some girls I know rave about London and how sad they are when a Season is over, but I've decided nothing can compare to Hampshire. The only thing missing is you, but I think I've found something else to amuse me. Father has agreed to take me to see some tenants tomorrow morning, and I'm very excited to learn more about what he does. We haven't told the duchess yet, but after being the Epitome of a Lady *all through finishing school and my first Season, I don't see how she could deny me this.*

—an excerpt of a letter from Elaina, written in June 1809, to Will, who was stationed in Portugal at the time

ELAINA STOOD ALONE in the corner of the drawing room, shifting her weight from foot to foot as she waited for Will to appear that evening. Montgomery seemed more than capable of entertaining the visiting duke and his daughter himself, and she somehow managed to sneak away from their threesome at the center of the room, which meant she'd be free to entertain who she would like instead of who Montgomery would like. Who she would like to entertain was Will, but he was nowhere to be found, leaving her to stand aimlessly in the corner.

With Will still missing—he must've been with his father, for the duke was nowhere to be found either—Elaina surveyed the room. Robert and Julia Winter, Montgomery and Will's cousins, stood with Mr. Hunt, who must have just arrived, as she hadn't seen him at luncheon earlier that afternoon. He smiled at her from across the room as Robbie told him something, and she smiled back.

Sighing, she supposed Mr. Hunt would make a good match for her. At the very least, he was intelligent and kind to her. In terms of title, he was a man of little consequence, but his family had made quite the fortune in banking over the years, with everything falling to him when his father died five years ago. With no brothers or sisters, the only person he had to care for was his mother.

In terms of looks, Mr. Hunt was an attractive enough young man of eight-and-twenty, though it didn't take much when one looked at other wealthy members of the ton. There were very few eligible bachelors with a full head of dark hair and all their teeth like Hunt, so she supposed she should consider herself lucky that he was interested in her.

He and Elaina had always been friends, and she had enjoyed his company over the years like she enjoyed Montgomery's, though she was admittedly surprised when he told the duke his intentions to court her. There was no spark between them, and now that she had seen Will again, the man seemed to pale in comparison.

While Hunt was taller and leaner than the average man, Will seemed to have become more robustly built in adulthood. Despite being small as a boy, he was now average in height. Although he may have been shorter than Hunt, Will's shoulders and chest seemed broader now, not to mention it was refreshing to see a man outfitted more ruggedly than someone like Hunt, who was always dressed impeccably. Meanwhile, Will had arrived at Blackmore wearing buckskins, Hessians, and a loosely tied cravat, looking all the more attractive for it.

She knew she should have tempered her attraction toward Will, especially after what her father told her in their sitting room earlier that day. She also knew the duke and duchess only wanted what was best for them, but would it be so horrible for her to end up with Will and he to end up with her? The Winters felt like family already, and they accepted her and her father for who they were—for the most part, anyway. She had a sneaking suspicion that some of their hesitation surrounding her being a potential match for Will had to do with her father's common blood coursing through her veins, not just her small dowry.

Still, it didn't escape Elaina's notice that the duchess had been showing off Will to all the single ladies and their mothers at luncheon, all of whom she knew had much bigger reticules than her. She knew she had nothing much to offer the Winter family, and God knew how much money they already spent on bringing her up to snuff in the eyes of the ton, but none of those fine, rich ladies could ever know Will the way she did. They had not prayed for him when he was away at war like she had.

"Do you normally stand by yourself in the corner at social gatherings?"

Elaina nearly jumped, not realizing Will had entered the room and somehow made his way to her undetected.

"Will!" she exclaimed, bringing one evening-gloved hand to the gold pendant hanging from her neck upon seeing him standing behind her. As his eyes grazed her figure, she smiled slightly. She had purposefully dressed in one of her finest evening gowns that night, hoping to impress him in a white silk gown with pink and cream floral embroidery across the bodice and waist. Her hair was done up with braids, woven with peach-colored ribbons.

"You startled me," she said with a slight laugh.

"Perhaps you would have noticed me had you not been staring at Mr. Hunt," he countered with a grin. He was dressed much more formally that night, wearing a gold waistcoat and black jacket. His buckskins and Hessians had been traded for more traditional breeches, stockings, and shoes. Judging by his more intricately tied cravat that evening, she guessed one of the servants had dressed him.

"Was I staring?" she asked. "I hadn't meant to. I was merely lost in my own thoughts."

"And what thoughts were those?" he asked, a playful grin on his face as he took a step closer to her. She didn't recall him being so unabashed in his youth, but she couldn't say she minded the change. She liked the way he grinned at her and said whatever he was thinking, so unlike most of the men she met.

"I'm afraid if I told you, I'd have to kill you," she responded in a low voice, her tone even with mock gravity.

"Oh, but where's the fun in that, especially when I've only just returned to England?" he asked.

"A fair complaint, I'll give you that," she replied. With a sigh, she nodded her head in Hunt's direction and said, "Mr. Hunt over there told your father earlier this spring he intends to court me."

"Has he?"

She nodded. "Oh, yes. There have been dances, flowers, afternoon strolls, and carriage rides through the park."

"Do you enjoy his attentions?"

"When you found me, I was in the middle of deciding as much for myself."

Will seemed to regard the man for a moment, his expression unreadable, though she couldn't help but wonder if anyone in her family mentioned Mr. Hunt and his intentions toward her. Turning back to her, he asked, "And what have you decided?"

"Honestly, I'm not entirely sure," she replied with a shrug. "Truthfully, I couldn't look at him this evening without thinking of you. I'm especially upset that your mother placed me next to him at dinner when I'd much rather be sitting next to you. I suppose such a confession does not bode well for mine and Mr. Hunt's matrimonial prospects."

Perhaps she was being too forward, especially in light of her father's earlier warning to tread cautiously in her dealings with Will, but she couldn't help herself, what with his own forwardness and the way they were standing so close together, like they were swapping secrets. There was finally a man in the room who she wanted to flirt with, and she wanted to take advantage of it at least once in her life, if only to experience the thrill of such a thing. She'd spend the rest of the party entertaining Hunt if she must, but she wanted at least one evening of nothing but Will's company. If his family insisted on keeping them apart under the guise of caring for her future, that was the least they could allow her.

"Luckily for you," Will drawled, leaning in closer to her, "I have an in with this evening's hostess, and she agreed to seat us together and put Hunt next to someone else."

Elaina couldn't help but smile. "Is that so?"

Will nodded. "I hope you're not too disappointed. If Hunt is a banker, then he must be wealthy, and I am nothing but a penniless retired army captain, though I like to think of myself as pleasant enough company for a young lady."

"Oh, I think you are pleasant," she replied with a laugh,

"and may I point out that you are hardly penniless. Although I'll admit you are not as wealthy as a banker, I'm sure the estate in Cambridgeshire will provide a handsome income. Besides, don't think for one moment that I didn't notice how the marriage-minded mamas and their similarly inclined daughters fawned over you at luncheon today. Your mother seemed to enjoy it, but I confess it filled me with jealousy."

"Fawned?" he asked, eyebrows raised. "Is that what they call it? I felt more like an animal carcass being circled by vultures."

Elaina stifled a snort. "Did you?" she asked. "I find that surprising, as most men would deem such attention to be flattering."

"Your words wound me," he replied with mock gravity. "I thought our close relationship as children and ongoing correspondence would result in a much different opinion of me—a much kinder one, if I'm being honest—for I am not like most men. I've never been one to find flattery in empty praise."

"And how would I know if you're not like most men? Do you really think a childhood friendship and years of correspondence is enough to really know a man's nature, particularly his best and worst qualities? For instance, whether or not he enjoys mindless flattery from desperate debutantes."

Will seemed to consider this. "Hmmm," he said. "Perhaps not his entire nature, but I do think, as you said, our childhood friendship and years of correspondences offer more credence to any courtship I may attempt as opposed to whatever Mr. Hunt has tried in the past or will try in the future."

Elaina stared at him for a moment, mouth slightly open. Had he just announced his intention to court her? Would he go against his parents' wishes and do such a thing? Perhaps she was being too encouraging, for the boy she once knew was terribly shy, and she seemed to recall being the one to initiate their first kiss on their last day together. She could have never pictured the thirteen-year-old boy she once knew making such forward remarks, but she supposed he wasn't a boy anymore.

"And is that what you're attempting right now?" she finally asked, her voice slow and careful. "Courtship?"

"Perhaps," he replied, a sly grin playing at his lips.

Remembering her father's words, she swallowed and turned away from him so their faces weren't so close. "I must advise you against such a thing, for your parents would hardly approve."

"Why not?"

"I am far less suitable for you than some of the other women in the room. As much as it pains me to admit such a thing and risk losing your affection, their fathers have much more to offer you than mine."

"But none of them are nearly as interesting as you," he countered, "so I must assure you that there is no risk at all."

Elaina laughed once. "You don't even know them."

Will pursed his lips, seemingly annoyed. "You're right, I don't—but would you rather me favor them and leave you to a man like Hunt, a ruthless banker who knows nothing of the way you wore your hair as a child or the name of your favorite doll growing up? Have you forgotten that Hunt bullied me as a child?"

"I have not forgotten, though I doubt he would have bullied you if it weren't for Montgomery. Keep in mind that once you left, I did not have much choice in companions, especially in London. Your brother and Mr. Hunt were my friends, even when Earl Gillingham and Viscount Fitzroy periodically snubbed me. They didn't have to be. They could have just pretended for the duchess's sake, but no. They were true friends."

Will made a sound of frustration, but Elaina couldn't help

but tilt her head to the side and smile slightly, unable to prevent herself from feeling touched that Will remembered things like the name of her favorite childhood doll. Still, she knew they could not be together. They would have to compromise.

"Let's not talk about such things tonight," she said quietly. "Tonight we will flirt with each other and share stories of our years apart. There will be no talk of courtship, though. I forbid it."

"You forbid it?"

She nodded once, determined to heed her father's warning, despite her pounding heart and the knot in her stomach that wanted something far different than what her mind was telling her to say. "I forbid it."

Will sighed. "I suppose I can at least attempt to honor your wishes. I make no promises, though. After all, I can't help it if you fall in love with me and want to marry me by the end of the night."

Her eyes widened, and she found herself on the verge of nervous laughter. "My, how you've changed!" she said. "I almost said so before and held my tongue, but now I'm afraid I can no longer do so."

"Is it such a bad thing, this change in me?" he asked, chuckling. "Or would you prefer me to be a boy of thirteen again?"

"No, but where was this self-assurance when you were that young?"

"I was a shy thirteen-year-old boy when I left this place, always considered second best to my brother," Will said with a scowl. "The problem was only exacerbated when I went to Eton and was forced to endure public humiliation at his hands—and Mr. Hunt's hands, if I may add."

"We agreed not to speak about that!"

"Yes, well, nevertheless, it wasn't until I joined the army that I gained my confidence."

Elaina frowned. "Well, you were never second best to me, with or without the army," she murmured, looking down as she did. She couldn't help wringing her hands as she said it. Such a confession indicated she desired much more than only one night of flirting.

"Somehow I think I always knew that," he softly replied, "but it means the world to hear you say it aloud."

"Never doubt it," she said, "regardless of what happens."

She knew she shouldn't have said the last part, but she did anyway. Eager to change the subject, she gestured to the door that led to the dining room and added, "I believe dinner is starting. Shall we go in together?"

Will managed to tear his eyes away from Elaina long enough to see his mother and father's guests begin coupling off. If she had meant to distract him with her beauty, she had succeeded, for he hardly even noticed the commotion in the room as the group readied themselves to go into the dining room.

Turning back to her, he offered her his arm. As she placed her gloved palm on the inside of his elbow, a sense of possessiveness ran through his veins, just as he happened to notice Hunt watching them. He couldn't help but smile deviously at Hunt, who was standing with his cousin Julia, for Elaina was by far the prettiest girl at the party—even prettier than Clara, if anybody were to ask him his opinion—and Will had snatched her away from him rather easily.

He had doubted Elaina's feelings when he entered the drawing room that evening and caught her staring at the man his parents deemed suitable for her, especially when Hunt was as tall and good looking as he remembered. He had almost been prepared to step aside if Hunt was what Elaina really wanted, but her reassurance was all he needed to continue his bullish pursuit, regardless of his family's disapproval.

This girl had carried him through war and boarding school—and Eton could be just as bad as war at times—and he wasn't going to let her marry someone else, especially not Hunt, who could never know Elaina like he did. He could care less about the size of her dowry, as he knew his father could afford to open the Blackmore coffers and support the new Cambridgeshire estate himself. The only person who might need more convincing of that was Elaina herself, but Will had just the thing in mind, especially as the heat seemed to grow between them as their time together passed.

He'd like to think seducing her would be a simple enough task, but he could tell she had her guard up around him, especially when she forbid talk of courtship. Someone must've warned her about the imprudence of a match between them. A penniless man marry a penniless woman? Everyone in the room would agree that nothing could be more injudicious. Perhaps even Will might agree in the case of a couple other than them, but this was him and Elaina, two childhood friends and longtime correspondents, finally reunited under the same roof. Keeping them apart would be like asking the Moon to stop orbiting the Earth. The idea of Will rejecting the natural pull he felt in her presence was complete and utter madness, and he knew she could not deny him, just like the tides of the ocean. From the moment he saw her outside the house that morning, he knew he must have her.

They sat down at the dinner table next to each other, the footmen helping them with their chairs. Unsurprisingly, his mother planned an impressive meal that evening, what with dinner being the first true event of the party. A cucumber soup made with heavy cream and garnished with parsley was the first course, followed by mutton with a caper sauce. After that, an artichoke and asparagus salad with potted cheese on the side. Another meat course followed, this time quail and watercress. Elaina told him that each of the vegetables were grown on one of the farms on the estate, and he couldn't help but smile as she recited the names of the farmers as well as what their wives and children were called.

Will was not used to the amount of food served at dinner and was quite full by the time dessert came around, but the banana ice cream was too decadent to pass up on, and it was difficult for him not to lick the bowl clean when he was finished with such a meager portion of deliciousness.

"Tell me," Elaina said toward the end of dinner, "what kept you and your father from joining the other guests earlier this evening?"

"He was eager to discuss the reason I've been asked to give up my commission," he explained.

"You mean the estate in Cambridgeshire?"

He nodded. "The very one."

"I assume he'll want you to go right away. When will you leave?"

"Right away, if my father gets what he wants," he grumbled. Noticing the way her face fell, he added, "I will stay until the end of the house party, of course."

"Of course," she said with a hasty nod, putting on a mask of indifference. "I suppose I've been silly. I thought you'd stay here forever, but I'm sure your father has a plan to make you feel successful in your own right. What is the name of the place you will soon become master of? I don't think anyone's ever told me."

"Master?" Will scoffed. "I'll hardly be the master. Father still owns the property. I'm only meant to oversee it."

Shaking his head, he added, "Anyway, to answer your question, the name is Larkspur Castle."

Elaina smiled almost wistfully. "It sounds rather romantic."

"Does it? I hadn't noticed, though I'm glad you think so. I have only been thinking about how much work it will be, especially if I must undertake it alone."

"I suppose you won't be afforded a land steward like my father."

Will shook his head. "My income will be whatever the new estate brings in, minus whatever my father decides to take for himself. I fear I'll be very poor as a result, especially at the beginning. I'm told the estate will need a lot of work before it's truly lucrative."

"It's a pity you can't take me," she mused, frowning. "I like to think if I were a man, I'd be an even more knowledgeable steward than my own father, but alas, I was born a woman and will be forced to marry and procreate instead."

"And why can't I take you?" he asked, daring to go there even when she warned him not to earlier that evening.

Elaina laughed, as if the question was some sort of joke, but he was serious. "That would hardly be appropriate," she said, "unless I went as…"

Her voice trailed off, and she put her spoon down, still holding a scoop of banana ice cream on it. She did not look at him, her gaze fixated on some unknown object on the dinner table. When it became clear she would not finish her statement, he asked, "Unless you went as what?"

"Well, unless I went as your wife," she murmured, finally turning to look at him. Her brow was furrowed, as if she was seriously considering the idea, despite what she said earlier about forbidding talk of courtship that evening.

Will decided to say as much. "I thought we banned all talk of courtship this evening. Then again, such an arrangement would allow you to marry, manage land, *and* procreate. My, I think you'd be a force to be reckoned with if you did such a thing."

She flushed, shaking her head and moving to pick up her spoon again. "I shouldn't have said anything," she said. "It's only a fantasy."

"A fantasy?" he asked incredulously. "Not many women fantasize about moving over one hundred miles from the home they grew up in to live in a derelict castle."

Elaina shot him a playful look. "Don't they? Isn't that what the fairy stories they tell us girls as children are all about? Princes and castles?"

"True," he said with a shrug, "but I think you would add much more value to Larkspur other than being a beautiful princess trapped in one of the towers, guarded by dragons. Elaina, you must realize that you belong in the country, tending your hothouse and visiting your tenant farmers."

"Perhaps—but I'm afraid it's just not meant to be. Middle-class girls like me are meant to marry other middle-class men, and we live in places like London and Manchester and Liverpool." Turning to look at him, she added, "I consider myself at least lucky enough to call Blackmore my childhood home, and I know I'll always be welcome here if I wish to get away from it all. And perhaps if my husband is rich enough, he'll buy me my own house in the country to raise our children."

Will felt frustration bubbling up inside of him, not only as she offered such ridiculous scenarios that didn't include him, but also as she continued to deny herself her own happiness in favor of what the duke and duchess wanted. Why should she do such a thing?

What frustrated him the most, though, was that his own parents were complicit in it all. If they could not bring themselves to care for Elaina's happiness, surely they could at least try to bring themselves to care about his, their son's.

"You'll be miserable if you marry Hunt," he warned through clenched teeth.

"You assume he will end up marrying me," she whispered as she bent closer to him, making sure no one else could hear her. She seemed to speak faster as she went. "Plenty of men have gone to your father and told them they wish to court me—and then they get cold feet at the last minute. Mr. Hunt is rich and handsome, and I am five-and-twenty—which is just three separate words for ancient—with a meager dowry, another phrase for dreadfully poor. He may very well meet someone else—someone better."

"He'd be a fool not to want to marry you," he spat, his voice equally as low. "Do not let your so-called old age or lack of dowry make you question your true worth to a man."

"The only fool here is you," she countered, nostrils flaring. "You'd have been better off sitting next to one of the other girls tonight. I won't let you put your future in jeopardy for some ridiculous childhood infatuation."

His voice seemed to rise as his anger did. "Is that what you think this is?" he asked. "A ridiculous—"

"What*ever* are you two talking about over there?"

CHAPTER FIVE

Your story about Robbie was a positively delightful diversion from an otherwise boring day here in Belgium. Please do tell me more about his perversions in your next missive. You'll probably want to hit me for that, but it's hard for me to picture Robbie as anything but my little cousin—yes, I know he's only a year younger than me, but I still picture him as a little boy. Do you still picture me as a little boy? I digress—we were discussing little Cousin Robbie becoming a rake! I hope I come home soon, if only to see him in action. (Do not worry, I have no plans to partake in any "rake-like" behavior myself.)

—an excerpt of a letter from Will, written in 1814 from Belgium, to Elaina

ELAINA LOOKED up to see Montgomery and Will's cousin, Robert Winter, who had been sitting across from them at the dinner table all evening, staring at them with an interested gaze.

Cousin Robert was the son of the duke's younger brother, Lord John Winter. Robbie, as his family called him, was younger than both Will and Elaina, having only finished his Oxford degree a year ago. His father, a barrister, wanted him to continue on to law school, but Robert said he had no more time for classes or books after such a strenuous stay at Oxford, resolving to live off his meager allowance until his father decided to cut him off and he was forced to find work.

From what Elaina knew of Robbie, this was not surprising, as he much preferred whoring and womanizing to hard work. She would describe him as a quintessential society rake, though she had somehow come to love him like family.

Like the other two Winter boys, Robbie was fair-haired and blue-eyed, though his features weren't as delicate as Montgomery or even Will's. His nose could be considered large and his lips were rather full, but neither unattractively so. His jawline was strong, but perhaps his most distinct physical traits were the two scars he had on his face: one just above his nose, in between his eyebrows, and the other on his upper right cheek, just below his eye.

Elaina heard they were the product of a fight at a secret and exclusive gaming hell in London, where one of Robbie's many romantic rivals pulled out a knife on him after partaking in too much drink. By all accounts, Elaina considered Robbie lucky to still have both eyes firmly in their sockets. Then again, she had heard women describe the scars as dashing in the past. Perhaps they would have liked an eyepatch as well.

Elaina looked from Robbie to Will, then back to Robbie. Will seemed to be struggling to come up with something to say, so Elaina decided to ask, "Would you like to know the truth, Robbie, or shall I lie and say that we were merely arguing over what the best flavor of ice cream is?"

"Oh, everyone knows chocolate is the best flavor of ice cream," Cousin Julia interjected from Robbie's left side. Julia was a young girl of nineteen, only recently introduced to society over the past Season in London.

Julia was pretty, but still young and slightly foolish, and took more after her mother with her dark hair and green eyes, and her features were the exact opposite of her older brother's: small and delicate, something like an attractive field mouse. As the youngest of the Winter cousins, she may have been picked on more by the three older boys than Montgomery ever picked on Will, though Elaina had taken a shine to her sweet nature from the moment they met.

"Although I must say," she added, "this banana flavor is quite delightful as well."

Robbie glared at his sister. "No one cares for your thoughts on ice, Julia," he said dismissively, shaking his head. Julia made a sound of protest, but her brother cut her off before she could say anything else, turning back to Elaina and asking, "I'll have the truth, Miss Walker. I have a feeling it'll be the most entertaining thing I've heard all evening."

Elaina smiled. "Lord William and I were only arguing whether or not my advanced age of five-and-twenty was a detriment to my... hmmm, how shall I put it?" She placed her index finger on her chin and looked up as she searched her mind for the right word. When she finally had it, she looked back at Robbie. "Marriageability."

Elaina heard a clank from her side of the table. Will had placed his spoon in his bowl of banana ice cream with some force, looking pained, clearly not wanting their private debate to become so public, especially when it was hardly appropriate dinner table conversation, though Elaina considered herself amongst friends.

Besides, there was something about being in Will's presence that brought out her more mischievous, childish side. She bit back a grin as she looked at Robbie, who seemed to be considering her question seriously.

"What do you think, Robbie?" she asked him. "Have I missed my chance? Am I too old now? Will I be destined to loneliness, eventually becoming some sort of intolerable spinster living here at Blackmore Park?"

Robbie crossed his arms, leaning back in his chair and studying her with a thoughtful gaze. Elaina tilted her head, studying him back.

"Miss Walker," he finally said, "if you weren't so beautiful, I might say yes, you are much too ancient to even hope for a marriage proposal at this point in your life, but you *are* beautiful, so I doubt you will end up lonely, though I sometimes wonder if that's not your goal, considering how much I know you to love it here at Blackmore Park. Why? I do not know. I find the country dreadfully dull, but if you were at all eager to leave, perhaps I would have seen you show even just a passing interest in one of the many gentlemen the duchess has introduced you to in London."

Elaina smirked at his response. "You know my secret, then. I do quite love it here, but I would like to know how you've come to decide that I only show passing interest in the gentlemen that the duchess introduces me to in London. Have you been observing me without my knowledge, Mr. Winter?"

"Perhaps," he replied, smirking right back at her. "I do find you rather fun to watch. If I weren't so determined to remain unmarried myself and I didn't see you as a quasi, sort-of sister of mine, I might offer for you."

"Careful, cousin."

Elaina turned to face Will then, who was glaring at his younger cousin. He looked up and over in Julia's direction, asking, "And what do you think, Mr. Hunt?"

She felt the color draining from her face as she turned in the same direction. She hadn't even noticed Mr. Hunt watching the entire exchange from Julia's other side. She could have died from mortification. She and Robbie had always loved to tease each other, ever since they were children, and she hadn't much considered what Hunt would think of it.

"Any fool could see that Miss Walker is quite the catch," he replied, his voice even.

"A fool, you say?" Will shot a pointed look at Elaina, who resisted the urge to roll her eyes at him.

"Indeed," Hunt confirmed. "In fact, I was rather disappointed when I wasn't seated next to Miss Walker tonight. She's the only reason I decided to come to Hampshire in the first place."

Elaina shifted uncomfortably in her seat. Beside her, Will seemed to be enjoying himself as he watched his point be proven to her.

"I'm sorry you were disappointed," she replied with a slight laugh. "You see, Lord William's only just returned from Brussels, and he implored his mother for the opportunity to reacquaint ourselves. Being his mother's son and so recently returned from war, she couldn't very well say no to him."

"No matter, Miss Walker," he said. "I understand." He nodded once at Will, adding, "I have not seen you since we were just boys at Eton. Army life seems to have agreed with you."

She looked back and forth between the two of them, but Will didn't bother to reply. She cleared her throat, desperate to change the subject from her eligibility, though she knew very well that she had brought it upon herself.

"Surely there are other reasons to come to a house party in the country than to sit next to me at dinner," Elaina finally said in an attempt to lighten the mood. "Fresh air, exercise, lawn games, shooting, horseback riding—all things you can enjoy at Blackmore."

Before Hunt could say anything, she thought she heard

Julia murmur, "Not to mention sit next to me, nineteen years young and very single."

Robbie laughed under his breath at his sister's comment while Hunt said, "I'm afraid I don't really like the country, Miss Walker. I much prefer the city. Hyde Park provides ample fresh air and exercise for me, which is all I really need for a happy life. The rest of it I'm sure I could do without."

"Sure, but—" Elaina shot him a puzzled look. Of course she realized everyone had their own preferences, but she couldn't help but ask, "You don't like the country? I didn't know that."

"Not at all, I'm afraid."

"I, for one," Julia interjected, "prefer the city as well. Mr. Hunt, do you often go out riding in Hyde Park?"

Julia seemed to reel in her dinner mate after that, and Elaina glanced at Will, who was regarding her with an unreadable expression, something like a mixture of sadness and triumph. How could she be friends with someone for six years and not know he didn't like the country?

"There, you see?" he murmured, leaning in close to her ear as he said it. "He will have you if you want him—he announced as much—but you will be miserable with him."

As much as she hated to admit it, she knew he was right.

WALKING out of the dining room with the other ladies, Elaina felt defeated. Will had been such lovely company—even when they argued about Mr. Hunt and her dowry and her age—and she was beginning to doubt her ability to truly give him up like her father asked and she knew the duchess wanted.

She could not deny Mr. Hunt would be the perfect husband for someone in her station in life, with his immense wealth and physical attractiveness, but she was beginning to realize how little they had in common. Would she really resign herself to living in the city when she preferred fresh air and the countryside? He would hate to visit Blackmore with her if they were ever married.

Meanwhile, Will would have an entire sprawling estate to manage. Not just any estate, either. An estate that sounded like it needed help. An estate that could have used someone like her, who would happily devote her life to making her tenants and parishioners content. Well, they wouldn't be her tenants. They would be Will's, but what better man could she imagine as her husband?

He wouldn't mind if she went out all day and came home with a muddied hem after a day in the fields like another husband might. With Mr. Hunt, it would be all about society parties and keeping up appearances in London drawing rooms. She wasn't sure if she would have the stamina for such a thing.

As she stood in the drawing room, feeling rather discouraged by her predicament, she noticed Lady Clara sitting by herself on one of the settees in the corner of the room, seemingly more interested in the floor than her surroundings. Remembering the duchess's request to look after the poor girl, Elaina decided to take a deep breath, push aside her own troubles, and approach her, but even as Elaina took a seat beside her, the girl remained lost in her own thoughts.

Elaina cleared her throat, and Clara eventually looked up, jumping slightly at the sight of someone suddenly sitting beside her. Recognition seemed to pass through her face when she noticed it was only Elaina.

"I took the liberty of joining you because you looked lonely," Elaina explained. "Do you mind?"

Clara shook her head. "No, of course not!"

Elaina smiled. "Good," she said. "With the men away for

the time being, I thought now would be the perfect time to start getting to know each other."

Clara smiled. At just eighteen, her face was still almost childlike. She had small features, but round cheeks, which were especially apparent any time she laughed or smiled. Her clothes were some of the finest Elaina had ever seen in her life, and she knew Clara's family must be awfully wealthy. They would have to be if the duke had insisted on Montgomery marrying the girl. Tonight, Clara was dressed in pinkish-red silk and white-satin evening gloves, the tops of which were trimmed with fabric to match her gown.

"Thank you, Miss Walker. I'm much obliged. I'm afraid I don't know anyone here except my father, really. My aunt could not come with us, and my mother… Well, my mother has passed."

Elaina frowned at her, knowing a girl's come-out was one of the times when she really needed her mother most. The duchess had mentioned that Clara's mother died while giving birth to her. Elaina's own mother had been gone over twenty years at that point.

For the most part, the pain was nonexistent. Some days she couldn't even remember feeling any pain at all, but every once in a while, it felt like something—or rather someone— was missing in her life, even though her mother had been gone so long that she barely remembered the woman. All she had were her father's stories about her.

She often wished that her aunt would have returned her letters as a girl or even as an adult after her grandfather had passed. She would have liked to know what her mother was like through her sister's eyes, not just her husband's. Perhaps Elaina would have felt closer to her that way, and she would have had a woman to look up to in life that wasn't just the duchess.

Looking at Clara's face, Elaina wondered just how much

pain she still carried from her mother's death. Even though Clara's aunt wasn't there, Elaina hoped the girl could confide in her.

"Did you know my mother has passed as well?" Elaina asked, the words tumbling out very suddenly. "During childbirth. I was five. My little brother was lost with her."

"How terrible," Clara whispered, looking down and shaking her head. "My mother died giving birth to me as well, though I suppose I'm lucky I survived."

Elaina shook her head, wishing to change the subject, and regretted having ever brought it up. She still had trouble speaking of her mother.

"Never mind all that," she said. "It was such a long time ago, and I approached you with the hopes of bringing you comfort, not sadness. You're in a strange place where you don't know anyone, and your only companion is your father." She paused as she considered her next words, not wanting to offend her, but curious to know if she was being forced into this whole marriage scheme against her will. "Do you like your father?"

Clara nodded vigorously. "He is often busy, but I do love what time we can spend together. I'm very lucky that he and Blackmore would arrange such a debut for me."

A debut with a guaranteed suitor and engagement—how convenient, Elaina almost said, but she stopped herself just in time, knowing how bitter she would have sounded.

"And do you like it here at Blackmore Park?" Elaina asked.

"I like it, but I'd be lying if I said I didn't miss Haywood House," Clara said with a wistful sigh. With a sudden nervous look on her face, she quickly added, "Please don't tell Montgomery I said that. When he asked me the same question, I told him that I did not miss home at all and I was thrilled to be at Blackmore Park."

"Why would you lie to him about something as silly as that?" Elaina asked with a laugh. "This must be your first time away from home, right?" Clara nodded, and Elaina smiled at her. "I'm sure he would more than understand if you are a little homesick."

"I know, but I'm so afraid of offending him."

Elaina scrunched her nose in confusion. "Why on earth would confessing to being homesick offend him?"

Clara shrugged, then laughed. "I'm not sure, actually! But I do know I need him to like me so I don't disappoint Papa."

"Oh," Elaina said, biting her lip. She hadn't considered what it'd be like to be Clara, venturing out to an unfamiliar home, all the while wondering if Montgomery would keep his end of the bargain or end up embarrassing her—and her father—by rejecting her.

If he rejected her, the ton might talk about the scandal all the way into next Season, maybe even two Seasons from now. The thought of such a terrible embarrassment would make any young society girl turn into a bundle of nerves.

Elaina ended up half smiling at Clara, leaning close. She wanted to make the poor girl feel better. "If you ask me, I think Montgomery is already quite smitten," she said. "He has not been able take his eyes off you all day long, and he spent the entire evening talking to you. He never does that. Usually, he likes to mingle."

Clara's cheeks flushed. "Really?"

"Really."

That made Clara perk up, and Elaina exhaled as her own thoughts started to drift toward Will, wondering what he was doing in the other room. Would the men come through soon? She hoped they did.

"Thank you, Miss Walker," Clara said, interrupting the other girl's reverie. "This conversation has made me feel *much* better."

"Has it?"

Clara nodded.

"I'm glad," Elaina replied, smiling as she looked up, noticing that the men had started to file into the drawing room and mingle with the ladies. Although she was hoping to see Will, she saw Montgomery and Hunt first, who noticed her and Clara sitting together and started heading their way.

She watched as Clara regarded Montgomery with a sort of wide-eyed wonderment. Elaina only hoped he deserved such regard from a precious creature like Clara, who seemed so keen on impressing her betrothed. It wasn't that Elaina thought Montgomery was a bad man. She only knew he cared much more about his duty and the legacy of Blackmore than any girl, hence why it was so easy for him to remain unattached while he waited for Clara to come of age.

Elaina and Clara stood as the men got closer. "Ladies," Montgomery said, bowing before turning to Mr. Hunt. "Have you met Lady Clara Haywood, Edgerton's daughter? Lady Clara, this is Mr. Giles Hunt, one of my bankers in London."

Being the demure lady that she was, Clara curtseyed and offered Hunt one delicately gloved hand. He took it, pressing a light kiss to her knuckles. Another eighteen-year-old girl might've swooned as a result, but Clara had been nothing but dignified in her social dealings at the party so far, especially when it came to the men. Elaina could only suppose she'd been training for this event her whole life, seeing as how her marriage contract was drawn up shortly after her birth.

"Lovely to meet you, my lady," Hunt said before eyeing Elaina, who was busy scouring over the tops of heads for a glimpse of Will in the crowded room and trying to avoid his gaze, still embarrassed over what happened earlier at dinner. "I must confess I've only approached the two of you with

Montgomery to ask Miss Walker if she would take a turn about the room with me."

Elaina stopped scouring long enough to look at Hunt, trying to remain expressionless as she did so. After all, it would not be becoming of her to express disappointment at his request, as he was probably her final opportunity to escape spinsterhood. She chose to smile at him, bowing her head slightly.

"Of course," she said.

He offered her his arm, she took it, and they began to walk. After a few moments, she carefully said, "Mr. Hunt, I fear I must apologize for any forwardness I may have displayed in my dealings with Mr. Winter earlier. As you are aware, Robbie and I have known each other since we were little children, and I've come to see him as a little brother of sorts. We like to tease each other, and I fear we might've forgotten our manners. I hope you weren't too disturbed by our very frank conversation."

"Do not apologize," Hunt said, shaking his head. "I understand your close relationship to the Winters. I have witnessed it myself for the past six years, in case you have forgotten. If I had found a fault in your behavior with them, I would not be here. I must confess seeing you all together makes me wish I had siblings, or at least close cousins, of my own."

"Well, you are so close to Montgomery that I've always thought of you like another brother to me," she said before cringing slightly, immediately regretting her words, remembering this man did not want to be her brother.

He smiled politely. "And is that how you feel about Lord William?" he asked.

She briefly hesitated. "Y-yes," she finally replied, hating the way her voice faltered. "He's known me since I was five. Of course he's like a brother to me—just like Montgomery."

"You must be excited, then, to have him back home safely from the war in France. Hopefully Waterloo will finally be the end of Napoleon."

"Oh, yes, I hope so, too," she said. Carefully, she added, "But I don't think I'm any more excited to have Will home than any of his other family members. We were all worried about him, of course. He was on the Continent for eight years. Can you believe that? There were plenty of times I thought—I mean, *we* thought—he might never return."

As Hunt gazed at her, she felt increasingly uncomfortable. He looked at her as if he could see right through her. Was her affection for Will that obvious? She tried to think of something to say to Hunt that would encourage him in his pursuit, or else the duchess and Montgomery would be very cross with her by the close of the party.

"I must say I felt very flattered when you said I was the reason you came to Hampshire," she decided to say when he offered no conversation of his own, "though I can't help but feel determined to convince you that the country isn't all that bad. Perhaps it's not as invigorating as city life, but I find Blackmore Park to be invigorating in its own way."

At this, Hunt finally smiled, if only slightly. "If you are so determined, could I be so bold as to ask you to show me more of the estate tomorrow, then? I know you like to ride."

"Oh, what a splendid idea! I'd love to take you."

"Good—we'll leave after breakfast tomorrow."

"What's this I hear about a ride?"

Elaina and Hunt stopped as Will seemed to approach them out of nowhere. She glanced at Hunt, who seemed annoyed—and rightfully so. Trying not to appear unnerved, she cleared her throat before addressing Will. "I only just agreed to show Mr. Hunt more of Blackmore Park on horseback tomorrow morning."

"I see," Will said, all the while looking at her expectantly.

She had to stop herself from sighing in annoyance. She knew he was expecting an invitation as well.

"You're welcome to come as well, of course," she finally offered, shooting an apologetic glance at Hunt before she did. "Perhaps Montgomery, Clara, Robbie, and Julia would all like to join us."

She didn't dare look at Mr. Hunt's face again. Of course he must've preferred if they'd gone just the two of them, but it was a house party, and she couldn't very well limit invitations to a bit of horseback riding.

"Splendid!" Will exclaimed, clapping his hands together and looking like the picture of civility as he grinned at Hunt. "Now, do you mind if I steal Miss Walker from you for a moment, Mr. Hunt? Nice to see you again, by the way, though we are much older now, aren't we? Anyway, the duchess was looking for her and asked me to retrieve her."

"Be my guest," Hunt said, though Elaina detected a hint of annoyance in his voice and reluctantly moved from one man's arm to the other. Will promptly led her out of the drawing room, straight past the duchess without so much as a word of explanation. Elaina glared at him, not even bothering to ask for an explanation behind his deceit.

"Where are you taking me?" she asked.

"You'll find out soon enough."

"Back so soon, Hunt?" Graham asked. He was in the middle of a conversation with Clara when his friend returned to them with Elaina nowhere to be found.

Hunt only shrugged. "Your brother said the duchess wanted to see her."

Graham frowned. His mother was standing across the room with a group of her friends. Elaina and Will were nowhere to be found. He gritted his teeth. Perhaps he should've expected his brother to act rashly, but Elaina? She knew better.

"What's the matter, Montgomery?"

Graham looked over at Clara and smiled. Her face was almost angelic in quality, and he liked that she was tall. She was polite and able to carry a conversation. All good qualities for a wife to have.

Why then, could he not stop thinking of Marianne?

He shook his head, forcing the thoughts of his mistress from his head. "Nothing at all. Why don't you tell Hunt that story you told me about your governess? Hunt, you have to hear this."

Clara grinned, and Montgomery became quite determined to do two things that night: one, fall deeply and passionately in love with Clara Haywood, and two, prevent his brother and Elaina from doing anything stupid.

CHAPTER SIX

Your father has commissioned an architect to construct a hothouse for Blackmore Park! He also told me that I can determine what we plant over the winter—isn't that exciting? By next spring, we'll have a whole collection of tropical flowers and fruit growing at Blackmore, and I'll be in charge of it all. Perhaps with Napoleon finally being banished to Elba, you will be able to come home and see it, too.

—an excerpt of a letter from Elaina, written during the summer of 1814, to Will

WILL KNEW he was being a fool by acting so rashly, but the sight of Elaina traversing the room with Hunt was enough to set him into ill-advised action. He would not let her throw herself away on that man, especially when Hunt could never appreciate Elaina like he could.

He would entertain her love of the country and of Blackmore for the length of the house party, but if he returned to London with a promise of marriage from her, that was where his consideration would end, and there was only one way to ensure Elaina would never face such disappointment.

He was leading her toward the library, which was empty and dark, making it and its adjacent conservatory the perfect spot for a secret rendezvous between two lovers—not that Will considered Elaina to be his lover. Not yet, anyway, though she would be soon enough.

He passed through the room with Elaina on his arm very slowly, careful not to bump into any furniture until they came to the double glass doors which led to one of the conservatories that flanked the south side of the house. This one was relatively small, making a half-circle shape over a floor of gray stone tiles. The roof was domed and made of glass, and the entire structure was framed out with white-painted iron.

There were some chairs, benches, and tables set out in the center of the room, each of them facing the house's southern gardens. Potted plants littered the perimeter of the glass room and its various surfaces. There was no light except for the moon, which was full that night, providing just enough light so that Will could make out Elaina's face while they stood together in the conservatory.

Coming to a stop near one of the settees, he looked down at her. He supposed he should speak first, but nothing quite came to mind as he looked at her, too transfixed by her beauty.

"What is the meaning of this?" Elaina finally asked, breaking away from him and placing her hands on her hips. She looked like some sort of defiant little warrior glaring up at him. "If someone finds us here, they'll think the worst, and I'll be ruined."

He couldn't help but grin at her, thinking to himself that such a discovery would be the best-case scenario, saving him much future trouble from trying to convince her they were made for each other. "Maybe that's the point."

"William!" she exclaimed, her eyes widening. He could only laugh at her outraged response. "How dare you say that! You are being ridiculous! We aren't children anymore, and we cannot just run off together whenever we please to wherever we please. I am going back to the drawing room."

She started to turn away, but he reached out and grabbed her forearm, sheathed in protective white silk, pulling her closer to him. Her soft body collided into his hard one, and she nearly yelped, her mouth slightly parted as she looked up at him with what seemed more like curiosity than annoyance.

He smiled, pleased with what efficiency he was able to get past her more sensible notions. Before she could say anything, he softly asked, "And why can't we run off together whenever we please to wherever we please?"

"Because… because…" Her lips twisted and pursed as her eyes darted across his face. She seemed to be struggling to find the words until they came pouring out of her all at once. "Because we have responsibilities now! Your father has expectations of you, your mother has expectations of me, and your brother has expectations of both of us. If we are caught together, think of all the people we'll disappoint! We'll be forced to marry, which is something no one wants."

"Do not say no one wants it," he practically growled, narrowing his eyes as he tugged her even closer to him. "I want it."

She shook her head, using her hand to push against his chest in a failed attempt to put some distance between them. He only grabbed onto her other forearm as a result, holding her still against him. She made a sound of annoyance before speaking again.

"And you're a fool for it," she said through clenched teeth.

"You could have any girl you want. You could have a girl with fifty thousand pounds! I'm sure there are plenty back in the drawing room. Why don't you try to seduce them?"

"Do you truly not understand, Elaina?" he asked, practically groaning the words. "Money is not what makes a man want to seduce a woman."

"I've seen enough of society to disagree."

"You are talking about society dandies who would never touch an innocent girl because they know the consequences of such an act. As for me, I'm no dandy. Unlike them, I know the consequences and am willing to face them for you."

She looked down, shaking her head slightly. "You don't know what you're saying."

"I've been fighting since I was sixteen. For eight bloody years, I've been fighting, and do you know what kept me going?" She looked back up at him, her jaw clenched, silent. When she did not respond, he shook his head and continued, his voice strained. "I fear I've misspoken. It's not what, but who. It was you, Elaina. The image of you, sitting at your desk, writing me a letter, smiling as you told me about your day taking care of all the tenants here with your father and the prospect of growing tropical fruit in the duke's new hothouse. I always knew I would return home eventually, and it wasn't because I was hoping my father would buy me an estate."

He sighed, letting go of her as he turned around and ran his fingers through his hair. "It was because I was hoping for *you*," he murmured, low enough that he wasn't sure if she even heard him. He moved to sit on one of the benches in the conservatory, facing the opposite direction of her and staring out the windows into the moonlit gardens. Looking back at her after a moment, he said, "I was hoping now that we were older, we could have a real future together. I suppose I wasn't expecting everyone to be so vehemently against us."

He turned away again, thinking perhaps he had been too bold with his feelings until he heard the shuffling of her skirts as she moved to sit beside him. She sniffed, and he turned to look at her. She pressed at her cheek with the back of her gloves. He procured a handkerchief from his pocket, handing it to her to use instead.

"Please," she said, her voice strained as she pressed the tiny cloth against the corner of her eyes, "please do not say such sweet things. It will only make everything more difficult."

"But why must things be difficult?" he asked, moving closer to her on the bench, so their knees were touching, skin separated only by two layers of thin fabric. He took her hands into his. "I know what my father wants, but I doubt marrying you will be the last thing I ever do that's against his wishes."

"I owe your parents my entire life," she said after a moment's pause, furrowing her brow as she shook her head, looking at the floor instead of him. She turned back to him, frowning. "I cannot disappoint them by coming in between you and what could be a great fortune."

"I do not want a great fortune, Elaina. I want *you*."

Tired of talking, especially when he was unable to talk any sense into her, his mouth covered hers, breathing in a little gasp from her mouth as he did. He half expected her to push him away, but she seemed to welcome his advances willingly—if not eagerly. This was no chaste kiss from memory. Soon his lips parted hers, and their tongues were intertwined.

Will released her hands to wrap his arms around her waist, pulling her closer to him to ensure she couldn't escape. Their torsos were facing each other, but their legs were still parallel as they sat next to each other on the bench. He moved his hand to grip one of her thighs, forcing both her legs up and over his so they were resting on the top of his lap.

When he finally pulled away from her to catch his breath, they stared at each other for a moment. She simply blinked at him twice until she kissed him again herself, bringing one of her hands to the left side of his face.

Smirking against her mouth, he slowly slid his hand back up her thigh and over her hip and waist, letting it rest just beneath her breast, forming a V-shape with his thumb and index finger. Her kisses were so warm and soft and inviting, and he couldn't help but slide his other hand lower, squeezing the plump skin where her torso met her buttocks. Using both of his hands, he grabbed her bottom and hoisted her upwards, positioning her so she was sitting directly on his lap. She yelped in response, their mouths breaking apart.

He managed to calm her by kissing her neck, finding that sweet spot where her jaw met her throat, causing her to tilt her head back and moan. He held her body steady by encircling his hands around her ribcage, just below her breasts. He savored her little sounds of pleasure as he explored her neck with his tongue and mouth. God, she tasted so good, better than he had ever imagined. His most devious daydreams could not be compared to reality. The pleasure was even more intense now that it was real.

He made his way back up from her neck to her lips, and she eagerly returned his attentions with her own mouth and tongue. He thought he may have felt her shiver underneath his hands, just as he started to gently pull and suck on her lower lip with his teeth.

Her eyes half closed and her cheeks flushed, he pulled her in deeper now, drinking her up, thoroughly enjoying the way she was becoming more and more daring as she explored his mouth with her tongue and her hands traced mindless patterns across his chest and back. He felt himself growing more and more hungry for her as she did, especially when she started to squirm in his lap in an attempt to move even closer to him.

She must've felt his growing erection underneath her bottom, as there was no hiding it at that point. He quietly groaned against her lips, the friction between them almost becoming too much to bear without the promise of some sort of physical release.

She broke away from him then, gasping and struggling to stand up, nearly losing her balance in her attempt to separate herself from him so quickly. When she finally made it to her feet, she moved away from the bench, looking down as she went. With her back facing him, he feared her expression would be one of regret.

"We should stop," she finally said, wrapping her arms around herself, still facing away from him when she spoke.

"Why?" he asked, standing up as well, his voice serious. He would keep her there for as long as it took for her to stop denying her feelings. She had to know marrying Hunt would be pure lunacy by now, especially after all that had just occurred between them.

"Because you are trying to seduce me, and I will not allow it."

He couldn't help but laugh at her overly pious tone of voice. "Well," he said, "you would not listen to reason. You gave me no choice but to seduce you. You had your chance to run away before, but you didn't. You stayed, and you played a willing part in my devious plan. You must marry me now—for propriety's sake."

"Your parents will never allow it, regardless of propriety."

"I will throw you in a carriage and take you to Gretna Green if I must!"

She spun around and glared at him. "How dare you threaten me with such a thing!" she exclaimed. "Stop acting like such a beast." Crossing her arms across her chest and sticking her chin up into the air, she said, "I will go nowhere with you. One kiss doesn't mean anything."

"One kiss?" he scoffed, stepping toward, closing the distance between them once more. "One kiss? That was much more than one kiss, Elaina."

"You're right, and I shouldn't have allowed you such liberties!" she nearly shouted back, clenching her fists into tiny little balls beside her. They stared at each other in silence, both of their chests rising and falling with vigor.

They stood like that for a long moment, staring at each other, all the while he fought the urge to take her into his arms once more. He wondered if she was struggling in the same way. Judging by the way her eyes kept betraying her by darting toward his lips, he didn't think it was too far from the truth.

When Elaina finally calmed down, she turned away and started to speak again, this time much more softly. "We ought to go back to the drawing room. Someone will have noticed we are gone."

He came in between her and the door that led back to the library. She wasn't getting off that easy. He bent over, whispering in her ear, "What are you so afraid of?"

She grumbled a few incoherent words under her breath, then said, "I'm *afraid* of being caught, and you should be as well!"

"What's there to be afraid of?" he asked, letting out a low laugh. "They'll have no choice but to let us marry—"

"And I will be subject to more shame and humiliation than I already have from being born to a fine lady and a lowly land steward, with a family who won't even speak to her in public or private!" she exclaimed, glaring at him. "Do you only think of yourself now that you're older? You say you're not like most men, but I see no difference in your character from any other. If you'll excuse me—"

"Wait," he said after she had already pushed him out of the way and was almost inside the library, feeling only slightly remorseful when he considered Elaina's precarious position in society. He would still stop at nothing to have her, but his intentions did not align with embarrassing or shaming her. "I'm sorry."

She shook her head, turning around and slowly walking back toward him. "I'm sorry as well, but it's just not meant to be. Surely you must realize that. I wish it were different... but it's not, and there's nothing either one of us can do about it."

He watched her as she practically ran away from him, his heart sinking like a brick in water. He paced the room, leaning over to pick up the handkerchief he had given her. At some point it must've fallen onto the floor of the conservatory. He folded the piece of fabric, slightly damp from her tears, and put it back in his jacket pocket.

He should've known she wouldn't be swayed with only some kisses and a few gentle caresses. She was much too logical to be overtaken by passion for too long. There was also the allegiance she felt toward his mother and father, who were like parents to her as well, and he considered for a moment that he might've been going about winning her hand the entirely wrong way.

Perhaps he had to convince his parents of the idea before he could convince her, but could he really count on them to listen to reason? They'd be perfectly content to watch her married off to Hunt, who was so completely and utterly wrong for the girl. Surely they already knew how miserable she would be living in London with him year-round. They just didn't care.

Frustrated, he sat back down on the bench. The air was

humid, and he swore he could still feel the lingering heat of their bodies clumsily intertwined there. Hunt may have been wealthier than him, but he could never match the passion he felt for Elaina.

Why should money have anything to do with marriage, anyway? Will believed matrimony should be a matter of the heart and the heart alone. Then again, perhaps his ideals were too high. He didn't know many people who married for affection and affection alone. Montgomery and Clara came to mind.

He sighed. He would not be like them, marrying due to the advantage of it alone. He could not be like them.

In the meantime, he had to get back to the drawing room. As he sat there and considered the rich society darlings currently gathered in his parents' house, he had an idea. If he would be forced to watch Elaina entertain the likes of Hunt, she would be forced to watch him entertain girls with much larger dowries than her. Perhaps that would make her think twice before throwing herself away on Hunt.

With a devilish grin, he stood up, smoothed his breeches, and then started to make his way back to the drawing room.

Elaina returned to the drawing room in a daze, unable to comprehend exactly what just happened between her and Will. The kisses they shared in the conservatory that evening were nothing like the one they first shared as teenagers over ten years ago. That kiss might as well have been nothing at all in comparison, for it had not left her shaky and breathless and feeling out of control with desire and need. She had nearly lost all her good sense with the touch of his lips.

Although she practically leapt off his lap to escape him, it took all of her remaining self-control to do so. Perhaps there was a bit of fear, as well, since she'd never been that close to a man before.

She had felt the growing hunger of his groin against her bottom, and she knew if they didn't stop, their secret rendezvous in the conservatory would have resulted in something she could not take back. She may have been an innocent, but she knew enough about sex to know how it could ruin a young woman—and she could not afford to be ruined.

She resolved then and there that it would not happen again. She would avoid him if she must, even if it pained her to do so. She did not find Hunt nearly as thrilling as Will, but he was the more suitable companion for the remainder of the house party, considering her position. In terms of marriage, Elaina could not offer what Will needed, and he could not offer what she needed.

Will's job was to marry and grow the Winter coffers, and Elaina's job was to marry so she could finally stop being their responsibility. If they married each other, neither responsibility would be filled, and she had decided she had already taken too much from them. How could she expect them to give her one of their sons as well?

"Miss Walker."

Elaina nearly jumped. She had not noticed Montgomery approach her from her side. "My lord," she said, taking a frightful breath but still managing to smile as she placed a hand to her chest. "You startled me."

He frowned. "I apologize. I didn't intend to."

"Where's Lady Clara?" Elaina asked, looking around the room for her, but she was nowhere in sight. Elaina frowned, hoping the poor girl was okay.

"She's already retired for the evening. She was tired after her long journey from Wiltshire today." He paused, then added, "I feel as if we haven't spoken at all this evening."

"You have kept yourself busy for most of it," she said, shooting him a sly look.

"Yes, well, the duke made it clear that anything short of a dream proposal for the girl would be considered a slight against Edgerton," he said. "Hopefully my intentions are clear now, as I have no desire to shirk my side of the deal."

"Of course you don't," Elaina murmured. "That's not quite like you, is it?" She paused a moment, then added, "For the record, I quite like Clara. She's as kind as she is pretty, and a good match for you, I think. Do you agree?"

He shrugged. "I can't help but wonder what it would have been like to set out to London one Season with the intention of marrying someone and choosing a girl for myself. Instead, I've been forced to be guarded in my emotions all my life. Attaching myself to someone who wasn't Clara would have been a recipe for disaster." He took a breath, as if being that honest all at once was too much for him. "Now, all of the sudden, I'm supposed to let down my guard and create lasting affection with a girl much younger than me who I've never met before this very day." He paused for a moment, half smiling, then added, "But you are right. She is pretty, and she is kind. It's just not as easy as one might think."

Elaina nodded once, her eyes drifting away, finding Mr. Hunt standing with some others across the room. Turning back to Montgomery, she said, "No, it's not."

Montgomery looked down, shifting his weight from foot to foot with his hands clasped behind his back. He looked as if he wanted to say something but was hesitating until he eventually blurted out, "You know I care about you, Miss Walker—right? I know I was not nice to you as a child, but I've come to think of you as a younger sister over the past six years."

She smiled at him. "Yes, Montgomery. I know—and I think of you as an older brother."

"Which is why I feel I must tell you to proceed with caution in certain matters having to do with the heart. I know it's exciting having Will home, but Mr. Hunt has traveled all the way here with the sole purpose of seeing you, and he's been courting you since the spring."

Elaina sighed, closing her eyes as she brought her thumb and forefinger to her temples. "You noticed Will and I were missing, didn't you?"

Montgomery nodded once.

"Did Mr. Hunt notice?"

"I think everyone might've noticed, Elaina."

"What will you have me do, then? Marry Will? Apologize to Mr. Hunt?"

Montgomery shook his head. "Neither—unless you think an apology is necessary. Spend time with him, Elaina. Open your heart to him. You might find he's not all that bad."

"I never said he was!"

"I know, but surely you know that no man wants to feel second best to another."

Elaina thought of Will. He often described himself as second best. Could she really shove aside her feelings just to make Montgomery happy? She didn't particularly want to make Will feel second best to Hunt, though she knew she might have to.

"You know, Elaina, if my brother doesn't marry well, his future might be in danger."

Elaina furrowed her brow. "What do you mean?"

"Has my brother told you anything about Larkspur Castle?"

"Only a bit," she admitted, biting her lip. Then, she shook her head. "Truthfully, not at all. All I know is it's in Cambridgeshire."

Montgomery nodded once. "That's right," he said. "My father bought it for a good price from an earl who desperately needed the money to maintain his dubious lifestyle in London. It'll take a lot of money to make it a successful estate, since I'm afraid it was neglected for so many years. There are barely any tenants left. Most of the land hasn't been farmed in years. The town is poor. The house lacks furniture and the more modern amenities of a house such as this. He'll need the dowry of a rich lady or heiress to make it successful."

Elaina pursed her lips, regarding him. She knew exactly what he meant. "Something I don't have."

Montgomery frowned. "Well, yes. Elaina, I'm sorry, but—"

She shook her head, effectively silencing him. "Can I ask you something, my lord? If all that was true, why would Blackmore buy the land in the first place? You make it sound like a lost cause."

"My father believes Will is up for the challenge."

"And part of that challenge is marrying well, I assume."

He nodded. "I suppose so."

She was silent at first, unsure of what to say. Why would the duke put his younger son in such a position? To test his devotion to the family name? Of course she didn't want to be the reason Will failed, but she also couldn't deny her strong feelings for him.

"I have no desire to be the reason your brother fails at his living," Elaina said. "I... I apologize for my indiscretion—"

"Elaina, you do not have to—"

"No," she said, shaking her head. "I apologize, and it will not happen again. Now, if you'll excuse me, I'd like to find Hunt and at least try to explain myself. Do not worry about me any longer, Montgomery. I have this all well in hand."

He half smiled at her. "You always do, don't you?"

CHAPTER SEVEN

Although my first Season was exciting, I'm finding my second more and more tedious. Your mother parades me around ballrooms like I'm a prize to be won. Some prize I am with only a thousand-pound dowry! I wish I could find some other girl here who finds the whole thing demeaning. I'm sure she exists. In fact, I'm almost sure most girls feel the same way as me, they're only too afraid to say something. At least Montgomery and his friend Mr. Hunt make for good enough company.

—an excerpt of a letter from Elaina, written in April 1810, to Will

WHEN WILL RETURNED to the drawing room, he immediately sought out his cousin Robert. If anyone could tell him the most eligible lady at the party with a fortune that could save Larkspur from ruin, it would be Robbie. Of course, he had not really known Robbie since Eton, but whenever he came up in Elaina's letters—and even his own mother's—he was always described with a tinge of disdain over his more rakish qualities. Will always gave him the benefit of the doubt, considering he was always much kinder to him at boarding school than Montgomery.

"Cousin William," he said when saw Will approaching him, a lopsided grin forming on his face. As a child, Robbie always had an easy way about him, a trait which only seemed to have been amplified as he grew older. He gestured to the man standing beside him. "Have you met my friend the Marquess of Seymour yet?"

Will shook his head. "I'm afraid not," he said. To Seymour, he gave a slight bow of the head. "How do you do, my lord?"

"Seymour, this is my cousin Lord William, the duke's younger son," Robbie explained. "He's just back from the war... well, today, actually. Isn't that right?"

"I believe I only arrived a few hours before the rest of the party did," he confirmed, studying Seymour as he did. Like his companion, the marquess was young and handsome, though a bit taller and thinner, with darker hair and no defining scars.

"Did you have any idea what you were walking into?" Robbie asked with a slight chuckle.

"I'm afraid not," Will replied, laughing as well. Looking around the room, he added, "I left my interview with the duchess this morning only to go to luncheon with her, where I was trumpeted around to every female here as if I were some sort of war hero. I'm afraid I'll only disappoint them when it comes out that I have no great battle stories to share with them."

"Ah, that's where you're wrong," Robbie said. "You'll only disappoint them if you insist on talking about yourself instead of asking them questions about their hair or their jewelry instead."

"Is your opinion of the fairer sex that low, Cousin Robert?"

Robbie nodded gravely. "Afraid so."

"Tell me, Robbie, if you had to pick one, whom would you choose?"

His cousin shuddered. "No woman here could possibly tempt me into the lifelong prison of marriage. I believe we've already established that Elaina would make for a fine wife if I didn't feel so much sisterly affection for her... and if you didn't nearly slit my throat with your dinner knife for saying so."

"Sorry about that," Will replied, shaking his head. "I'm afraid I'm a bit overprotective of her, especially now that I'm here to witness it all. The idea of a so-called marriage mart was much more bearable when it was only relayed in her letters, especially when I was still picturing her as..."

"An untamable tomboy?" Robbie filled in for him.

"Well, yes," he said with a slight laugh.

"She has changed, hasn't she?"

Nodding once, he slowly realized he would talk about Elaina all evening long if he didn't change the subject then. He turned to Seymour, asking, "And what about you, my lord? Who do you find to be the most eligible lady here?"

He shrugged. "I'm afraid your brother has claim over the most eligible lady here. Lady Clara is the daughter of a duke *and* uncommonly pretty, not to mention in possession of a sizeable dowry."

Will nodded once, unable to deny that the girl was pretty, beautiful even, though she was nowhere to be found now, not to mention unsuitable for his purposes. If he hadn't been mesmerized by Elaina since his return, perhaps he would have been jealous of his brother, for it wasn't so often that arranged marriages saw not one, but two handsome people joined together in matrimony. Standing together, Clara and Montgomery appeared to be equals in every way, both tall, slender, and fair, with the type of looks that made one wonder if they ever had a bad day in their lives, though Will had a sneaking suspicion that Clara's heart was much larger —not to mention much more giving—than his brother's.

"Fifty thousand pounds just to marry her," Robbie said, corroborating Seymour's point. He whistled, turning to Will. "Even I, who despises the idea of marriage, can think of much worse fates. Fifty thousand pounds! Can you imagine?"

Will shook his head. "As a mere second son, I'm afraid I cannot. The duke tells me I must marry for money, though I'm not sure what rich woman would settle for a courtesy title."

"Ah, yes," Robbie said, nodding his head as he took a sip of the amber-colored beverage he had been nursing, "I heard my uncle demanded you home so he could unload some disastrous estate in Cambridgeshire on you. I tried to tell him there were much smarter investments to make in this day and age, but he insisted on purchasing the property for you."

"If only he had listened to you," Will replied with a grimace. Not wishing to talk of Larkspur, Will quickly changed the subject back to that of eligible ladies, this time being less discreet in his request. "Tell me, if I were looking for a rich girl who wasn't my brother's intended fiancée, is there anyone you'd recommend?"

Robbie seemed to consider this. "Well, that depends. If you're looking for money and money alone, look no further than Miss Margaret Arnold. Mr. Arnold was a wealthy merchant and left everything to his two daughters when he died, though I should probably note that the youngest is illegitimate and has yet to leave the schoolroom. Thanks to money and connections on her mother's side, Miss Arnold was able to claw her way into fine society. Her cousins are actually your neighbors, which is why she's here for the party."

"You mean the Mortons?" Will asked, furrowing his brow.

Robbie nodded. "They're how she's been able to secure an invitation to your parents' house party every year. If you're looking for rich, she's it, though I wouldn't describe her as good looking myself. She's a funny, peculiar sort of girl. Very short and much too thin. Features a bit mouse-ish, not unlike my sister. Not at all attractive, if you ask me."

Seymour snorted then. "He's only saying that because he's been on the receiving end of Miss Arnold's barbed tongue more than once in his life."

"Oh?" Will asked.

Robbie grinned, as if he was remembering something funny. "We like picking on each other, me and Miss Arnold. I think it's become a bit of a pastime for both of us. Don't you think, Seymour?"

Seymour clucked his tongue. "Whatever you say, Robbie."

"She sounds like a gem," Will interjected as the two other men shared a laugh. "Will you introduce me?"

Robbie nodded, looking around the room and stopping when he appeared to have found the woman in question. "She's over there. Come along."

Upon seeing her, Will immediately decided his cousin was wrong in his assessment of her looks. Miss Arnold *was* good looking, though she was short and slight in stature. Her hair was brown, done up in the typical curls and ribbons that he guessed were fashionable nowadays. Her eyes matched her hair. Her features were delicate, sharp, and strong, and she stood with a quiet authority. Thin nose and lips, but full cheeks. Yes, she did have a bit of a mouse-like quality to her face, just like Robbie said. He'd very much like to see his cousin on the other side of Miss Arnold's so-called barbed tongue.

"Miss Arnold," Robbie said, "have you met my cousin yet?"

She looked at Will and smiled at him, one corner of her mouth seeming to go up higher than the other, revealing a previously hidden dimple on her left cheek. "I have not, Mr. Winter. I arrived late today, so I'm afraid I wasn't at luncheon. I'm sorry to have missed it, for meeting Lord William is all the ladies have been discussing tonight. Is this him?"

"It is," Robbie replied.

"How do you do, my lord?" she asked, curtseying. "I am Margaret Arnold." With a bit of a smirk, she added, "Though I suppose I should've let Mr. Winter introduce me. He'll blame my vulgar habits on being a merchant's daughter, of course."

Robbie raised his hands in mock offense. "I would never say such a terrible thing," he said. He then leaned closer to Will, mock whispering in his ear, "Seymour did tell you she had a barbed tongue."

"I resent that, my lord!" she told Seymour. "I would have expected better from you."

Turning back to Will, she said, "I'm sure Mr. Winter and Seymour have already told you, but my cousins the Mortons are your neighbors."

Will nodded once. "I'm afraid I haven't been home in years, but I remember the Mortons fondly and was happy to see them here tonight. They would let me and Miss Walker raid their orchards whenever we wanted as children."

"My little sister is fond of those orchards as well," she said with a slight laugh. "She lives at Morton House with my cousins."

"Does she like it there?"

"Very much so," she replied. "I think she may prefer the country to the city, actually. I'm afraid I can't relate. Now, Lord William, the ladies tell me you are a war hero."

"Hardly," he said with a slight shake of the head. Meanwhile, his eyes had wandered to Elaina, who was quietly speaking with Montgomery in the corner of the room. He quickly looked back down at Miss Arnold, determined to go through with his plan. "Though I will lie and say it's true if it impresses you."

She laughed at him. "I'm afraid to tell you that my company may have benefitted greatly from the conflict with France that kept you away from your home and family."

Will shrugged. "We all must make a living somehow. Don't we, Miss Arnold?"

She nodded, seemingly in agreement. "And how will you make your living now that you've decided to retire, my lord? It is true that you've decided to retire, right?"

"That's right," he replied. "I sold my commission a month ago at my father's behest, shortly after the battle at Waterloo."

"The duke bought my Cousin William a castle," Robbie interjected. "Could there be a better homecoming gift, Miss Arnold?"

"My, did he, really? A castle?" she asked. She furrowed her brow. "What does one *do* with a castle, exactly?"

Will laughed. Miss Arnold was indeed a funny, peculiar girl, just like Robbie said, easy to talk to with bits of her sense of humor showing up intermittently. If he had to feign interest in someone, he supposed he should be glad it was her. She would be no bore.

"I believe I'm meant to fix it up and make the land surrounding it profitable again," he explained.

She crinkled her nose, looking to Robbie and Seymour. "Some gift that is!"

"This may be the first thing we agree upon, Miss Arnold," Robbie remarked.

"I suppose there really is a first time for everything."

"Do you ride, Miss Arnold?" Will asked after watching her and Robbie exchange a glance that made him question whether or not his cousin truly despised her as much as he said he did.

"I do—not well, though. I actually learned while staying with the Mortons during my summers as a child there. Why?"

"Earlier today I overheard Miss Walker and Mr. Hunt planning a ride tomorrow morning and decided to invite myself," he said. "I'd love it if you would join us." Turning to Robbie and Seymour, he added, "You're welcome to come as well, gentlemen."

"What is a country house party without a good ride?" Miss Arnold asked. "What time will you leave?"

"Shortly after breakfast, I believe."

Miss Arnold nodded once. "Then shall we convene again in the entrance hall tomorrow morning, gentlemen?"

"I would be delighted," Robbie said. "Shall we have a rematch of last year's horse race, Miss Arnold?"

She snickered. "Only if you would like to lose again, Mr. Winter."

"Cockiness does not become you, Miss Arnold."

"Nor you."

AFTER SPEAKING TO MONTGOMERY, Elaina made a point of devoting the rest of the evening to being by Hunt's side. She was pleased when he didn't mention the earlier scene with Will, or ask what the duchess had wanted, especially when it was clear to both of them that she had just been missing with another man for at least fifteen minutes.

In turn, he seemed pleased when she listened attentively to what he had to say, to her and to others, and even more so when she laughed at his jokes. They had a charming evening together, and any error on Elaina's part seemed forgotten.

She did find her eyes wandering at one point, looking for Will, almost out of instinct. She could not deny that she was almost subconsciously drawn to him, but he seemed to have found company with Robbie, Lord Seymour, and Margaret Arnold. She quickly looked away, frowning. It appeared he had found his rich heiress.

That was the only time she lost focus on Hunt.

She found herself wondering later that night, after she had retired to bed, whether or not she could live with being Hunt's wife. Truthfully, she and Mr. Hunt had always had a pleasant time together, even when she thought he only saw her as Montgomery's younger sort-of sister. He'd be a better husband than most, that was certain.

Marrying him would make the duchess happy. It would even make the duke happy. Her father would no longer have to worry about her, nor would Montgomery. Although she wished to live in the country, she'd find something to do in London. Perhaps there was a charity she could involve herself in, and after that there'd be babies to worry about.

As for Will and Miss Arnold… Well, she supposed Will had to marry someone. She liked Miss Arnold well enough. Surely she and Mr. Hunt could be friends with them.

But having babies with Mr. Hunt! What a thought.

There was also the question of how he actually felt about her. Did he love her? She didn't think so. How could he? Unless he had been hiding some sort of secret yearning for her over the past six years.

And did she love him? How could she? If she loved anyone, it would be…

She forced that idea from her mind. She would have to forget about that. If she married anyone, it would have to be Hunt. She would just have to accept that. She turned in bed in an attempt to make herself more comfortable, willing her mind to be silent so she could finally fall asleep.

When morning finally came, she felt like she hadn't slept at all. She saw her father in their shared sitting room before going down for breakfast. Like usual, he was reading a newspaper, enjoying his morning coffee and a piece of buttered toast. He looked up at his daughter, smiling at her.

"Did you have a nice evening, Elaina?"

She hesitated. Had he noticed her sudden departure from the party with Will? Dreading a lecture from her father about such things, she decided to pretend she had done nothing wrong the previous night. "Yes, I did, Papa. I'm beginning to think Mr. Hunt would make a fine husband."

"Are you?" he asked, still holding the newspaper.

She nodded. "We always have such a nice time together, me and Mr. Hunt, and I feel he's less two-faced than some of my previous suitors." She nodded again, this time with more certainty. "Yes, I think he will come up to scratch."

"And you will really say yes to him when he proposes?"

Her father was staring at her in such a discerning manner from over the top of the paper that she froze. Perhaps the façade she had worked to create all night was not as impenetrable as she thought when she awoke that morning.

"Oh, Papa." She sighed, falling on the settee across from her father. "I feel I don't have much choice. Hunt and I are similar. He is an outsider like me. He is not a fine lord, just as I'm not a fine lady. Perhaps we belong together. Perhaps together, people will begin to accept me in truth instead of just show."

He lowered his newspaper on his lap. "What do you mean?"

"Oh, please, Papa," she said dismissively. "Surely you must notice it, too. How in the undercurrent of everyone's niceties toward me, and even you, we still don't really belong."

He sighed, nodding his head slightly. "Yes, I understand what you mean."

"I keep hoping…" She shook her head. "No, it's too silly to say out loud."

"What is it, my dear?"

"I keep hoping that my cousin Gillingham will write to me and tell me he wishes to accept me as part of their family. Perhaps he would be able to…"

"Offer up something more than a meager thousand pounds for you?"

She bit her lip, nodding. "Then perhaps the duke will want me as a daughter-in-law."

"My dear Elaina," his father said, frowning at her. "You should not waste your thoughts on such hopeless dreams. Whatever you decide to do, I will support—whether that's pursuing Mr. Hunt or Will. You know that, right? I was only trying to give you advice yesterday."

"Yes, I know, but I cannot discount the fact that it was good advice."

He frowned. "But it would be dishonest of me not to say how happy I was when your mother did not follow the advice of her father. If you truly care for Will—"

"No," she said, shaking her head firmly, still thinking of his family more than her own father. Why did she care so much for their opinion? She sighed. "We must not consider it as a possibility. I will go downstairs and align myself with Hunt for the rest of the party—not Will."

Mr. Walker hesitated, then nodded slightly. "Whatever you think is best, dear. I will support you either way."

She nodded once, standing up to press a kiss on the top of her father's head. "Thank you, Papa."

· · ·

IT WAS as beautiful of a morning as ever for a ride. The sun had yet to reach its apex, hanging low in the sky and leaving the air cool and pleasant for a late August day, and there was still a low mist rolling over the fields of Blackmore. The grass was wet, long blades of it sticking to Elaina's riding boots as she walked to the stables with the others.

Elaina wore a white muslin skirt with a long train that day, presently bustled in the back, with a matching shirt and spencer jacket made of robin-egg-blue velvet. Its V-shaped neckline revealed her shirt's high collar and ruffled front. The look was made complete with a black top hat and a short green veil that fell behind her.

What started out as a ride with only Mr. Hunt turned into a ride with many of the young people at the party, including Will, Montgomery, Lady Clara, Cousins Robert and Julia, Robbie's friend Lord Seymour, and Miss Arnold.

Will seemed to pay extra attention to Miss Arnold. Elaina refused to allow herself to become jealous as a result. She had practically begged him to take an interest in anyone but her at the party, and now her wish was complete. If he was trying to achieve a reaction out of her, though, she was determined not to give him one.

As she rode side by side with Hunt, refocusing her attention on him rather than Will, she took the time to point out the various landmarks along the way.

"You know Blackmore very well, don't you, Miss Walker?" he asked about halfway through their ride.

She nodded once, smiling out of pride. "I like to think I know it better than even Montgomery."

"Will you be sad to part with it one day?"

"Do you mean if I eventually marry?"

He nodded once.

"Yes, but I like to think I'll remain friends with the Winters and be able to visit occasionally. Besides, my father lives here as well. He will want to see me even after I've gone, even if the Winters grow tired of me."

She laughed, and Mr. Hunt smiled at her. "You know, Miss Walker, I don't think I've ever seen you half as happy in the middle of a Season as you are right now."

"It's a shame you don't like the country. Then you might see me this happy all the time."

"I'm finding I don't find the country nearly as boring with the right company. Perhaps you are the right company."

"Perhaps," she replied. A growing anxiety rose up within her, probably due to the nature of their conversation. She looked behind her to see Will watching her as he rode beside Miss Arnold. She immediately turned away, looking back toward Hunt. "Are you sure you aren't just humoring me, Mr. Hunt?"

He shook his head. "Never, Miss Walker," he replied. "You have me wanting to buy my own big country house and plot of parkland somewhere with the way you talk about it so passionately."

"I suppose a man with your wealth could do such a thing, couldn't he?" she asked, raising a brow. "Would you get any use of the place, though, with all your business in London?"

Elaina knew Mr. Hunt operated one of the biggest banks in London. Did a man like him ever get a day off?

He shrugged. "A man in my position could also afford to hire help. Perhaps it's not a bad idea. My mother often says I work too much."

"Does she?"

He nodded. "Yes. In fact, she says I'd have a much better chance at finding a wife if I did not spend so much time at the bank. Despite not taking part in society, she's not so different from the duchess and the other marriage-minded mamas of the ton."

"But if she does not take part in society, she must not like balls. In that case, she's very different from the duchess and her friends."

"My mother had her day in the sun. Then she married my father."

Elaina furrowed her brow. "What does that mean?"

He shook his head. "Nothing. I shouldn't have said anything."

Elaina found his secretiveness peculiar, but rather than fall into an uncomfortable silence, she asked him, "And why haven't you married, Mr. Hunt?"

"I suppose I just haven't met the right woman, just like—"

"I haven't met the right man," she finished for him, smiling. "My favorite excuse. I use it all the time with the duchess."

"Is that your only excuse, Miss Walker?" he asked, looking at something—or someone—in the distance behind her. Somehow she knew he was looking at Will. She forced a smile.

"I'm afraid so," she murmured.

They rode a leisurely six miles before they stopped, resting for a picnic at the top of St. Catherine's Hill, the former site of an ancient fort built some thousands of years ago from which one could observe the city of Winchester below. An overgrown, old mizmaze was also located on the hill, and it was a bit of a local mystery as to who made it in the first place. Supposedly, one of the students at Winchester College had been banished to the hill for misbehaving one summer and made it out of boredom. Elaina found it to be a rather farfetched explanation, but she enjoyed the mizmaze nevertheless. When she finished her food, she stood up and announced her intention to traverse the maze.

Irritatingly enough, Will was the first to volunteer to join her. Mr. Hunt remained unmoved upon the other man's declaration, though she looked at him hopefully, while Miss

Arnold did not cease her conversation with Robbie and Seymour, leaving Elaina and Will to go off on their own.

GILES WATCHED as Elaina and Will walked toward the mizmaze with a sense of calmness. After Elaina showed so much interest in him last night and that morning, he knew her mind was with him. Her heart was another matter altogether, but he didn't take Elaina for the type of woman to allow passion to override her more logical senses.

Montgomery must've felt differently, judging by the way he stalked over to him shortly after Elaina and Will left.

"Why did you not go with them?" he asked softly. Out of all the Winters, Montgomery seemed the most worried about Elaina's future. For some reason, the marquess did not want Elaina to end up with his brother. He said he only wanted her and his brother to have successful futures with their own respective well-to-do spouses, but Giles suspected something else may have been going on. Perhaps the man was afraid his brother would end up getting what he wanted while he was forced to follow his father's orders and marry a girl he barely knew.

"Don't you have other things to worry about?" Giles asked, eyeing Clara, who was now sitting by herself, over Montgomery's shoulder.

"Yes, but right now I'm worried about you."

"Don't worry, Montgomery," Giles said coolly. "I have it well in hand."

"Funny. That's what she said last night, yet here we are."

"Don't you trust her?"

"Not with him."

Giles shook his head. "She's an intelligent woman. She won't throw her life away on him and some estate in Cambridgeshire."

"For her sake, I hope you're right."

"Are you enjoying the outing?" Will asked when he and Elaina were out of earshot of the others.

"Yes," she replied as she ran her fingertips over the tops of long grass, maneuvering her way through the narrow and winding path of dirt. "One couldn't ask for a more beautiful morning for a ride and a picnic. What about you? Are you enjoying yourself, my lord?"

"My lord?" Will echoed. "I don't think you've ever called me that." When she didn't bother to respond, he added, "I am enjoying myself, *Miss Walker*. Miss Arnold makes for very fine company, though I suspect she is more interested in Cousin Robert than me."

"Robbie?" she asked incredulously. "Those two never stop bickering whenever I have the displeasure of being in both of their companies. Apart, they are fine, but together..."

Elaina made a face, and Will laughed. "Is bickering not a sign of affection?"

Elaina tilted her head, considering such an idea. "I suppose in some cases, yes," she replied, "but it could hardly make for a happy marriage to be constantly arguing about the most minute things."

"I suppose you're right," Will said. "In that case, do you think *I* have a shot at winning Miss Arnold's heart?"

Elaina suddenly stopped, causing Will to bump into her back. He lightly gripped her waist for balance, and she spun around, pushing his hands away, too easily reminded of the passionate kiss they shared only the night before. She looked over his shoulder. Although they were out of sight of Montgomery and the others, she could still hear their conversation from last night in her head. She refused to be the reason Will failed. He would not throw away his life due to some unfounded, ridiculous obsession with her.

"You mustn't touch me like that," she scolded in a low voice. "If Mr. Hunt sees—"

"Firstly, you're the one who abruptly stopped in front of me," Will said, his tone irritated. "Running into you could hardly be avoided. Secondly, so what if he sees? You'll be forced to marry me then, and I will win this game you insist on playing."

"This is not a *game*!"

They stared at each other for a moment, Elaina's chest rising and falling with rapidly growing frustration. He had to know that both of their futures were at stake here. Miss Arnold could be the perfect companion for him, but he was being too stubborn to see it.

"And what of winning Miss Arnold's heart?" she finally asked. Shaking her head, she added, "You reveal yourself much too easily, Will. If you're going to attempt to make me jealous, you should try committing to the act of preferring someone's company to mine for longer than only one morning."

"Ah, now we're back to Will," he said. Moving closer to her, he slipped a hand behind her waist, palming her closer to him. "Perhaps I have given up my act too quickly, but tell me, Elaina, have I succeeded at all in making you consider what your life would be like if you were with Hunt and I were with another woman?"

"Yes, you have," she replied. She took a deep breath, knowing her next words must be firm and resolute in tone, though they might not have been completely genuine. "And I've determined I would be quite happy. Mr. Hunt is agreeable enough, and I think I could enjoy Miss Arnold as a friend as much as I enjoy you as one."

"Friend?" he scoffed. "Surely that's not all you see in me, especially after what we shared last night."

She was sure she was blushing, very aware of how close they were standing. There were mere inches separating their lips, and his open palm on her back felt hot against her. Repeating what happened last night would have been easy. All she had to do was close the distance between them and invite him inside, but she could not. She would not for his sake. She could care less if she married him and ended up impoverished living in a drafty old castle, but he did not deserve the burden of a penniless wife.

"That's all I see in you, my lord," she finally said, her tone even. He looked away, sharply inhaling, as if her words stung him. "We should return now. Me to Mr. Hunt and you to Miss Arnold. She is a smart match for you, you know."

He abruptly let go of her then, causing her to almost lose her balance. "Is she?" he asked. "How do you mean?"

"She is pretty, clever, and wealthy," she replied, tilting her chin upwards with a slight look of indignation. "What more could a man ask for?"

He laughed once. "I'm afraid there's much more a man could ask for, Miss Walker," he said, taking off his hat and rubbing a bead of sweat from his temple with the back of his hand before turning around and walking back to the party at the top of the hill.

Giles was probably the first to notice Will coming back from the mizmaze. Montgomery's younger brother looked frustrated, and he couldn't help but smile as a result. He knew Elaina would not give Will what he wanted, especially if he continued to appease Elaina's own desires with talk of country houses.

If Elaina wanted a house in the country, he would gladly

provide it to her. Although he could not imagine himself loving her—or anyone, really—he would do what he could to make her happy if she became his wife.

She returned from the mizmaze shortly after Will, and when she saw Giles standing on the hillside looking out at the city of Winchester, she joined him immediately. She smiled up at him, and in that moment, he felt he had absolutely nothing to worry about.

CHAPTER EIGHT

I find myself worrying about you more and more as time goes on, especially when I do not hear from you for long stretches of time. I know that's not your fault, but I selfishly wish you wrote more, even just to tell me that you are alive and well. I enjoy being at Blackmore during the summer and winter, but I do find there is much less to distract me here than in London during the Season. When there's less distraction, I tend to worry even more. Please know that I pray for your safety, morning and night. I do not know what I'll do if you don't come home.

—an excerpt of a letter from Elaina, written in the winter of 1811, to Will

WILL RETURNED to the party at the top of the hill dejected, out of ideas to win Elaina's heart if she would not listen to reason. How could he possibly convince her that her lack of wealth did not matter when the rest of his family had convinced her otherwise?

He looked at Montgomery, who was enjoying a tête-à-tête with Clara on one of the picnic blankets while the others stood at the edge of the hill, inspecting the city of Winchester in the distance. He had hoped the resentment he held for his brother would diminish as they grew older, but watching him seemingly fall in love with Clara while Will lost his hold on Elaina only served to kindle his dislike. Will was sure Montgomery was filling her brain with some sort of nonsense about him when he saw them speaking the night prior.

Why should Montgomery always be happy while he was always miserable? Will had joined the army to gain a certain sort of agency outside of being a Winter, but now that his father had tasked him with Larkspur, he was back to being where he started, explicitly tied to all the rules and expectations of the peerage. He half wondered if Elaina would have had him if he were a captain in the army and the Larkspur question had never come into the equation. Plenty of the officers had wives in Brussels. Would she have liked being so far from home, though?

A disheartening thought crept into his mind. He hadn't believed her when she said she only saw him as a friend, but perhaps she was telling the truth. If she cared about him at all and wanted to be with him, wouldn't she have been willing to give something up for him? Marrying each other may have resulted in the temporary disappointment of his family, but they would have come around eventually. Surely she knew that. His father would not let them go destitute, and he wouldn't let Larkspur fail, either, regardless of what money Will gained from any marriage he sought.

He watched as she returned from the mizmaze and joined the others at the edge of the hill, taking her spot beside Hunt. He had thought she would be miserable with him, living in the city as the wife of a banker, miles away from her beloved country home, but perhaps money mattered more to her than he originally supposed. She had lived so comfortably from the age five and onward that perhaps the idea of giving up that comfort for him and his drafty estate in Cambridgeshire wasn't appealing at all to her.

If that was the case, he decided that he didn't know her at all. If that was the case, their childhood friendship meant nothing more than the relationships he shared with the members of his regiment. If that was the case, the correspondence they shared—the letters he swore kept him alive during the most difficult times of war—meant even less.

Watching her smile and laugh at Hunt made him increasingly angry. He could not bring himself to flirt with Miss Arnold anymore, and he remained silent on their ride back to the house as he contemplated his next move.

ELAINA WAS DETERMINED to keep her distance from Will, though she couldn't help but notice the way Will sulked throughout the remainder of the party. She was convinced he would move on from her rejection once one of the many young ladies that the duchess kept pointing in his direction finally caught his eye. Soon their fondness for each other would be nothing more than distant memories for them both.

Mr. Hunt proved himself to be a more than amiable companion time and time again, subjecting himself to all the things he claimed to hate about country house parties, including games of bowls on the lawn and charades after dinner. He was intelligent and quick-witted, and he made her laugh, all the things Elaina supposed one could want in a man, and he seemed genuinely interested in her opinions and life at Blackmore. Even her father seemed to like him, and he tended not to like anyone who attended the Blackmore annual party.

As the days passed, she had fewer doubts that Mr. Hunt

would be a very good partner in matrimony. She could see him being a very giving spouse, especially to her, not always caring if she didn't fit in perfectly with the ton, seeing as how he didn't either. He would humor what some of her peers would call her more masculine tendencies, like her desire to remain well-read and learn about the world around her (why those should be deemed traits of men and not women, she did not know). And he was friends with Montgomery, so she envisioned frequent trips to Blackmore to visit him, the duchess, and her father. Perhaps one day he would even buy a house in the country for himself nearby.

All of those dreams for the future inspired pleasant feelings inside of her, but one thing she struggled to conjure up for the man was passion. When she looked at him, she did not feel the same things she felt when she saw Will. She had been a stranger to passion until Will returned home and she ran into him standing outside of Blackmore. She found herself becoming distracted as the days of the house party dragged on, her eyes sometimes wandering to him across a crowded room.

For some reason, he always seemed to catch her staring at him, sometimes long before she even caught herself. He'd always smirk at her when he did, as if he was winning some sort of competition, causing her to turn a shade of red and quickly turn away.

Clara was with her one time while this happened. They were standing together in the drawing room before dinner on the third day of the party, and there had been a lull in conversation.

"Do you and Lord William often stare so longingly at each other?"

Elaina's mouth nearly fell open. "I beg your pardon?" she asked, not sure if she heard the younger woman correctly.

"You heard me," Clara replied. "I constantly see you

staring at him, or him staring at you, or both of you staring at each other. I wonder why you waste your time with Mr. Hunt."

Elaina ignored the first part of Clara's statement. "Mr. Hunt means to marry me. Why wouldn't I spend time with him?"

"Why? Because you don't love him, of course. It's clear to me that you love Will."

"Do you always speak your mind so freely, Lady Clara?"

"Amongst friends, I do." Clara paused for a moment, her face suddenly falling. "We are friends, aren't we? I hope I haven't—"

"We are friends," Elaina said quickly, shaking her head. Clara had not offended her. Elaina had only hoped no one else had noticed the longing way in which she and Will looked at each other. She had done her best to push her feelings aside, but they were still there, bright as ever.

"Then may I say something to you as a friend?" she asked.

Elaina nodded in response.

"I do not have much choice in who I marry, but you do, and I think you should take advantage of that—for my sake, at least. I'd hate to see you waste the most important choice of your life on the wrong man."

"Is that how you feel? Like you are wasting the most important choice of *your* life?"

Clara shook her head. "Not at all. I quite like Montgomery. I was nervous when I first came here. My father told me I should keep my expectations low, but I… I'm quite taken with the man. Can you believe it?"

Elaina smiled. Sweet, precious Clara. She only hoped Montgomery felt the same way. "I can," she replied. "Montgomery is kind when you get to know him, though he is not always so understanding."

"Is that why you insist on allowing Mr. Hunt to court you?"

Elaina shook her head. "I allow Mr. Hunt to court me because he's the best possible husband I could hope for."

It was a lie, of course. But without Montgomery or his parents' support, she could not in good faith align herself to Will.

"But—"

"It's the truth, Clara. Must we speak on this anymore?"

Clara sighed. "Of course not, Miss Walker. I only hope you aren't making a grave mistake."

Me too, Elaina thought. *Me too.*

ON THE LAST day of the party, the morning before the grand ball, Elaina took a stroll with Mr. Hunt through the same north gardens that she did with Will the day he arrived home. They walked arm in arm, the same as she did with Will that day, and willed herself to feel something from his touch or the growing intimacy between their two minds. Instead, there was nothing but a growing emptiness inside of her as she came closer and closer to her fate of becoming engaged and then married to him. Everything about Mr. Hunt was so pleasant, but there was no passion, and that seemed to be what Elaina craved, no matter how much she tried to deny it.

She showed him the duke's hothouse, taking him on a similar path as she did Will, ending at the red carnations.

"What do you think, Mr. Hunt?" she asked, looking around the structure, taking in the mixture of heavenly smells and exotic sights. Walking through the greenhouse was like leaving England altogether. "Could you find some-thing as extraordinary as this in London?"

"Perhaps not quite so big," he said, tilting his head as he

considered it. "Don't you think London has charms of its own, though?"

Elaina shrugged. "I believe I thought so when I was nineteen," she said. "Not so much anymore, or maybe it's only because there's so much for me to do whenever I go there. Perhaps it wouldn't be so bad if I could have a quiet life in the city. Do you think that's possible?"

"Maybe not," he replied, "but we could try."

It did not escape her notice that he said the word "we." She found it difficult to think of her and Mr. Hunt that way, though she knew very well that was where they were headed.

"Elaina," he said, "may I ask you something?"

She swallowed, her pulse quickening. She was afraid to say yes, but afraid to say no as well. If she said yes, he might propose. If she said no, the opportunity might never present itself again, even if she felt more ready in a month, more past the subject of Will.

"Yes," she finally said, her voice quiet. She cleared her throat. "What is it?"

"I can't help but notice the way you and Lord William look at each other when you think no one's watching," he said, his voice tentative and slow, as if he was choosing each of his words very carefully. There seemed to be no judgment in his gaze, but she still feared what he might say next. "I was quite determined to ignore it at first, but I'm not impervious to developing certain insecurities. I know the two of you are fond of each other, but I need to know... should I be worried?"

"Worried?" she asked, furrowing her brow.

"Yes," he said, nodding once. "I think you know what I mean."

How could she explain it? Yes, she felt a certain passion for Will that she was sure she would never feel with Hunt.

However, that would not—could not—impact her choice in husband.

"Will and I, of course, grew up together, as you know, but we also maintained a correspondence while he was away," she finally said. "With Montgomery being older than the both of us, we were very close before he went to Eton, and the army after that. We are only friends, though, if you're worried about some sort of deep attachment."

"You say there's no deep attachment," Hunt said slowly, "but does he feel the same way?"

They gazed at each other for a moment, and Elaina pursed her lips, struggling to lie any further. "I don't think Will knows what he feels. He's been away for so long."

"But he—"

"I do not wish to speak of this anymore, Mr. Hunt," Elaina sputtered, shaking her head, breathing heavily as she gazed up at him. He looked troubled by her response. She didn't blame him as she looked away, flushing. "I beg you to change the subject."

"Of course," he said, nodding once. "Shall we go back inside?"

She nodded, shooting him a wary glance. His lips were pursed, his jaw set. She could tell he was annoyed. Still, he took her by the arm, leading her back to the house.

"When do you plan on proposing? I think you should do it soon."

Giles looked at his friend, surprised. They sat in Montgomery's private study at the back of the house, enjoying a glass of cognac together before the ball.

"Soon?" he asked. "How soon?"

Montgomery shrugged. "Tomorrow morning. Before you leave."

"Wouldn't that be stealing your thunder?"

Giles knew Montgomery intended to propose to Clara that night at the ball. The whole thing could have been considered an engagement party. Everyone knew Montgomery and Clara had been promised to each other as children. It would be downright shocking if they didn't become engaged tonight.

Montgomery waved his hand nonchalantly. "You don't have to announce it. You only have to secure her hand. That would prevent my brother from doing anything rash."

"And what about her?" Giles asked. "What if she says no? She seemed rather upset today when I tried to question her on the subject of your brother."

Now it was Montgomery's turn to look surprised. "You asked her about my brother?"

Giles nodded. "I don't wish to make a fool of myself for her, Montgomery. I don't even love her."

"That's beside the point." Montgomery's tone was dismissive. "All that matters is that she doesn't marry my brother."

Giles furrowed his brow. "Why are you so against them, anyway?"

"It's not that I'm *against* them. I only wish the best for them. Will needs to marry an heiress if he's to make Larkspur a success."

"I could procure a low-interest loan for him instead," Giles offered. He was growing tired of this game. He had approached the duke last spring because he was genuinely interested in Miss Walker. Now he only felt like a pawn in Montgomery's plan to ensure his brother's unhappiness. "Something that would help him get started."

Montgomery shook his head. "He wouldn't accept it."

"Why not?"

"You're a rival for Miss Walker's affections. No, a loan will not do. You must propose to her tomorrow morning, ensuring that Will ends up with someone else. Someone more suitable."

Giles sighed. "You act as if you care for his future, but I can't help but feel like you only want him to marry for duty because *you* must marry for duty. For as long as I can remember, you have resented your brother simply because he has more freedom of choice than you. Are you really that hell-bent on taking it away?"

"My father agrees with me."

Giles realized then that his friend would not see reason on the subject. He finished his cognac and stood up. "I think I'll join the others in the ballroom."

"You have not told me whether or not you will propose tomorrow morning."

Giles hesitated, then nodded once. "Yes, I'll do it."

"Good." Montgomery smiled. "I'll join you soon, then. There's one more person I'd like to speak to before I go in."

Elaina was in her sitting room by herself, trying to gather the nerve to go downstairs and mingle with the other guests. Her father had already gone down some time ago.

She knew Hunt would be at her side within moments of entering the ballroom, and she was still struggling to decide how that made her feel, especially after their exchange that morning in the greenhouse. She still thought Hunt was a fine enough man. She only wasn't sure if she truly wanted him for a husband.

At least she didn't have to worry about him proposing that night. The only people becoming engaged that night would be Montgomery and Clara. Hunt wouldn't dare take any attention from his friend.

As she considered these things, she heard a light rapping

on her door. She stood up, going to answer it, and found Montgomery on the other side.

"My lord!" she exclaimed, ushering him inside. She went to sit on one of the settees, and he sat down across from her. "I was just thinking of you."

"Is that so?" he asked.

She nodded. "Tonight is a big night for you, is it not?"

He half smiled. "I suppose it is."

She frowned at his lack of excitement. "I hope you aren't getting cold feet. I cannot say enough how much I like Lady Clara."

"I know," he replied with a nod. "I like her as well. I just can't help but feel like my life is about to change forever."

"Well, isn't it? Marriage is not something to take lightly. I'm not surprised you feel nervous. I know I feel nervous whenever—" She stopped herself. She did not want Montgomery to know she was still struggling to decide if she should marry Hunt or forgo him and his family's desires and pursue Will. "Never mind. How do you intend to do it?"

Montgomery raised an eyebrow. "Do what?"

"Why, propose, of course."

He looked as though he might laugh. "I don't know," he said with a shake of his head. "I suppose I haven't given it much thought."

"You haven't?" Elaina knew she shouldn't have been surprised. This was Montgomery. Being affectionate was not his strong suit, but someone like Clara... Well, she deserved affection, and Elaina would see to her receiving it. "Perhaps you should."

"What would you advise, then?"

"Well, you cannot ask her as if you are striking up a business deal, which I'm sure is what you might do."

Montgomery gave a little snort. "I resent that."

"Nevertheless, you should give her an earnest display of

affection. Let her know that you want to marry her because she's *her*, not just because she's a way of fulfilling your duty to your family."

He seemed to consider this, crossing his arms and tilting his head while he sat on the settee. "Do you really think one can develop affection for someone after only such a short time of knowing each other?"

She shrugged. "Maybe. Perhaps the seeds of affection can be planted in a short time. Now you must work on watering them, that way they actually grow, and then cultivate whatever blooms appear, or else you're in for a very long and unhappy life indeed."

"Do you really think that?" he scoffed.

Elaina felt taken aback. "Do you disagree?"

"There are ways to find happiness outside of marriage."

"Forgive my bluntness," she said, frowning, "but fulfilling your duty to your family will only make you happy for so long."

He chuckled, low and deep. "That's not what I meant, Miss Walker."

She flushed. "Oh." When he didn't say anything else, she shook her head and added, "Well, nevertheless, I don't see why you couldn't fall in love with your future wife, though it's perhaps too early to feel or even express such sentiments to her. That being said, she seems like a good enough girl who's more than worthy of your feelings."

Montgomery sighed. "I'm not sure I'm capable of producing the feelings you speak of, but I will try for your sake."

"Don't try for my sake. Try for Clara's."

"Right," he said with a smile and a nod. "Shall we go down now?"

Elaina nodded, standing up. "Why did you come up here,

anyway? Were you sent to fetch me by your mother or something?"

Montgomery shook his head. "I came to discuss Mr. Hunt, actually," he said, standing up as well. He took Elaina by the arm as they left the room and walked to the ballroom.

"Oh?" she asked.

"I know you are conflicted, but perhaps you could heed some of your own advice. Mr. Hunt is a good enough man who's more than worthy of your feelings as well."

Elaina swallowed. She did not want to disappoint Montgomery or appear hypocritical, so she nodded and smiled. "You are quite right. I will try to remember that tonight."

WITH THE BLACKMORE ball that night and Larkspur upon him the next morning, Will knew he had one last chance to change Elaina's mind about having a potential future with him.

He had spent the majority of the party avoiding her, though he couldn't help but occasionally watch her as she entertained Hunt. He would sometimes catch her watching him in return, which always led to a smirk on his part. Perhaps his hold on her wasn't as loose as he expected the day after the outing to St. Catherine's Hill.

Will knew his brother planned on proposing the last night of the party, but Will also vowed to make one last proposal of his own. He could not leave for Larkspur without one more attempt at winning Elaina's hand, despite the mounting gossip that Montgomery and Clara wouldn't be the only couple to become engaged that night, but Hunt and Elaina as well. Will hated the idea of it, though the gossip may have been correct. He had seen them walking alone together to the northern gardens that morning. If they had to become engaged, he hoped they'd at least do him the common courtesy of doing it some other time, preferably when he was at Larkspur, far, far away from them. In any case, he figured he had one more chance to stop it.

Blackmore Park's ballroom was one of the finest rooms of the house, with salmon-colored walls and light wood floors that seemed to glitter and sparkle under the light of the crystal chandelier hanging from the ceiling. Portraits of Winters past, along with large gilded mirrors, hung on each wall of the room, reflecting back scenes of dancing people and a small orchestra that the duke and duchess commissioned for their party every year. The ball was a mixture of London society and people from the country that the duke and duchess deigned important enough to attend. He watched as Elaina took refreshment from one of the side tables, finally approaching her after days of silence.

She saw him coming, and her face turned to concern as she frantically looked around the room. Did it really make her that nervous to be seen with him?

"Miss Walker," he said, bowing slightly. She curtseyed in response. He detected a bit of uncertainty in her motion but continued anyway. "Would you do me the honor of dancing with me?"

They both knew she had no choice but to say yes. It would be impolite to reject him without just reason, and he knew she had none. Slowly, she nodded, taking his hand as he led her to the floor. The dance was a waltz, and she seemed to be resistant to the way he was holding her at first, but as the music started, her body seemed to become more and more pliable, as if it was melting into his as they twirled and swayed around the dance floor.

Her dress that night was made of white muslin with threads of dark blue embroidered into floral patterns throughout the fabric. The sleeves were cut short, positioned to reveal a scandalous amount of shoulder. The bodice of the dress itself was low cut, and her white evening gloves only came up to her wrists. All her bare skin was a distraction, and he found himself almost unable to speak as they danced.

"You've been avoiding me," she finally murmured, looking up at him through dark eyelashes.

"Isn't that what you wanted?" he asked.

She frowned. "No. Yes. I mean…" She bit her lip, and he felt that familiar longing to kiss her again begin to take over his senses. If only he had the power to kiss away all of the uncertainty so clearly written on her face. "Is it so hard to believe that what I want and what I think is right are two completely different things?"

Looking down at her, he nearly laughed. "And what makes you think what you want isn't right?"

"My mind will not allow me to consider anything else, I'm afraid," she replied. "To take what I want without thinking of the consequences… well, that's just selfish, isn't it?"

"And do you ever wonder if what you think is right is the product of other people being selfish? Why should you or I live for the whims of anyone but ourselves?"

"What your parents and brother want aren't mere whims," she passionately replied. "Larkspur Castle will be your legacy. It will be what you pass down to your children. I will not stand in the way of your success, and I will not marry only to remain a burden to your family as a result. I will free them of their responsibility of me."

"But—"

"I will not speak of this anymore. Not here while everyone is watching." Her eyes seemed to wander around the room, and Will knew who she was looking for. "Especially not Mr. Hunt."

He pursed his lips. He found himself hating that man more and more with each passing day. "Then let's speak of it elsewhere. Montgomery and Clara will be announcing their engagement any moment now. We will be able to escape to the library during the commotion that follows. Will you meet me there?"

She hesitated. He thought for a moment she might say no. *Please don't say no*, he thought. He stared at her, begging her with his eyes as best as he could. Finally, she nodded. "Fine," she said. "I will meet you there."

GRAHAM INVITED Clara to take a walk with him through the gardens, which had been illuminated that night with hanging lanterns along the edges of the walkway that traversed through the greenery. They were both quiet. Conversation had not come as easily to them that night as it had for the rest of the party. Graham supposed they were both just nervous.

Nervous. Graham could have laughed at the thought. Him, nervous? He couldn't remember a time he had ever been nervous in his life. And why should he be nervous? She was required to marry him anyway.

Still, Elaina's advice weighed heavily on him. He did want his proposal to be affectionate. He wanted to make Clara happy, but images of his mistress Marianne haunted his mind. He had no intention of giving her up after he and Clara were engaged, or even after they were married. As a result, his affection felt like a lie.

"May I ask you something, my lord?" Clara asked, breaking the silence between them.

Graham smiled at her. "I feel I must insist on you calling me Graham, but go ahead. What is it?"

She blushed. "I was only wondering why you are so against Miss Walker and Lord William being together. I know Mr. Hunt is your friend and much wealthier than your brother will ever be, but shouldn't Miss Walker's feelings be taken into account? Surely you can find it in your heart to support her in what she wants."

Graham gritted his teeth. This was not the conversation he'd wanted to have when he brought her to the garden. Knowing his true thoughts would only upset her, he was desperate to change the topic. "Come now, Clara. I did not bring you out here to discuss my brother and Miss Walker. You must leave her to make her own decisions, and I believe she sees the benefits of marrying a man like Mr. Hunt, regardless of her feelings for my brother."

"I do not deny that there are benefits, but—"

"I'd rather talk of our future than hers." He came to an abrupt stop, and she looked up at him, her lips slightly parted in surprise. He wondered what it would be like to kiss her. Perhaps he should. Perhaps that would purge the thoughts of Marianne from his mind. He swallowed. "Over the past few days, you have shown yourself to be everything I could want in a wife. You are kind and intelligent and polite—not to mention beautiful as well."

She looked away. He took her chin between his thumb and two fingers, gently forcing her to look at him. He smiled. "What I'm trying to ask, Clara, is will you marry me? I know neither of us knows each other very well, and we've been thrown together by our fathers without much say in the matter, but I think we have a real shot of being happy. Do you feel the same way?"

She smiled, nodding. "Yes," she said. "Yes, I do."

"Then will you marry me?"

"Yes."

He exhaled. He hadn't even noticed he had been holding his breath. "I'm going to kiss you now, Clara. Is that all right?"

Slowly, she nodded, and he brought his face down to hers,

their lips meeting where she stood. They kissed, and for a moment, Graham forgot all about his mistress Marianne, as well as the subject of Miss Walker and his brother and Hunt.

ELAINA FOUND herself walking around the ballroom in a daze, watching others around her make merry while she felt utterly miserable. She and Will would have their reckoning while Montgomery and Clara announced their engagement, though she wasn't sure what difference it would make. Still, she had agreed to meet him anyway.

Meeting Will in the library again that night could only result in more heartache and suffering. She knew he would leave for Larkspur tomorrow morning. She was dreading saying goodbye to him, knowing there would be no more letters once he left. Not after she became engaged to another man, which was looking all the more likely as her closeness to Hunt grew. Perhaps she would be lucky enough to see Will at Christmases, but probably not. The Hunts would have their own family traditions.

Still, she couldn't bear to say no to one last secret liaison with him, not when this could be their last night together as two single people. Surely Will would go and see Larkspur for himself and realize what had to be done if Montgomery's account of the place was at all accurate. He would give up his senseless pursuit of her as a result, realizing he must marry well if he was to succeed. Maybe then they could hope to be friends again one day, once clear sense had overtaken their mindless passion for each other.

After the orchestra went silent and Elaina noticed Montgomery and Clara standing at the front of the room together, gathering everyone around them, she discreetly slipped out of the room and headed to the library.

.   .   .

WILL STOOD in Blackmore's library in between one of the settees and the unlit fireplace. The room was illuminated by candles instead, as he had snuck away to the servants' quarters to find matches before going there.

He was hopeful that Elaina was beginning to see reason since she agreed to meet him there, for he could not bear to leave for Larkspur the next morning without knowing if she would be his.

When Elaina appeared in the doorway, his breath caught. She looked like an angel come to save him from the hell of the past few days, standing there in the yellow-gold glow of candlelight. He knew then that he could no longer control himself.

"Shut the door," he commanded before she could say anything. She did as she was told, and he practically ran to her then, taking her face into his hands and kissing her lips like a drunkard finally quenching his thirst. He needed to feel her against him, no matter how determined she was to marry Hunt. She braced herself against the back of the door as he crashed into her, though she made no sounds of protest. After a moment, she managed to break away from his voracious mouth.

"Will," she said, her voice breathless. "We shouldn't be doing this. I only came here to talk."

"How am I supposed to only talk to you when I feel the way I do? I have nothing to say but how much I want you."

She shook her head. "I should've known it would be this way. In fact, I think I *did* know it would be this way."

He broke away from her then, taking her hands into his and guiding her to one of the settees. "But you came anyway."

"Oh, Will," she breathed as they sat down together. "You must know how I feel about you, but we cannot marry. It's not right."

"Who cares if it's right?" he growled. He kissed her from

where they sat, clutching the back of her head with one hand and placing the other one on her taut waist. How he longed to undo her hair and run his fingers through the silky strands, especially when her mouth was more than inviting. He playfully nipped at her lower lip with his teeth before pulling away to admire her. Her lips were slightly swollen and parted, and her creamy skin looked almost golden under the faint glow of the candlelight.

The hand he had on her waist traveled to her breast, hoping to feel her heartbeat. He wondered if it was pounding as rapidly as his. She reached up with one of her hands, placing it over his, confirming that yes, she was just as excited—and maybe just as unsure and frightened—as he was. They stared at each other for a moment before he kissed her again, cupping the back of her head with his hand once more and lowering her so she was beneath him on the settee.

He became more daring with his kisses then, trailing them from her lips to her chin to her neck, all the way down to her breasts. She only encouraged him to explore further with her pleased little moans, so he roughly pulled the layers of fabric covering her down, not bothering with the buttons on the back of her dress. She was exposed then, two aroused rosebud-like nipples greeting him. He stared at them, then back at her face. Her cheeks were slightly flushed, her lips still parted.

"You are exquisite," he whispered before bending down and taking one nipple between his lips, gently sucking and twirling his tongue around it. His desire only intensified with each of her soft moans. He peppered kisses across the valley between her breasts until he found her other nipple with his mouth. He gently took it between his teeth while brushing the flat of his thumb against the one that was already wet with his saliva. She moaned again, this time even louder than before.

"We must stop this madness," she breathed, though she hardly sounded convincing, especially when she was writhing beside him with what he hoped were intense feelings of pleasure. "Someone will catch us."

He groaned, lifting his head from her breasts to look her in the eye. How could he stop when she looked so tempting? How could he stop when he *wanted* to be caught? Her chest was flushed with want, and she held her arms tight to her torso, a position that made her two breasts look even more delicious than he already knew them to be.

But part of him knew she was right. He was a gentleman, and she was a lady. Maybe not in title, but in upbringing. Gentlemen and ladies waited until their wedding night to copulate, and he couldn't imagine what kind of cad it would make him if he took her virginity on a settee in the library.

"You're right," he finally said out loud, albeit reluctantly, reaching over to fix her chemise and stays and then the bodice of her dress, despite the fact that his groin was still aching with want. When he was done, he took her hands into his. "Surely you must see now that we cannot be parted. We must marry, Elaina. We were made for each other. Even as children, we were made for each other."

She shook her head. "But how? Regardless of your feelings or my feelings, your family would never approve. We would disappoint them greatly, and I don't know if they'll ever recover as you say they will."

"Run away with me," he begged. "Before I leave, I'll arrange for the servants to prepare a carriage for you tomorrow night. Instead of going to Larkspur in the morning, I'll head north to Oxford. I'll wait for you there, and when you arrive, we can be off to Scotland before anyone notices we're gone."

"Oh, Will," she said, still shaking her head, "do you hear

yourself? Do you care nothing for the scandal it will cause? The damage it will do to your family?"

"Dash my family, Elaina! I like to believe at least a small part of them loves me and loves you enough that they wouldn't want to see us spend the rest of our lives in misery. They will forgive us for this, and if they don't, I will purchase another commission, and they can deal with Larkspur themselves."

"What about me?" she asked. "What will they say about me?"

Biting her lip, she turned away, and he wondered what she was thinking. He knew her cousins and aunt had never supported her, even after her grandfather had died. What could he say that would convince her the loss of the Winters' good graces would be temporary?

He lifted one of his hands to the cheek facing away from him, gently forcing her to look at him. Her brown eyes were rimmed with tears. "Do not cry, my sweet," he said. "The more likely outcome is they will come to accept us, and we will come to live happy, peaceful lives in Larkspur—together. You will be able to help me make happy lives for our tenants and parishioners." He laughed then, adding, "I'm convinced you are the only person who can make the place a success. I will only muck it up without you."

He lifted her knuckles to his lips, pressing light kisses on them. "My sweet, sweet Elaina. After so many years apart, do not deny yourself happiness for their sake, for you know you will not find it in the arms of Giles Hunt or any other man like him."

When she still did not speak—she was still too unsure, still too afraid—he resorted to begging. "Please, say something."

"I—"

CHAPTER NINE

*I feel very lucky that my father supports me in whatever I do. I
sometimes think of all the times my cousins have treated me with
disdain at parties in London and feel an emptiness inside of me.
My father, however, fills all of that up when I return home to
Blackmore. He's always willing to take me out riding to teach me
about farming, and I find I'm finally learning something useful. I
only hope it doesn't go to waste whenever I get married.*

—an excerpt of a letter from Elaina, written in the summer
of 1810, to Will

WILL LEFT at dawn the next morning. He had already spoken
to the drivers of the two carriages his father had given to him
for his expedition to Larkspur. The driver with the majority
of his personal effects would be going straight to Larkspur,
where he would deposit them at the house before returning
to Blackmore.

The driver carrying him and only one of his trunks with a
week's worth of clothes and toiletries would be going to
Oxford.

Despite the uncertainty of what laid ahead, Will found himself sitting in the carriage with a smile on his face as he watched Blackmore Park disappear into the distance. Somehow, perhaps by the grace of God himself, Elaina had agreed to his scheme to elope. She would follow him in her own carriage after everyone had gone to sleep that night. He had already arranged everything with the servants, securing their silence with a guinea for each of them. He feared that if anyone—especially Montgomery or the duchess—discovered their plot, they might easily talk Elaina out of going.

It wasn't that Will didn't believe Elaina really wanted to be with him. He only knew that the opinion of the duke and duchess and his brother—who had become *her* family more than *his* while he was in the army—meant a great deal with her. The idea of losing their good opinion forever terrified her, no matter how many times Will reassured her that they would come around to the two of them being together, especially once they showed them what a success they could make Larkspur. There was also her father to consider, who may find himself disappointed in his daughter's choice, but Will had made her promise that she wouldn't divulge their plans to even him.

"I can't even leave him a letter?" she asked, face full of concern.

Will shook his head. "The whole idea of eloping is to *not* tell your parents what you're planning on doing."

This seemed to pain her greatly. Elaina had always been close to her father. Both were untitled, yet they had been thrown into a world of peers and money and good society, always expected to behave a certain way in a never-ending effort to prove their deservedness. Will only hoped that taking Elaina away would not damage the close relationship between father and daughter. If it did, he thought that might become his only regret over the whole scheme. Everyone else could go to hell.

The journey to Oxford took about eight hours, not including an hour-long stopover in Newbury, where Will stretched his legs and enjoyed an early luncheon at the local coaching inn. The horses were watered and fed as well, and Will took the time to pay close attention to their care with one of the grooms, knowing the team had a long journey ahead of them. The journey between Oxford and Gretna Green was nearly three hundred miles. If they were to use the same team throughout, it would take them at least two and a half days to get there.

The length of the journey worried Elaina as Will divulged his plan to her the night prior. "Won't Montgomery be able to catch up to us if we take two nights of rest at coaching inns?"

She had a point, but there was no other way. Will couldn't afford to hire and switch out a team of horses every thirty miles so they could travel nonstop. He was banking on his father letting them go without sending anyone after them, hoping the duke would be content to watch them fall victim to what he would have deemed their own senseless folly to anyone willing to listen.

By the time Will reached Oxford, it was late afternoon. As the carriage rolled by the city's ancient university, Gothic architecture abound, Will considered a life where he had gone to university like his brother instead of joining the army. He supposed he would have been as miserable there as he was at Eton, and despite the hardships of war, he was glad for the decision he made eight years ago. He doubted he would have had the bollocks to run away with Elaina if he hadn't.

Eventually the carriage stopped at the Angel Hotel, where he'd be staying for the night. He had directed Elaina to meet him there the following morning, telling her to use a false name when she arrived.

"My wife, Mrs. Talbot, will be meeting me here sometime tomorrow morning," Will told the man at the front desk as he was checking in. "Will you send her to my room when she arrives?"

"Certainly, sir," the man replied as he handed him the keys to his room.

Will's room was on the fourth floor. It was a small room with a low ceiling, but well-appointed for a single night's stay, plus the most he could afford on the meager allowance his father gave him. He imagined the sum would only become smaller once he eloped with Elaina, despite the fact that he'd be managing a large estate for him.

Sighing, he fell backward onto the bed, closing his eyes as he reminded himself it would all be well worth it.

ELAINA WOKE that morning with a knot in her stomach. Will would have already left for Oxford, and the rest of the house party guests would start gathering for breakfast soon, just before they finally departed Blackmore Park.

Those party guests included Mr. Hunt, who she knew she would have to say goodbye to without revealing her plans with Will. But how? By now, everyone thought *they* would also become engaged at the end of the party, just like Montgomery and Clara the night of the ball.

Prior to her retiring for the previous evening, Mr. Hunt had asked to take one last stroll through the gardens before he returned to London the next morning. She couldn't very well say no to him after paying him so much attention these past few days. Still, she had already made her promise to Will.

She would run away with him. Nothing Mr. Hunt could

say would stop her, but she met him in the entrance hall anyway. He looked as he always did: handsome, pleasant, and amenable. She imagined one day he would make a woman very happy—just not her.

He took her by the arm and led her outside, this time toward the south gardens, which were connected to the same conservatory where Will kissed her the night after he returned home. She blushed when she thought about it, knowing there would be plenty more kisses like that when they were married—and even more than that.

"You are quiet this morning, Miss Walker," Mr. Hunt observed.

"My apologies, Mr. Hunt," she said, shaking her head. More sunnily, she declared, "You must be happy to return to London today."

"Is that what you think?" he asked, tilting his head to the side.

She paused for a moment, knowing she said the wrong thing by his tone of voice. She tried to lighten the mood. "Well, yes, but with that response, I suppose I've managed to warm you to the idea of the country, then."

"I suppose you have." He stopped walking. He let go of her arm to turn and face her, his face serious. Her heart started to pound, and not out of want, but out of dread. She did not want to hurt this poor man. "Miss Walker, there is something I must ask you before I go. I—"

"Don't," Elaina said, cutting him off. His mouth hung open, suspended mid-sentence. He promptly shut it, giving her a quizzical look. "I hate to disappoint you, but... don't."

He stepped closer to her. "What do you mean... don't?"

Elaina swallowed, trying to find her wits. She clenched and unclenched her fists at her sides and took a breath. "I mean I think I know what you intend to ask, but I wish you wouldn't, as I do not wish to hurt you by..."

Her voice trailed off, a sudden fear of being too presumptuous coming over her.

"Saying no?" he asked.

Hesitating, she met his eye, then nodded once.

He sighed. "I cannot say I'm not disappointed, Miss Walker. I thought…"

"I know. I've used you badly. You came here with the sole intention of getting to know me better, and I encouraged you. And I'm sure Montgomery encouraged you as well. And to think you are my first suitor to actually follow through with proposing, and now I must say no!"

"You must?" he asked.

She had said too much. "Forgive me," she said, shaking her head and looking down. "Please say nothing to Montgomery. Please."

"I already told him of my plans to propose."

"Then leave before he can ask you if you succeeded. If you care for me at all, let us pretend this never happened, and if Montgomery asks, tell him you got cold feet."

Mr. Hunt stared at her for a moment before nodding. "Very well, Miss Walker. If that's what you wish."

As they walked back toward the house, he asked, "I hope we can remain friends, Miss Walker, despite all this. I think very highly of you and always will. I hope you know that."

She smiled slightly. "I don't see why. I fear I've used you very badly."

"I'm not entirely surprised it turned out this way," he admitted with a sigh. "I've always known you had strong feelings for someone else, feelings that became all the more clear while I was here. I do not know what your plans are, but I hope you will call on me if you ever need anything. I already told Montgomery that I could offer Lord William a loan with favorable terms if he does not manage to find that heiress everyone is hoping for."

"You are much too kind, Mr. Hunt. I do not know why."

"We have been friends for six long years, haven't we? This does not change that."

Elaina nodded. They arrived at the front of the house, where his carriage was being loaded with his things by the servants. "Thank you, Mr. Hunt."

"I will part ways with you here to avoid seeing Montgomery," he said. He took her hand, bringing her knuckles to his lips, pressing a kiss there. "God bless you, Miss Walker."

AFTER ALL THE guests had gone, Elaina found herself wandering through the house in a daze, knowing she would be leaving Blackmore that night without knowing when she would return. She was walking by Montgomery's study when she heard her name from inside. When she came to the doorway, she found Montgomery sitting inside at his desk. She swallowed. She would have to tell him about Mr. Hunt.

"Please, come in," he said, pointing to the chair across from him. "Sit down."

Elaina did as she told, willing her heartbeat to slow down. Unprepared for how to broach the subject of Hunt, she decided to ask Montgomery about Clara. "I saw Lady Clara this morning," she said. "She seemed very happy with how things turned out. I trust that means you proposed in a satisfactory manner."

Montgomery smiled. Elaina couldn't help but smile back. She didn't often see Montgomery genuinely happy. "Yes, I believe so. And what about you, Miss Walker? How was your walk with Mr. Hunt this morning?"

Elaina sighed. That distraction didn't last very long. "Mr. Hunt is a very good... friend."

Montgomery's face fell. "Did he not come up to scratch?"

Elaina shook her head. Montgomery's face twisted. She

supposed genuine happiness could only last for so long. "Why, I—"

"Please, don't be mad at Mr. Hunt. It's not his fault. I did not necessarily encourage him."

"You spent the entire party with him!"

"I mean this morning. I did not encourage him this morning."

Montgomery pursed his lips. "Well, there will be other opportunities for you two to see each other. Perhaps we could plan a trip to London before it gets too cold, or he could spend the holidays here. With my brother in Larkspur, there will be less distraction, and perhaps you will be more encouraging then."

Elaina did not bother arguing with him. There was no point, especially since she intended on running away that night. She only hoped Montgomery could forgive her. "Yes, perhaps we could go to London next month. I'm sure Mr. Hunt would be more than happy to entertain us."

They smiled at each other, and Elaina wondered if Montgomery had any idea of what was to come.

ELAINA DID NOT HAVE her maid undress her and put her in her nightdress the evening before she was supposed to depart for Scotland via Oxford.

Although Elaina knew Ferguson was aware of her clandestine plans to elope—she was one of the ones Will had paid a guinea in exchange for her silence—she did not dare speak them out loud. She only had the maid draw her a bath and then help her change into more comfortable traveling clothes, consisting of a short-sleeved gingham-printed cotton dress and a matching maroon-colored cape. After she was dressed, all there was left to do was sit on her bed and think, all the while listening to her father move about their shared sitting room next door.

As could be expected, the wait felt excruciatingly slow, despite being only a couple of hours long. All the while she wondered if her father suspected anything. She thought he might have, especially when he commented that Elaina seemed unmoved by Will's departure to Larkspur earlier in the day. She only shrugged in response when he remarked on it, asking him why she should be sad. After all, he was only just a friend, and they would see each other at Christmas.

Her father seemed thoroughly unconvinced, begrudgingly returning to his paper after studying his daughter with a discerning gaze. He looked at her a few moments longer than would make her comfortable enough to believe he lacked any sort of suspicion on his part.

Eventually, the noise in the study ceased, and she thought she heard the closing of his bedchamber door, indicating that he had retired for the evening. Fifteen minutes passed after that, and she stood up from her writing desk chair and began to pace. She had considered leaving her father a letter explaining herself while she sat there, but Will had advised so strongly against it that eventually she also decided against it, determinedly pushing the idea far from her mind, despite the large amount of guilt that accompanied such an action.

An hour later, her bedchamber door opened with Ferguson appearing on the other side.

"It's time to go, miss," she whispered. Swallowing, Elaina nodded, conflicting senses of uncertainty and resoluteness swirling in her belly. Ferguson grabbed Elaina's simplest straw bonnet from the dressing table, taking it and placing it on Elaina's head, fastening the red ribbon around her chin with a bow. Elaina was sure the maid must've thought she was trembling terribly as she did so.

The two women were at the doorway leading from the

sitting room to the corridor when Elaina heard someone call her name. Her heart dropped as she turned, seeing her father standing just outside his bedchamber wearing his night-clothes and dressing gown, his hair disheveled with sleep underneath his nightcap.

"Elaina?" he asked again, pulling his spectacles out of the front pocket of his dressing down and placing them on his nose. "Is that you?"

Swallowing, she turned to Ferguson. The maid's face had gone white with the appearance of Mr. Walker. "Leave us," she said. "I will meet you out back."

After hesitating a moment, the maid nodded, closing the sitting room door behind her. Elaina turned to her father then, his face full of concern.

"Papa," she said. "You're awake."

He shook his head. "I'm afraid I was never asleep. Where are you going with Ferguson at this hour?"

Elaina frowned. "Surely you know, Papa." She paused before adding, "Do not make me say it."

They stared at each other for a moment, until a look of realization appeared on her father's face. "Oh," he said, moving to sit down on one of the settees as if the wind had been kicked out of him. "You are running away. You mean to meet Lord William somewhere and elope." He shook his head. "I should've guessed by your lack of sadness over his departure this morning."

"Oh, Papa," Elaina replied, fighting back tears as she went to where he sat, kneeling beside him so her face was just under his. She took his hands into hers, squeezing them. "Surely you must understand. Everyone was against you and Mama as well, but you did it anyway, didn't you?"

"Selfishly, yes," he said, nodding. "But look what happened to her. Her family ostracized her. She lost her dowry, and now her daughter will be nothing as well." Pausing, he asked, "Are you sure you don't want to marry Mr. Hunt? You will be a rich woman if you do."

Elaina quietly laughed. "I'm sure Mama had her own Mr. Hunt as well. Did you ever ask her such a question before you married in secret?"

Her father half smiled. "No, but maybe I should have. I'm afraid I might have been being rather selfish at the time."

"I'm afraid in this day and age, if any of us are to have a love match, we must be a little selfish. Oh, Papa. Please tell me you won't disown me after this, even though I was planning on running away into the night without saying goodbye."

She could not bear the thought of her father disowning her. She had already lost her mother and her mother's family. She had come to accept that the Winters would be disappointed in her for a while. But her father? She couldn't stand the idea.

He shook his head, making a gruff sound of dissent. "Disown you?" he asked incredulously. "Of course I won't disown you—what a ridiculous thing to say!"

"Then I suppose I'm lucky to have a better father than my mother."

He looked at her ruefully. "Now, I'd be a dishonest man if I were to sit here and reassure you that the Winters will accept you as their daughter-in-law. They love you—I am sure of it, after everything they did for you—but their kind thrives off advantageous marriages. Why do you think Blackmore went through all the trouble of arranging a marriage for Montgomery when he was a mere lad of ten?"

"I know that, but..." She bit her lip. "Oh, Papa. I cannot marry Mr. Hunt. Please do not ask me to. He's a nice enough man, but I'll be forced to live in London, which you know I hate. With Will, we will live in Larkspur and take care of the land there. I will be good at that, regardless of what difficulties the estate finds itself in now. Marriage for a woman shouldn't be just about who we like best or who will make us the richest. It should be about which man can offer us the life we most want, especially when society has put us in the position where we can't do it ourselves."

Her father sighed. "If that's the case, then I don't think the Winters could ask for a better daughter-in-law. You'll make Larkspur a success, regardless of money. I only hope they can eventually see it the way you and I see it."

"They will someday," she said softly, though she still struggled to believe her own words. "Maybe not at first, but someday. If I cannot have faith in that, what do I have?"

He nodded once. "I will tell them you aren't feeling well," he said. "That should stall them at least a day in going after you."

She shook her head. "Oh, Papa, please don't do that. I wouldn't want you to risk your position here. Pretend you haven't seen me at all, and you had no idea of our plans. Be as outraged as Blackmore will be!"

"He will be outraged," her father said, nodding, "though I don't think at you. At William, he will be."

She bit her lip. She hated the idea of coming between Will and his father, not that they ever had a peaceful relationship in the first place.

"You both must know there will be no handouts from him —not at first, anyway. You will only have the income from the estate, as meager as it is right now. That's it."

"I know, Papa."

He sighed once more. "Fine. Go. I will not tell anyone that I knew when you are discovered missing in the morning." Taking a look around the sitting room, he said, "I suppose I will have to give this up after you leave and move back to one of the cottages on the grounds. I won't mind, though. A cottage will be nice for an old man like me."

"Oh, Papa," she said, tears now flowing freely from her eyes. She stood up, taking her father's face in her hands as she did, placing a firm kiss on his wrinkled forehead. "What did I do to deserve a father like you? I will give word once we are married and once again when we've arrived safely in Larkspur. Maybe one day you can come and see it for yourself."

"One day," he said, patting her arm with his hand. "Now go. You cannot risk anyone else discovering you. Montgomery or Blackmore—even the duchess—will not be so kind."

Elaina nodded, giving him one last kiss on the cheek before turning and leaving the room. She tiptoed down the second-floor corridor to the back stairs, making her way to the servants' quarters. The carriage was waiting for her at the back service entrance, as was Ferguson, who began crying upon seeing Elaina.

"I thought you'd never come, miss," she said in between tears.

Elaina shushed her. "There, there, Ferguson. All is well. Now, go back inside and don't speak a word of this to anyone if you want to keep your position here. Thank you for your help."

"Shall I come to Larkspur eventually?" she asked, her voice hopeful.

Elaina had known Ferguson since she was a little girl, back when Ferguson was just a scullery maid, not much older than Elaina was now. She was simply Gracie then, and Elaina and Will would sneak downstairs for sweetmeats when they grew tired of their lessons. Young Gracie was always more than willing to indulge them, and when the duchess told Elaina she must take a lady's maid when she turned nineteen, she requested Gracie—now Ferguson, as was appropriate—despite her lack of experience, which was why it pained Elaina to say her next words.

"I'm not sure," she replied, frowning. "We will have very little money at first and no budget for even a valet, let alone a lady's maid. I will send for you as soon as we do, though."

Ferguson nodded, throwing her arms around Elaina and embracing her tightly. Seeing the maid's tears made Elaina doubt herself. If she married Hunt, she could take Ferguson with her and even give her a raise.

Their final goodbye over, Elaina climbed into the carriage, where she promptly burst into tears, watching Blackmore fade into the distance through the window as the carriage rolled northward.

"Have you seen Miss Walker this morning?"

Graham had popped into his mother's sitting room, where the older woman was reading a book. She closed it, leaving her thumb in between the pages to save her spot, a concerned look on her face.

"I haven't, actually. Why do you ask?"

"I've been looking for her, but none of the servants have seen her. She's not even in her room."

The duchess frowned, standing up. "Have you spoken to her father?"

Graham shook his head. "He's out with Father looking at some of the farms."

"You don't think—"

Graham shook his head, effectively silencing her. He would not believe that she ran away to be with his brother. He could not. She would not be so irrational. That was not the Elaina he knew. "Will you wait with me downstairs for them?"

The duchess nodded, following Graham downstairs to

one of the drawing rooms. His mother sat while he paced. It was already late afternoon, so he knew they would be home soon. Surely she wouldn't have left without speaking to her father. Mr. Walker must know where she went.

It was another fifteen minutes before the duke and Mr. Walker arrived. "Has something happened?" Blackmore asked, looking between his wife and son.

"Miss Walker is missing," Graham said, his gaze focused on Mr. Walker instead of his father.

"What do you mean she's missing?" Blackmore glanced at his land steward. "Did you know about this?"

Mr. Walker sighed, taking a seat in one of the empty armchairs. He used his index finger to adjust the bridge of his spectacles. "Elaina left last night. She intends to elope with Lord William."

Graham felt as if the wind had been knocked out of him. How could she have been so foolish? And how could she have not told him? He spent six years protecting her, defending her honor to anyone who dared to even mention the names of her cousins on her mother's side of the family.

"And you didn't think to mention it?" Blackmore asked while Graham remained speechless. His father's face had turned red.

"I trust my daughter to make her own decisions."

Blackmore made a sound of disbelief, and the duchess let out a sob. "Another scandal! I should've known. She's too much like her mother."

Graham had to think. There was a way to fix this. He would go over after them and prevent the whole thing from happening. He'd be able to talk some sense into her, even if his brother was being senseless. "Do you know where they went?" he asked Mr. Walker.

The older man shrugged. "I assumed they were going to Scotland."

"Yes, but they must've chosen a place to meet not far from here so they could make the journey together."

"I don't know. I did not ask."

Graham could have strangled the man. How could he be so careless with his own daughter's reputation and safety? He turned to his father. "I will go to London. Perhaps they met there."

Blackmore shook his head. "No. You won't go anywhere. You will stay here and allow your brother to make his own mistakes."

"And what of Miss Walker?"

"She is more foolish than I ever thought."

He left then, muttering something about having work to do. Graham watched him go before looking at his mother, who was crying. He procured a handkerchief from his jacket pocket and handed it to her.

"She was like a daughter to me," she sputtered. "Why would she not tell me?"

Graham frowned, wondering something similar. She was like a sister to him. Why would she not tell him? He could not abide by his father's rules. Not this time. "I will go to London to see if I can gather information." He turned to Mr. Walker. "Will you come with me?"

He shook his head. "I will not help you bring her back. She will be miserable without him. Can't you see that?"

Graham pursed his lips. "Fine. I'll go by myself."

WILL'S night alone at the Angel Inn in Oxford was restless, especially as he considered all the things that could possibly go wrong before Elaina even arrived.

One of the servants could have told Blackmore about Elaina's plans to escape in the middle of the night. There was no question his father would have intervened in that case, and even if Elaina remained steadfast in her desire to elope with him, they would have locked her in her bedchamber until she agreed to stay with them at Blackmore. Their next chance at marriage wouldn't be until spring, and only if Will could persuade his father to allow the match after moving him with his steadfast devotedness to Larkspur throughout the fall and winter.

There was also the chance someone would awaken in the middle of the night and catch Elaina trying to leave. Her father might've allowed it—the man married outside his own class almost thirty years ago himself—but someone like Montgomery or his mother would have been much less forgiving.

Elaina herself might have even decided against the whole plan after he left. He half expected a courier to arrive in the middle of the night, holding nothing but a letter filled with her regrets. When no courier came, he began to worry about highwaymen instead, cursing his own rashness in letting a young woman travel alone in the middle of the night and early morning.

When a knock finally came at his door around ten o'clock in the morning, Will was half expecting the worse. A feeling of calmness finally set in when he found Elaina standing on the other side of the door, looking tired with dark bags under eyes but nevertheless smiling brightly when she saw him, a sigh of relief passing through her lips. He pulled her into a tight embrace before shutting the door behind her. Perhaps the hardest part of their journey was over. From there on out, they would not be separated again.

"Did you manage to sleep at all on the way here?" he asked when he released her. She shook her head, and Will embraced her again. "I wish I could let you rest all day here, but I'm afraid we must leave right away if we are to make it to Gretna Green by Friday morning."

She nodded. "Of course," she said. "I think I'll be able to rest in the carriage now that I'll have you with me."

Will had his men ready the team after that, and once Elaina's things were loaded into his carriage, they were off. The couple sat across from each other at first, sharing uncertain smiles as they regarded each other. Will wished he knew what she was thinking. He only hoped she didn't regret coming—not yet, anyway. He suspected there might be moments in the future where she would, especially during the coldest and most drafty nights in Larkspur. She might end up wishing for the comforts of places like Blackmore Park or Giles Hunt's home in London. He would not blame her for such wishes, especially when he knew the challenges that inevitably lay ahead. He opened his arms then, urging her to come sit beside him in the carriage.

Silently, she moved next to him, letting him hold her close to him, cradling her head against his chest. He took the liberty of removing her bonnet and placing it on the seat next to him, running an open palm over the top of her head.

"Sleep, my darling," he murmured. "We will not stop again for another four hours."

She made a mumbled sound of contentment, and soon enough her eyes fluttered shut until she was resting peacefully against his body. He tilted his own head back then as well, letting himself shut his eyes until they were both sound asleep.

CHAPTER TEN

I find myself dreaming of you more and more often these nights, especially when I know I am close to returning to you. I wonder what you look like now. Are the miniatures you send me anything like your true likeness? I must confess I find myself thinking of more than just your face, though. I fear I've said too much. I should probably burn this letter. Sending it would only embarrass me.

—an excerpt of an unsent letter from Will, written in July 1815, to Elaina

GRAHAM ARRIVED in London the next day, visiting every hotel and stage station that he could possibly think of, giving out descriptions of his brother and Elaina, asking if anyone had seen them. When he found himself with no leads, he went to the bank, seeking out Mr. Hunt.

His friend saw him right away. Hunt looked at him with concern. "What brings you to London, Montgomery? You look pale."

"We believe Miss Walker ran away with my brother."

"Oh," Hunt said, moving to the sideboard in his office to

procure two glasses and a bottle of brandy. Montgomery couldn't help but notice that the man didn't sound surprised at all.

"Did she mention anything to you?" he asked, his eyes narrowing with suspicion.

Hunt shook his head as he poured two glasses of brandy. He handed one to Graham, who slumped into one of the chairs across from Hunt's desk. "She didn't, but I'm not surprised. I was going to offer for her two mornings ago, but she wouldn't hear it."

Graham nearly choked on the amber-colored beverage he was currently guzzling. He placed the glass on the desk and wiped his mouth with the back of his sleeve. "She told me that you didn't propose at all."

Hunt laughed once, sitting down at his desk. "She was probably only afraid to tell you the truth." He took a sip of his brandy. "You are not the most understanding sort of fellow."

"Can you blame me?" Graham grumbled. "Why should I have to follow the rules while Miss Walker and my brother do whatever they want?"

"And do you always follow the rules, Montgomery?"

Hunt's gaze was discerning, and Graham fidgeted in his seat. "I proposed to Clara last night, didn't I?"

"You did," Hunt said, nodding once, "but where do you plan on staying tonight?"

"I suppose I'll go to Marianne's since I'm here. I haven't seen her in a while." There was a moment of silence between the two men. Hunt stared at him thoughtfully. Graham fidgeted again. "You didn't expect me to give up my mistress just because I became engaged, did you?"

Hunt shrugged. "No, I suppose not. I only worry about Lady Clara."

Graham laughed. "I had no idea you were so virtuous, Mr. Hunt."

"I only think that perhaps you shouldn't judge Miss Walker and Lord William so harshly for eloping if you are going to see your mistress three days after becoming engaged."

"*I* am not breaking any rules."

"It would appear we do not agree on the rules, then."

"Apparently so."

Graham finished his glass of brandy quickly, putting it down on the table before standing up. He looked down on his friend who had judged him so harshly. "I'm sorry you will not have Miss Walker for yourself."

"It's fine. I've already come to terms with it. You will marry while I remain a bachelor with no more single friends."

Graham laughed once. "My cousin likes you, you know."

Hunt raised his brows. "Miss Winter, you mean? She's much too young for me."

Graham did not bother pointing out that his cousin was one year older than Clara. He did not wish to broach that subject with Hunt again, especially when Hunt had made his feelings about Marianne clear. "I'll leave you to your work. Good evening, Hunt."

THERE WAS no denying that the journey to Gretna Green was long and exhausting for both Elaina and Will. They only stopped every four hours so the team could rest and they could stretch their legs. They took food and refreshment at whatever coaching inn they found themselves at and used whatever archaic facilities were available to them.

They finally stopped for the night just south of Birmingham. Will estimated they were nearly 130 miles north of

Blackmore Park, and he supposed by now the estate was settling down for the night after a day of panic due to Elaina's disappearance.

Despite Elaina's protests, Will booked the largest suite of rooms available at the coaching inn.

"You do not have to put on airs for me," she said to him after the innkeeper showed them to their apartments. They were standing in the middle of a sitting room, where they agreed to take their dinner that night. "It would have been far more economical to share a room, and seeing as how we are to be married in two days, does it really matter if we consummate the relationship a bit early?"

He shot her a devious grin, walking toward her and placing two hands on her waist. "You act as if consummation is merely a chore we must do, like taking down the laundry from the clothesline or cleaning the stables," he joked.

She glared at him. "That's not what I mean at all. I'm only saying if you want to, I—"

"I want to take my time with you," he murmured, leaning in close to her ear. He thought he heard her breath catch as he did, which made him smile. He wanted their first time making love to be something that excited her instead of being something that frightened her, so he continued. "I have no desire to be rushed. I have no desire to be tired, either, after a long day of travel. When I finally take you, I want it to be something you remember for years to come—and I want to be married. Do you understand?"

Slowly, she nodded, her cheeks red. He pressed a kiss to one of them. "Good," he said.

A collection of cold meats, cheeses, bread, and some sweetmeats was brought up for supper. A glass of ale was poured for Will, and Elaina watched him as he drank it.

"I don't think I've ever seen you drink ale," she said.

He smiled. "Oftentimes it was the only drink available to

me overseas. My regiment didn't have the pleasures of things like my parents' cognac or champagne very often."

"Can I try some?" she asked, eyeing the frothy beverage in between them.

He pushed the tankard toward her. "Be my guest."

She took it to her lips and tasted a small sip, smacking her lips as she did. "That's quite good, actually."

He laughed. Something about the way she looked as she said it reminded him of the Elaina he knew as a boy. "I'll order another round. It'll help you sleep tonight."

"I suppose we must leave at dawn again."

He nodded. "We cannot risk anyone catching up to us."

"I… I don't think anyone will come," she said, her voice uncertain. "I should've told you earlier, but my father caught me leaving last night. He seemed to understand my desire to go, and if anyone can influence Blackmore in our favor, it's him."

"Was it hard to say goodbye to him?" he asked, frowning.

"Yes," she replied quietly. "But I'm glad I had the chance to do so."

Will nodded once, understanding. Another round of ales was ordered, and eventually the two of them went to their separate rooms to sleep a few hours before waking again to leave in the early morning hours. Elaina came to Will's room just as he was finishing dressing himself.

"Can you help me?" she asked as she turned around, revealing her unlaced stays and the unbuttoned bodice of her dress. He paused tying his cravat for a moment, too busy staring at her bare back to even think, let alone move or breathe.

He swallowed in an effort to find his voice. "Of course."

With every ounce of self-control he possessed, he laced her stays and then buttoned the bodice of her simple cotton traveling gown. When she turned around, she smiled at him.

"Thank you," she said. "It's a wonder how I made do before Ferguson became my maid."

They left shortly after that, traveling for almost fifteen hours before stopping for the night. Elaina had been napping against his arm when he woke her. "Where are we?" she asked.

"I believe we're just northeast of Liverpool," he said.

Like the night before, Will booked another suite of rooms, these ones smaller than the ones at the coaching inn from the night before. The ale that night was flat, and the bread was stale. Elaina looked wearier than ever, her clothes crumpled and her hair falling out of its pins.

"Do not worry, my dear," he said, extending his hand to hold hers from across the table where they sat and ate their supper. "We will be in Scotland soon enough."

It was another two days before they arrived in Gretna Green. They stopped another night in some small town only thirty some miles south of the Scottish border. Elaina begged Will to continue, but he told her the horses had to rest, and it was a small miracle that they made it this far with none of them throwing a shoe or becoming injured.

She supposed he was right, but she was eager to have the business over and done with. Once they were married, his family wouldn't be able to separate them, not to mention she had been thinking of their wedding night ever since she rejoined Will in Oxford. She was more excited than nervous. Will had a way at putting her at ease, so all that was left was her own desire, which she was truthfully still coming to terms with.

When they finally arrived at their destination and she stepped out of the carriage, Elaina was shocked. "Are we to be married by a blacksmith?"

Will nodded, a flicker of a smile playing at his lips. "Didn't you know? That's the way they do it here." When Elaina didn't reply, choosing only to look at the blacksmith's shop with uncertainty, he softly asked, "You aren't having regrets now, are you?"

Resolutely, she shook her head. "Of course not. Let's go in."

Inside the smithy's shop was small and dark, and the name of the man who married them was David Lang, a so-called anvil priest who had them recite their marriage vows over a literal anvil and demanded they call him Bishop Lang in return. Their witnesses were his son, Simon, and assistant, a man called Elliot. The whole ceremony cost three guinea—not including the simple ring that Lang swindled Will into purchasing, despite Elaina's protests she didn't need one—and Elaina had dissolved into fits of laughter by the end of it.

"I could barely understand a word of what he was saying," she said to Will as they made their way to the coaching inn where their driver brought the team to rest. "Are you sure we're really married, or did you just lose three guineas for nothing?"

Will tapped the folded piece of parchment inside his front coat pocket. "This piece of paper here says we are. I'm afraid there's only one thing left to do now."

She flushed as he regarded her, a feeling of anticipation growing inside of her when he booked only one room at the inn that evening. "Are you hungry?" he asked as he worked to remove his coat after they were shown to their room by the innkeeper.

Elaina removed the cloak she was wearing as well, hanging it on the nearest hook she could find. She then shrugged. It felt like butterflies had taken up most of her stomach at that point, though she hadn't eaten all morning. "A little, I suppose."

"They'll bring our luncheon to us shortly, and then we'll have the whole day to ourselves," he said. "I asked for champagne as well. I was surprised they had it all, but they must keep some on hand for occasions like this. We must celebrate the new Lady William as much as we can."

She smiled. "You know I don't want for much."

He reached for her hand, pulling her close to him and planting his hands firmly on her waist. He rested his forehead against hers, his eyes closed. "I still want for very much, I'm afraid," he said, his voice low. Her heart started to pound.

He opened his eyes then, leaning his head away from her to inspect her face. She was sure she was blushing, based on how hot she felt underneath his gaze. He cupped her face in his palms, this time leaning forward with his mouth. He pressed his lips against hers, and she almost gasped. That feeling—his mouth against hers—still felt so new, though she'd lost count of how many times they had kissed by then. Perhaps it only felt different because they were married now, and she knew one kiss could go much, much further.

A jolt of anticipation raced through her veins, and she leaned into him, urging him to go deeper, to explore more. Without breaking the kiss, he removed one hand from her cheek and pressed it against her lower back, pulling her toward him until she was wrapping her own arms around his waist.

Both of his hands were now cupping her bottom, lifting her into the air with ease. She instinctively wrapped her legs around his waist and let him carry her to the bed, where he deposited her on the freshly made linens. He climbed on top of her as he continued his loving assault on her mouth.

He kissed her jaw and her neck and her collarbone, and soon enough she was gasping for air, wanting to be free of her confining clothes, but there was a knock on the door.

"Luncheon," she said breathlessly, looking up at the door.

"You said you weren't hungry," Will replied, his voice muffled against her lips.

As much as she wanted to continue—his lips were greater than any meal a little coaching inn in some small village could ever serve—she didn't want to be rude, either.

"You should answer it," she said, her voice just as muffled.

He stopped, sighing. "Fine."

He moved to the door, and Elaina sat up, attempting to straighten her dress and hair, though there was really no use in doing such things. She reminded herself that they were married now, and there was nothing to hide or be ashamed about.

When they finished receiving their meal and the door was finally closed, Will extended his arm to the trays and plates on the small table that the servants had brought in. "Shall we eat?"

Elaina bit her lip. The food looked hardly appetizing at all when compared to the man standing in front of her. "I..."

Her hesitation was all the invitation he needed. He came around the other side of the bed, and she turned around to watch him. He was taking off his shoes, so she quickly did the same, then turned back to face him. He was crawling on all fours behind her, taking her by the waist and pulling her closer. She yelped at the sudden tug, and he laughed as he peppered kisses across the back of her neck and shoulder blades.

"How I've longed to undress you like this," he whispered in her ear. His breath tickled, causing her to shiver.

He unworked each button at the back of her bodice slowly, not because he was struggling with it, but because he seemed to want to savor each patch of new skin being revealed. He kissed her all the way down her spine until she was able to slip her arms out of her sleeves. He stopped her from moving any further, kneeling behind her and tracing up and down her bare arms with his fingertips. He reached around to her front, cupping her two breasts, still covered by her stays and chemise, and squeezed them. He groaned.

"You feel so amazing," he said. Something fluttered in her stomach, and she felt something pooling inside her where her thighs met. "I wonder…"

He let go of her breasts and started to unfasten her stays, discarding the piece of fabric on the floor beside the bed. He allowed her to stand up then, just so she could step out of her dress and petticoats. He lifted her chemise over her head himself from where he was kneeling behind her on the bed. When she turned to face him, there was nothing covering her chest, and she was left in only her drawers and garters. As she watched his eyes drift up and down her body, his mouth slightly slack, she shifted uncomfortably from foot to foot.

"I forgot how beautiful they were," he said, leaning forward to steady her, kissing the top of each breast as he did. "I've only seen them once, after all."

She closed her eyes, tilting her head back and getting lost in the feel of his mouth on her. She felt his hands slide from the side of her drawers, up her waist, and onto her breasts. He slowly moved back to her lips with his mouth while taking one of her nipples, already swollen with desire and wet from his previous kisses, between his right index finger and thumb, lightly pinching it. She gasped, and she felt him smile against her mouth and then bite her lip.

He placed his free hand on her lower back, gently forcing her to lift her legs one at a time, until she was kneeling on the bed with him. He grabbed her by the waist, lowering her onto the pillows. He hovered over her, making his way down her neck to her breasts with his lips. He took the left one in his hand, bringing its rosy head to his lips. She moaned as he swirled his tongue around its sensitive tip.

While he did that, his free hand drifted between her

thighs, finding the opening in her drawers and touching her in a place no one had touched before. She gasped when he did, looking down at him to find his eyes on her as he played with her nipple with his tongue. He stopped long enough to grin at her, as if she'd caught him doing something bad, and he was just daring her to tell him to stop.

"Do you like that?" he asked breathlessly as his fingers found an extra sensitive spot at the top of her cleft. She nodded slowly, almost unsure of the pleasure she was feeling from just the tips of two of his fingers gently moving round and round. They slowly drifted downward, and she tensed as she felt him insert one finger inside of her. He moaned as she gasped.

"You're so wet," he said, his voice was almost like a growl, "and tight."

She threw her head back, not wanting him to see her blush. "I-I wish you wouldn't say things like that. It's embarrassing."

He removed his finger then, shifting his body on the bed so they were face-to-face. She saw the concern in his eyes as he brushed her hair away from her face. Most of it had fallen out of its pins since they went tumbling onto the bed.

"Oh, darling," he said, kissing her on the top of her nose. "There's nothing embarrassing about it. It's wonderful."

He kissed her again, cradling her face with his hands and focusing on just her lips for the time being. As she felt herself relaxing and growing more confident, she lifted her hands to start exploring the clothed muscles on his back until she was pulling at his shirt, trying to remove it from his breeches.

He laughed against her lips again and then kneeled back. "Allow me," he said, taking his shirt off over his head with one quick movement.

Although her initial reaction was to look away, she allowed herself to stare at his bare chest and abdomen, which was more defined than she had expected. She sat up and reached out to him, using her fingertips to trace a line from the middle of his chest to his belly button, where there were the beginnings of a thin line of hair leading to the waistband of his pants. He grabbed her hand before it could reach his breeches, though she would have to be blind not to notice the growing bulge there.

Folding her hand into her bare chest, he leaned over and kissed her again, pushing her back onto the pillows with the force of his mouth on hers. "Can I do something for you?" he asked. "You might be embarrassed at first, but I swear you'll like it."

She nodded slowly, nervous anticipation still boiling up inside her. He smiled, kissed her one more time on the lips, then started to make his way down her body with his mouth. He stopped at her bellybutton, lingering on her lower stomach before kneeling back and working to remove her stockings. He did each one slowly, kissing the inside of her thigh, the top of her kneecaps, all the way down her shinbone as he worked them off. She felt she might die for wanting. He seemed to enjoy the way she was biting her lip, watching as he finally removed her drawers.

He lay down again, hooking her legs over his shoulders and leaning forward to kiss her… well, there. She gasped at the invasion of his lips and tongue in that place, using her hand to grab his head and instinctively push him back.

"Will!" she gasped.

He looked up and shushed her, licking his lips. "Relax." When she didn't look convinced, he added, "Trust me."

Slowly, she nodded, allowing him to kiss her there again. He focused most of his attentions on that same sensitive spot from before, and she found herself lifting her hand to her mouth, hoping no one would hear her moan. He kissed and sucked and licked until she was throwing her head back and saying his name—this time not out of shock, but out of pleasure.

It was like he'd found a coil inside of her. He had wound it up as tightly as he could until all that was left for it to do was snap and release. Her legs shook. Her breathing became haggard. She thought she might've seen stars on the ceiling above her. The feeling became so intense that she tried to inch away from him, but he continued until she had nothing left to give.

When he stopped, he started taking off his breeches with such ferocity she was sure he might rip them. It didn't take long until he was on top of her again, positioning himself at her slick entrance. He stopped his frenzied movements to massage her cheek with his palm.

"You are so beautiful," he whispered. "I want you, Elaina. I want you so badly. This might hurt, but I promise to be as gentle as I can be."

She nodded, and he kissed her, giving him leave to slowly slide inside her. She winced at his slow and unfamiliar invasion as his breathing became labored. "God, you feel so good," he moaned. "Am I hurting you? Please tell me I'm not hurting you."

She shook her head, not wanting to admit that he was. She only wanted to give him the same pleasure he had given her.

He continued to move further and further, only stopping when he was fully sheathed by her. There was pain, yes, but as he slowly started to thrust in and out of her, her pain turned to pleasure. He kissed her as he did, and she couldn't help but want more and more. She pressed her hands on his lower back, urging him deeper. He groaned, taking her hands off his back and holding them above her head.

"If you do that, this might not last very long," he said through gritted teeth. She wrapped her legs around his waist then, using the heels of her feet to nudge him along. She had to use her body, for she couldn't speak her desires. If she opened her mouth, she might simply cry out instead. All she wanted was more of him.

"You're going to be the death of me, Lady William," he said, his voice low and gravely beside her ear.

"Stop talking and kiss me."

Will did as he was told, and Elaina decided right then and there that she had made the right decision. Perhaps that was base or vulgar or thought only out of lust, but she couldn't imagine sharing her bed with anyone but him.

She felt herself reaching the point of no return once more, crying out when that senseless wave of pleasure overtook her body. He seemed to be going through the same emotions, the same physical torture, as he took one last plunge inside her before groaning her name and collapsing on top of her. A feeling of warmth—his warmth—filled her, and she knew if she died that very moment, she would die feeling happy and complete.

They lay like that for a moment, perspiring and blistering hot, yet neither of them minded their bodies being intertwined at all as they panted, trying to catch their breath. When they succeeded in regaining their bearings and moved to lay beside each other, Elaina smiled at her husband as he played with the loose strands of the damp and sweaty hair that framed her face.

"I think luncheon can wait a little while longer," she said. "Don't you?"

He laughed, planting a kiss on her lips. "I do, Lady William. I do."

PART TWO

CHAPTER ELEVEN

*My brother and Miss Walker have eloped, or at least that's what
we think. We've neither heard from nor seen either of them for the
past three days. They are probably in Scotland now or perhaps on
their way to Larkspur, already married. I know you were fond of
Miss Walker when you met her, so you can write to her there. I
must caution you on aligning yourself too strongly with her. My
father is beside himself on what to do about the pair of them; he
considers what they've done to be the ultimate betrayal...*

—an excerpt of a letter from Lord Montgomery to Lady
Clara, early September 1815

WILL and Elaina spent their first day of wedded bliss in bed,
making love twice before falling asleep for the entire afternoon. Neither of them had realized what a toll their long
journey had taken on them after such an eventful morning.

Their luncheon was ice cold by the time they even
considered eating it, so they drank the champagne that was
delivered to their room while Will rang for dinner instead.

Elaina had changed into her nightdress and dressing gown by the time it arrived, much to Will's disappointment.

He had decided he rather liked Elaina's nude form, and when she returned to the bed after finishing her meal, he became determined to divest her of her garments once more. She was lounging on top of the crumpled bedclothes, her elbow bent and head in her hand, watching him eat the remnants of his dinner.

Without finishing, he stood from the table and slinked over to her, pressing a kiss to her lips. He decided to lay behind her on the bed, tugging at her hips so her bottom was cradled at his groin.

"Are you tired?" he asked, feeling a familiar twitch underneath his breeches as he absentmindedly played with a strand of her curly brown hair.

She bit her lip, smiling at him. She must've known he wasn't talking about the sort of exhaustion that required sleep. She had been a virgin until that morning. He knew she must've been at least a little sore after their first two lovemaking sessions.

"A little," she admitted. "I'm not sure if I'll be able to just go back to sleep, though. We slept all day, and I have so much on my mind."

"What sort of things?" he asked, nuzzling the crook of her neck from behind, kissing and tickling her with his hot breath until she couldn't help but giggle.

"You're downright insatiable."

"I don't disagree," he said in between kisses.

"Where did you learn to do all of this, anyway?"

"Call it instinct," he replied.

"William…"

He sighed. He hadn't entered their marriage a virgin like her, but he was hardly a rake like Cousin Robert. There had been girls at Eton before he left school, ones he bedded mostly due to pressure from his schoolmates and a desire to fit in with the other boys, but those were hardly great love affairs.

"Would you like me to admit that most of what I've done to you I've only heard about secondhand?" he asked. "Wartime does not leave much opportunity for love affairs, especially when one is pining away for his childhood friend back in England."

He was still lying behind her, so she turned her neck to look at him over her shoulder, eyebrows raised. "Pining away?"

He nodded. "Did you know that you're actually quite easy to pine for? What with your letters and the miniatures you sent me every year on my birthday."

She bit her lip, grinning. "Then my scheme worked. I hoped you would come back one day if I could make you want me enough."

"Oh, I wanted you. Every time you wrote to me about some ball you attended and all the men you danced with, I half considered deserting my regiment and racing home to be with you instead. My biggest fears were that you didn't care about me half as much as I cared about you and that you wouldn't wait for me, especially when I knew my mother would have preferred you with a man like Hunt or even Seymour. I can only imagine how I would have felt if someone had proposed and you said yes. I doubt I would have lasted another battle after I found out."

She frowned. "I hope you know that if anyone had proposed, I would have said no. Your mother would have been livid, of course. She always said I wrote to you too much."

He laughed once. "You would have said no? But I nearly had to throw you over my shoulder and drag you to Gretna Green."

"Well, I hadn't expected everyone to be against us like they were when you returned," she said, glaring at him. "I wonder what they all must be thinking now. They never did come after us, did they?"

He shook his head. "No, they didn't, but even if they did, no one could have stopped you from becoming my wife, especially now that I can do this."

He flipped her from her side so that she was lying on her front. As he climbed on top of her, the inside of his knees trapping her by the waist, he leaned down to kiss her on the neck. She attempted to turn around from her waist so she could see him, giggling as he trailed kisses from across her shoulder blades to down her spine.

"What are you doing?" she asked.

"I have not adequately shown my love to your back. Take these off, will you?"

He tugged at the hems of her robe and gown, helping her to untie them and then dragging them upwards and over her head so she was completely bare again. He softly moaned at the sight of her. Her delicate shoulder blades, the inward curve of her waist, her perfectly round bottom. He wanted to touch all of it, with his hands *and* his mouth.

"Let me see you," she said, struggling to turn around. He only tightened his grip around her waist with his knees and shushed her. He reached around his back, rubbing her bottom and then using his fingers to gently prod the welcoming slit between her thighs.

Feeling her wetness resulted in his manhood hardening almost immediately, especially after she turned her head around again, revealing a pair of hooded eyes and her slightly open mouth. He bent down to kiss her on the lips.

"Are you sure you aren't too tired?" he asked breathlessly.

"I'm sure," she whispered.

"Then let me love you this way."

She watched as he hastily removed his clothes and then scooted behind her, gently spreading her legs so he could fit comfortably between them. He grabbed a pillow from the top of the bed and gingerly lifted her hips, placing it beneath her lower stomach before positioning himself at her entrance. He took a breath as he entered her, refusing to exhale until he was certain he wouldn't spend himself right then and there. This position only served to make her even tighter, but he would try to withstand it for as long as he could for her own pleasure.

He began to move—back and forth, back and forth—causing her to groan. He watched as she closed her eyes and moved one of her arms to cover her mouth with her hand. He, however, wanted to hear her, so he grabbed that same arm, bringing it behind her back, tugging her—closer, closer, closer—to his own body. He took his other hand and snaked it underneath her front, first caressing her breast, then dragging his hand down her belly until his fingertips found the sensitive bud just below where their two bodies joined.

His fingers circled there, and her body responded in kind. Her insides became damper and damper until he felt her convulse around him, her legs shaking with her climax. She arched her back, causing her bottom to look even plumper and more delectable as she came to rest on her forearms. Her breasts were now lifted off the bed with her repositioning, so he removed his hand from where their bodies met to hold on to one of them, applying gentle ministrations to her hardened nipple. He used his other hand to grab a fistful of her hair, gently pulling it backward with every thrust.

He bent down to whisper in her ear. "I'm not hurting you, am I?"

"N-no."

He grinned, yanking her hair a bit harder than before. She moaned. "You like it, don't you?"

He moved his hands to squeeze her buttocks as he continued his relentless rhythm of in and out, in and out. Lightly spanking her once, she moaned in response, and he thought she might've come again, judging by the way her intimate muscles repeatedly tightened and untightened around his cock. She looked behind her and let out a dreamy sigh upon seeing his face above her. Her delirious state was enough for him to allow himself to start climbing toward his own peak. He gripped the side of her hips firmly, taking her roughly until he was riding out his own waves of pleasure. He shuddered as he spent himself inside of her.

When he finally unsheathed himself, he toppled over beside her, head on the pillows, panting.

Elaina turned to face him, deeply flushed and giggling. "Have you finally been satiated?"

"Mmm," he said, nodding with his eyes closed, suddenly feeling tired. He wondered what time it was. "You're satiated as well, I trust?"

"Yes. A bit sore, actually."

Immediately sitting up and frowning, he said, "I was too rough with you. I should've known better. I should've been gentler. I should've—"

Her eyes twinkled as she reached out a finger and touched his lips, effectively silencing him. "Gentler?" she asked, a devious look on her face. "Where's the fun in that?"

They both laughed. He leaned down and gently pecked the side of her mouth. "Come now," he said. "Time to get under the covers and go to sleep."

"Must we?"

"Afraid so. As much as I enjoy your eagerness, we must pace ourselves. We're married now and will have all the time in the world to make love."

She pouted. "Fine, but I won't be so easily turned down

tomorrow night. Perhaps *I* will climb on top of *you* and have my own wicked way with you."

As much as he liked the sound of that, he had nothing left to give after three sessions of lovemaking in one night. "Is that supposed to be a threat?" he asked.

"Not a very good one, I guess," she said with a laugh.

"No," he agreed. "One doesn't typically have pleasant dreams about threats, but I suppose there's a first time for everything."

"Sweet dreams, then, husband."

He kissed the top of her nose. "Sweet dreams, wife."

ELAINA AWOKE LATE the next morning. Will was already dressed, enjoying a cup of tea while looking out the window of their room at the inn. When he heard the sheets rustling, he turned and smiled at her.

"Good morning," she said sleepily. A feeling of slight embarrassment crept over her, seeing him and remembering the intimacies they shared the night prior, but she reassured herself that such activities were natural, especially between a husband and wife.

Which was what they were. She grinned happily.

Leaving the cup of tea on the windowsill, Will made his way to the bed, leaning over her and planting a firm kiss on her lips. "Good morning, my darling."

She moved to sit up more, peering out the window closest to the bed. With only a few clouds in the sky, the sun was shining brightly, and she wondered how long she had been asleep. "What time is it?" she asked, furrowing her brow.

"It's half past ten."

Gasping, she asked, "Why did you let me sleep so late?

Oh! We should've left hours ago. Larkspur is a two-day journey at least, and I've only delayed us."

He chuckled. "There's no hurry. You looked so peaceful sleeping that I couldn't bear to disturb you. Besides, after all you indulged me last night, I thought you deserved the extra rest."

She only blushed in response, biting her lip.

"Shall I call for breakfast?" he asked.

She shook her head. "I'll get dressed, and then we can leave."

"Not until you eat breakfast as well. There's another long journey ahead of us, and you must be well-fed. We'll be less than halfway there by the time we stop at the next coaching inn this evening."

Reluctantly, she nodded in agreement, and the newlyweds ate breakfast together in a private dining room downstairs. After one heavenly day of rest, they were back in their carriage, happily on their way to Larkspur.

The journey took them three days, and when the castle finally came into sight, Elaina couldn't help but gasp. She had never seen such a large house before.

"It's larger than Blackmore Park!" she exclaimed.

Will seemed just as surprised as she was, perhaps wondering why his father had entrusted him with such a piece of property.

The castle was three stories of white stone with a large portico at the center, complete with four Doric columns that extended from the bottom to the top of the house. Their carriage stopped in front of a flight of steps leading up to the entrance. A woman stood waiting for them, watching as their driver came around the side of the carriage to open the door. Will stepped down first, helping Elaina out next.

Elaina suspected the woman was in her midfifties. She was slim, with brown hair and a long face, and she seemed to be giving Elaina and her new husband a once-over. She spoke to Will first.

"Are you the new master?" she asked.

Will nodded once. "Yes, I am Lord William Winter. You are?"

"Mrs. Harding," she replied. "Your housekeeper." She glanced at Elaina before turning back to Will. "I was expecting you five days ago. You're lucky I happened to be looking out one of the windows and saw your carriage coming, or else I wouldn't have known to wait outside for you."

"My apologies, Mrs. Harding," Will said. Elaina caught him looking at her out of the corner of her eye. She could tell he was nervous.

"I am Elaina Winter, Lord William's wife," Elaina said, smiling at the woman in an effort to lighten the mood. She seemed unimpressed by the statement. "You may call me Lady William."

Mrs. Harding turned back to Will. "The duke did not tell me that you had a wife, Lord William."

"We were only recently married," he explained.

Mrs. Harding nodded once. "Very well," she said. "Would you like to see the house? Your driver can bring your things into the main hall."

"A tour would be wonderful," Elaina replied.

Mrs. Harding took them up the steps through the main door. The entrance hall was large but empty, with one fireplace and collections of dust where impressive portraits must've once hung on its white walls.

"I apologize for the dust, Lord and Lady William," Mrs. Harding said. "The former master let go of most of the staff and sold most of his paintings and furniture before the duke bought Larkspur." She glanced at Will. "I hope you aren't too disappointed."

"I'm not quite sure either of us knew what to expect," Will replied with a sheepish grin. "Have you been here all by yourself?"

Mrs. Harding nodded once.

"Why didn't my father hire back the old staff?"

"I wrote to him about it, but he insisted his son would handle it once he returned from Belgium."

"You must be relieved that we are here!" Elaina exclaimed. When Mrs. Harding's expression gave no indication of relief, Elaina frowned.

"I will be relieved once more help is hired," she replied coolly. "Most of the old staff have already found placements elsewhere, but there are a few that still linger in the village, still looking for work. I will take you to see them tomorrow, if you'd like. The rest you can advertise for in the newspapers."

"Yes, let's do that."

Elaina swallowed nervously. Hiring the staff would be her first big task as lady of the house. She was happy that Mrs. Harding was willing to help, but the woman's judgmental gaze did not go unnoticed by Elaina. She wondered what the housekeeper was thinking. Perhaps that her and Will were much too young to run an estate like Larkspur, which seemed to be a shadow of its former self the more and more Elaina saw of it.

The house had three drawing rooms, only one of which was outfitted with furniture. The salon on the south side of the house was much like the entrance hall, large but void of anything interesting. Elaina nearly breathed a sigh of relief when they reached the dining room and found that there was still a table and chairs. She had started to fear that they would be forced to eat their supper that night on the floor.

As for entertainment, there was none. The billiards room, as Mrs. Harding called it, was not much of a billiards room at all, considering it had no table to play upon. As for the library, the books were all gone, and all that remained was a desk and three chairs. Elaina couldn't help but notice the way Will looked upon the room with a sadness in his eyes, as if he hadn't imagined he'd be doing business in such an unimpressive room.

Larkspur, though large, was nothing like Blackmore. It was an empty vessel, and Elaina tried to let that excite her, knowing the possibilities were endless for how they could decorate the house for themselves, but then she reminded herself they had very little money. There would be no trips to London, or even Cambridge, for new books, paintings, and furniture. They still hadn't seen the entire estate, and the land was much more important than their own comforts at home.

She only hoped that Will wouldn't become too discouraged. When Mrs. Harding led them upstairs, she only bothered showing them their bedroom.

"This is the only room with any furniture remaining," she said, taking them to a room with wood paneling and floors, partially covered by a red-and-gold floral-patterned carpet. The bed was large, complete with four posts holding up a canopy, placed adjacent to a fireplace. "I can bring up a wash basin later if your driver is willing to help."

"I will bring one up with him later, after dinner," Will replied. "I do not want you to hurt yourself. We'll hire proper footmen soon enough."

Mrs. Harding smiled slightly at that. "Thank you, my lord. I am not the best cook, but I can have dinner ready within the hour."

"That would be wonderful, Mrs. Harding," Elaina said.

After Mrs. Harding left, Will and Elaina stood in the center of the room, inspecting their surroundings. She wondered if he had expected separate bedrooms. She remembered her parents sharing a room in the cottage that they lived in before her mother died, but she knew the duke and duchess did not, as was custom for couples in their position.

"Are you terribly disappointed?" Elaina asked when Will's gaze stopped wandering and landed on her. She bit her lip, and he smiled.

"What is there to be disappointed about?" he asked, moving closer to her and taking her into his arms.

"Well, if you had a rich wife, you could have this house properly outfitted within a week, and you would have your own bedchamber, and—"

Will brought his finger to her lips, effectively silencing her. "I have no need for a rich wife. I have you, and you are worth a thousand rich wives. At least I'll have you by my side tomorrow, when we go out to survey the land. God knows I have no idea what I'm doing. I'm still trying to understand why my father thought this was a good idea."

"He's only trying to challenge you."

"I suppose I failed the first test by stealing you away."

Elaina smiled. "I'm rather glad you did—despite how empty this house is. It's almost eerie, isn't it?"

"Good thing I'm here to protect you from any ghosts."

Elaina laughed, and he kissed her. "Do you think there's time before dinner…?"

"There's always time," she replied, kissing him back, leading him toward the bed.

CHAPTER TWELVE

I'm happy to report that Will and I married in Gretna Green some four days ago, and we have now arrived at Larkspur Castle, where the housekeeper Mrs. Harding was waiting for us. I think she was a little surprised to find that there was not only a master of the house, but a mistress as well. I'm sure this missive is much shorter than you would like, but we have a busy morning ahead of us surveying the estate and visiting our tenants, and I must get going. A longer letter will follow—I promise.

—an excerpt of a letter from Elaina to her father at Blackmore Park

ELAINA AWOKE EARLY the next day, eager to see the rest of the estate. While Will remained in bed, she put on her dressing robe and slippers and went downstairs to the library in search of materials with which to write a letter. She knew her father must be worried about her, and she wanted to make sure he knew they were married and arrived at Larkspur safely.

Although she was happy to be married, she wondered

constantly about the inhabitants of Blackmore. She could only imagine how angry Montgomery was at her. She thought of writing him as well, but perhaps it would be better if she allowed him to reach out to her first.

When she found nothing of use in the library, she went belowstairs, looking for Mrs. Harding. She found the woman stoking the fire in the kitchen. She looked up when she heard Elaina on the stairs, seeming somewhat surprised.

"You are up early," she declared, standing up and wiping her hands on her apron. "I suppose you need help dressing?"

Elaina tilted her head to the side. "I suppose it would be nice to have some help, but I was actually wondering if you had anything to write with here. I'd like to send a letter to my father to let him know we arrived safely."

Mrs. Harding nodded once, leaving the kitchen to enter the corridor. Elaina followed her, entering a room which she assumed was the woman's office. Much like the rest of the house, it was furnished sparsely, with just a few chairs and a desk. She procured what Elaina needed quickly.

"How long have you worked here, Mrs. Harding?" Elaina asked, lingering in the office. She knew all of the servants so well at Blackmore. She'd like to know Mrs. Harding, too, if the woman was to be her housekeeper.

"Oh, for at least thirty years," Mrs. Harding said.

"So you worked for the family that owned this house before the duke?"

The housekeeper gave Elaina a suspicious look. "Surely my history doesn't interest you that much, my lady."

"Oh, but it does, Mrs. Harding! If we are to live under the same roof, I'm afraid I must know a few things about you."

Mrs. Harding glanced at the parchment paper, quill, and ink pot in Elaina's hands. "Is your father a duke like Lord William's?"

Elaina shook her head. "Oh, no. I'm afraid my father is nothing more than a land steward."

Mrs. Harding looked a bit taken aback by this, and Elaina bit her lip. The last thing she wanted was to lose her housekeeper's respect.

"I see," was all Mrs. Harding said. She took a seat at the desk. Elaina remained standing, watching her. "I hope your husband takes better care of this place than the old earl. He inherited it from his father when he was around your husband's age. He was a selfish man, if you don't mind me saying, Lady William. He let the place go to ruin. Now most of the tenants have left, and I'm afraid I'll be without a job."

Elaina frowned. "Surely you must have more faith in me and my husband than that."

Mrs. Harding raised a critical brow. "You are both young —just like he and his wife."

"I know we are young, but trust me when I say we have every intention of making Larkspur a success again. I meant what I said about going to the village with you. We will hire as much as the old help as we can afford."

"Afford?" Mrs. Harding echoed. "Surely a lord and lady such as you and your husband can outfit a house such as this very quickly."

"I'm afraid not, Mrs. Harding. You see... Lord William and I... well, the duke did not approve of our marriage. He will not give us much to live on, and until we make the land profitable again, I'm afraid money will be tight."

Mrs. Harding pursed her lips. Elaina swallowed, afraid she might have said too much. Perhaps ladies did not have such frank conversations with her housekeepers. She should've known she'd be terrible at this. Why hadn't she paid more attention whenever the duchess planned her grand house parties?

"Well, I'll be going back upstairs now." She held out the

letter-writing materials. "Thank you for procuring these for me, Mrs. Harding."

Elaina couldn't have left the woman's office any quicker. Unable to think from embarrassment, she scrawled a short missive to her father in the library and sealed it with an old wafer she found in the back of one of the desk drawers. Perhaps if Mrs. Harding wasn't too ashamed to serve her, she would go to the village to post it after Elaina and Will had left.

Letter in hand, she went back upstairs to find her husband dressed and ready for the day. He smiled when he saw her.

"There you are," he said, crossing the room to bring her into his arms and kiss her. Elaina had come to enjoy how affectionate Will had become. She was sure she would never grow tired of being married. He looked down at the letter in her hand. "Is that for your father?"

Elaina nodded. "Yes, Mrs. Harding was kind enough to spare me some parchment and ink. I fear I've made a fool out of myself in front of her, though."

Will furrowed his brow. "What do you mean?"

She sighed. "When I told her I was writing a letter to my father, she asked if he was a duke like yours. You should've seen the look on her face when I told her he was a land steward. She must be livid to serve a woman such as me!"

"I'm sure it's not so bad, my darling. If she has a problem serving you, we'll only hire another housekeeper."

"That's other thing," Elaina said, breaking away from Will to sit on the edge of the bed. "I may have told her we have no money."

Will laughed once. "Well, isn't that the truth? She's bound to find out sometime." He went to sit beside her, pushing a loose strand of hair behind her ear. He smiled kindly at her. "You fret too much, my dear. I'm sure Mrs. Harding thinks nothing of it. If anything, she's probably thankful for your honesty. I can only imagine what it was like to serve the old earl, watching him let the estate go to ruin."

The sound of someone clearing their throat caused them both to look up. Mrs. Harding was standing in the doorway.

"Mrs. Harding!" Elaina exclaimed. She hoped the woman hadn't heard them talking about her.

"It's been a while since you were belowstairs, my lady, and you hadn't rung, so I thought I'd come and help you dress you."

"Oh, you don't have to—"

"I insist."

Elaina and Will exchanged a glance. He grinned at her, as if to say *I told you so.* Elaina looked back at Mrs. Harding. "Very well," she said, standing up as Mrs. Harding entered the room.

"There's breakfast in the drawing room, my lord," she said to Will. He nodded once, smiling at Elaina before leaving the room.

Mrs. Harding gestured at the letter in Elaina's hand. "I can post that for you while you and Lord William are out today, if you would like."

Elaina smiled, handing the letter to her. Perhaps the woman wasn't too ashamed to serve her after all. "Thank you, Mrs. Harding."

ELAINA AND WILL took to their horses for the rest of the day, surveying the land Will had been tasked with managing. The entire parish of Larkspur was over five thousand acres, most of it being pasture for shorthorns, though some seven hundred of it was arable farmland. What Elaina and Will found that day was a disturbing lack of farmers and cattle.

What farmers they did meet lived in dilapidated cottages

with their families. When they discovered that Will was the new squire, they rattled off lists of things that needed repair, including broken cottage windows, crumbling pasture walls, and leaky barn roofs. Elaina listened carefully to each interview and spoke to the farmers' wives as well, entertaining their children as she did. Dealing with the tenant farmers of Larkspur was no different than dealing with the ones of Blackmore, though they had been woefully neglected over the years. They all wanted the same thing: money to pay their rent and fill the bellies of their children. Elaina silently cursed the old earl for leaving them in such a way.

Other than the farms, there was a long-forgotten forester's lodge and lumberyard on the estate as well. Elaina and Will decided immediately the estate's four groves were where they would make their money to pay for the repairs to the farm buildings, though they'd have to move quickly if they were to attract enough tenant farmers in time for the spring planting.

"There will be an advertisement for a woodcutter in every newspaper in Cambridgeshire by the end of next week," Will said on their ride home. Amazingly, the sun was beginning to dip underneath the horizon, though it felt like they'd only just set out from the castle.

"I only hope there are enough strapping young men in the village to help Harding *and* said woodcutter," Elaina teased.

"Yes, we will need a footman or two as well," he replied with a grin. "Perhaps we can go to the village with Mrs. Harding tomorrow."

"I'm sure she would be more than happy to help. I don't think she's as unimpressed with me as I originally suspected."

"I'm not surprised. You are hardly an unimpressive woman. You will make a great lady of the house once you have a staff."

Elaina frowned. "You don't expect to only worry about

the house, do you? I think we should worry about the land first."

"You're right," he replied with a nod. "But you should let me worry about that. The fields are no place for a lady."

Elaina narrowed her eyes. "Do you really think I'll let you keep all the fun to yourself? I'll be out here with you, of course, whether you like it or not. Surely you did not expect me to sit around doing nothing all day."

"The lady of the house cannot be seen clearing weeds and fixing fences," he scoffed. "I will not allow it."

"How else will I make up for my lack of dowry? You could have had a woman with—"

"Elaina—"

"How about this," she said, not wishing to argue with him. "If I can beat you back to the stables, you will let me help you. If not, I will remain in the house where I will make up lists of all the furniture we must buy but cannot afford. Deal?"

She didn't let him answer. With a click of her tongue, she was off. She had left her hair half down that day, not bothering with any sort of hat, and tangles of brown curls flowed in the wind behind her. She arrived at the stables well ahead of him, bringing her mare to a stop before jumping down without the help of a groomsman. She looked up at Will and laughed.

"I told you I would win," she said.

"You had a head start," he grumbled as he got down from his own horse. "I suppose you can help me, but you must go to the village and hire enough people to keep Mrs. Harding content. We can afford a few extra hands around the house, and the last thing we need is our housekeeper leaving us for a much more impressive estate than ours."

Elaina sighed. "Fine."

As they ate dinner that night, Mrs. Harding appeared in

the dining room with a stack of letters. "I picked these up when I was posting your letter, my lady," she said to Elaina, handing them to her.

Elaina took the stack of letters, knowing right away they'd be from Blackmore. There were two for Will and four for Elaina.

"Shall we take turns reading them out loud?" she asked after Mrs. Harding had left, her voice nervous.

Will nodded solemnly, tearing open the first letter. "I'll start," he said. Looking down at the piece of parchment, he added, "It's from my father."

William,

I suppose by the time you receive this, you'll be at Larkspur with your new wife. If you've come to regret your decision upon seeing the place, I only hope you do not take it out on poor Miss Walker, now Lady William. She is a foolish girl—like most girls are, I suppose—saddled for life with an even more foolish boy as her husband. You will have your standard allowance and whatever income the property makes—which won't be much. You should know that you will have no handouts from me as you embark on your new mission in life: the management of Larkspur. Do not disappoint me like you have in your choice for a wife.

Blackmore

"How dare he speak of you in that way," Will said, crumpling the short missive and letting it land on the floor beside the dining table.

Elaina bit her lip, thinking perhaps they had been foolish to think Blackmore would ever accept them, but knowing she couldn't let his lack of support discourage her. The house would be difficult to manage, yes, but the land was something she had already decided she could handle, and handle well, as long as Will let her. She felt at ease when they visited the tenants that day, even though there was plenty of work ahead of them.

"I'm sure the next one will be much more pleasant," she said sunnily, opening the first letter from her stack of three. She tore it open. "It's from your mother."

Dearest Elaina,

I have always thought of you as my daughter, but I suppose it's official now that you've married my son. I have decided I'm not angry with you—your mother would hate me if I was—but I do wish you would have told me what you intended. Perhaps then we could have gone about the affair in an entirely different way. The family name is now engulfed in scandal, with the name "Elaina" firmly at the center of it. You of all people should know how such a scandal can ruin a woman's reputation, but I suppose you have already made your decision. I only hope you can live with the consequences. It saddens me that I will not be seeing you for a while, but please know that you and William are still welcome here at Christmastime.

Love,
   Helena Blackmore

"I suppose that's slightly more positive than your father's note," Elaina said, laying the letter flat beside her dinner plate.

"Why should your name be at the center of the scandal, though?" Will asked. "I was the one who asked you to run away with me."

She shot him a pointed look. "Surely you know the answer to that, my dear." She wondered if the news had made its way to London yet, and if Earl Gillingham and Viscount Fitzroy had learned of her marriage. Would they be disappointed or proud? She had married a son of a duke, after all.

She eyed the next letter beside Will's hand on the table. "That looks like Montgomery's writing. What does he have to say?"

If anything, Montgomery's note was more disdainful than his father's.

William,

I know I shouldn't be surprised by your selfish behavior, seeing as how you first deserted your family for the whimsy of being a soldier eight years ago now. I only wish you wouldn't have roped poor Miss Walker into it. What she sees in you I will never understand. If Father had allowed it, I would have chased after the both of you and dragged her back to Blackmore to marry a more suitable man. It was what she deserved.

Montgomery

"Do not listen to him," Elaina said, shaking her head. "He's always been a fool when it comes to you."

He sighed. "At least it's my last one," he replied. "You still have three more. I only hope they're letters of support, not ridicule."

The next one she opened was from Lady Clara Haywood, surprisingly enough. It read:

Lady William,

Allow me to offer you felicitations on your recent wedding. Montgomery will probably be disappointed when he discovers I went through with writing to you, but you were so kind to me when

I came to Blackmore that I couldn't resist, for I was so happy when I heard the news. I often noticed the way you and Will looked at each other during the house party, and I always thought you and he would be a much better match than you and Mr. Hunt—no offense to Mr. Hunt, of course. I rather like him with Miss Winter, don't you? Anyway, Montgomery and I are to be married in the spring. It won't be as romantic as an elopement in Scotland, but I have no close female relatives of my own, and seeing as how are to be sisters-in-law, I was hoping you would be my maid of honor. Do say yes?

Your friend,
   Clara Haywood

"Maid of honor?" Elaina asked incredulously after reading the letter, still staring at it. She looked at Will. "I hardly know the poor girl."

Elaina liked Clara well enough, but surely she had a closer relative she could have asked.

"I suppose you made an impression," Will replied. "I'm not surprised. Now read the next one."

My dear Elaina,

I know you said you would write to me when you safely arrived in Larkspur, but I couldn't wait to send you a short missive of my own. Although it is well known by the wretched ton that you lack any sort of sizeable dowry, I have enclosed the paperwork that transfers your one thousand pounds to Will. I know you will use it wisely and turn Larkspur into a lasting success.

Always yours,
   Papa

"At last," Elaina said, "some money we can use on the estate—even if it's not much, it will certainly help."

Will frowned. "We should invest that money. You can use the interest as pin money."

Elaina cocked an eyebrow at her husband as she put her father's letter in her pile of correspondence. "I'm sure I have no use for pin money, and if you insist upon investing it, I will spend all the interest on the estate rather than myself."

Will grunted, and Elaina moved to open her fourth and final letter. She gasped when she saw who it was from.

Dear Lady William,

Please do not be alarmed at receiving this letter from me. I write only to offer my congratulations on your marriage and my ongoing friendship. After six years of knowing each other, how could I not? Montgomery tells me that he is disappointed in your decision, but I cannot say I'm all that surprised. Should you or your new husband ever find yourself in need of a loan, please do not hesitate to reach out to me.

Always your friend,
  Giles Hunt

"Give me that," Will said. She extended the letter in his direction. He promptly snatched it from her.

"William!" she exclaimed as he watched his eyes race over the parchment, reading the whole thing again after she already recited it out loud. He promptly crumpled it into a ball, letting it join his father's and Montgomery's letters on the ground. "Why would you do that?"

"You have no use for his assistance or friendship," he grumbled in response. "You have a husband for that."

Elaina rolled her eyes. "Do not be so primitive. Cleary

there are no hard feelings on his end. I'm obligated to reply to such a nice missive. Besides, he's right. We have been friends for some six years."

"You are obligated to do nothing. You are married now. Must I remind you to whom?"

"I know very well who I married, but I will respond to Mr. Hunt whether you like it or not. There's a good chance we *will* need financial assistance before winter's end."

Will shook his head. "Even if we do, he's the last banker in London that I would go to for help."

"The last banker you will go to, yet perhaps the only one who will give you any sort of credit at a fair interest rate," she said, nostrils flaring. "I did not expect you to be such a jealous fool, especially after I risked my entire reputation by running away with you."

She rose from the table then.

"Where are you going?" Will asked.

"I am tired," she said.

"Then I will go with you," he replied promptly, standing up as well.

She shook her head. "I'm not in the mood tonight, Will."

"Not in the mood?" he asked, stepping closer to her, pinning her in between his body and the doorframe of the dining room. She glared up at him as he bent his face down to nuzzle her neck. His breath was hot against her body, and she stifled a sigh filled with desire. "Surely you cannot resist such a primitive, jealous husband."

"Surely I can," she countered between clenched teeth.

"I think I like you even better when you're angry," he mused, taking a strand of her brown hair and twirling it between his fingers. "There's something remarkably alluring about it."

She began to roll her eyes in response, but he lifted her up and threw her over his shoulder. She pounded at his back. "What are you doing?" she yelled.

"This is how primitive husbands take their wives to bed," he replied matter-of-factly.

"William! Be serious. Put me down!"

"Absolutely not—to both requests."

He carried her all the way up the stairs, describing all the "primitive" things he planned on doing to her when they arrived at their bedchamber. By the time they were halfway there, she was laughing so hard she could hardly breathe, and when they finally reached the bedchamber, she had forgotten all the reasons she had been cross with him, making love to him any which way he wanted, "primitive" or otherwise.

As they lay in bed together, their naked bodies intertwined, Elaina's thoughts wandered to the letters Will received from his father and brother. She frowned.

"Does it hurt when your father and brother are so dismissive of you?" she asked.

Will seemed to consider this for a moment. "I'd be lying if I said it didn't affect me, but I've learned not to dwell on it. I know what I'm worth. The army taught me as much. I do not need my father or brother's approval to know such things."

"But surely it would be nice to hear them say they are proud of you?"

Will sighed. He ran his fingers down the side of her body. "I'm much more worried about making you proud of me, Elaina."

She smiled. "I already am proud of you, Will. I always have been. I only believe that how our families treat us influences our self-worth greatly."

"I hope you don't let *your* family's treatment influence your thoughts about yourself," Will countered.

Elaina could only frown in response. Sometimes she did, but she couldn't bring herself to admit it out loud.

Will must've noticed her troubled demeanor because he asked, "Have you tried writing your aunt again?"

Elaina shook her head. "There is no point. She will not answer me, even if I am a real lady now. Gillingham and Fitzroy wouldn't either."

Will pulled her closer, pressing a kiss on her forehead. "Then let's agree that we won't dwell on our families for as long as we're here. Larkspur will be a new start for us, something that can be completely our own."

She closed her eyes, enjoying the warmth of her husband's body. "That sounds like a wonderful plan."

"When will you learn I only have wonderful plans?"

Opening her eyes, she smiled. "When Larkspur becomes a success."

"A fair challenge. Do you think I'm up for it?"

"Of course," she replied. "Do you think I am?"

"More than anyone else I know."

They fell silent, holding each other close until they both drifted off to sleep.

CHAPTER THIRTEEN

Thank you for your kind letter. I am sorry I have not returned it sooner, for it was probably the kindest one we've received. As you can imagine, the Winters aren't very happy with us right now, most of all your future husband. Are you sure there is no one else you can think of to be your maid of honor? I would hate for you to offend Montgomery, nor would I want to usurp someone you may have known longer just because you grew fond of me over the few days we spent together at Blackmore...

—an excerpt of a letter from Elaina to Lady Clara at Haywood House, Wiltshire

WILL and Elaina visited the village the next day with Mrs. Harding as their guide. Will sought men in the village to help begin his work in the groves, while Elaina interviewed potential footmen, a cook, and three maids. She hired all of them, surprising Mrs. Harding.

"We can make do with two maids," she mumbled as they left their last interview. "Three will be much too expensive."

Elaina smiled at her. "I couldn't very well give two an income and leave one without an offer. Don't worry, we can afford it."

Will might be upset, but Elaina would just explain the same reasoning to him. They'd have to go without something to support the third maid.

While the extra help made Larkspur feel more like Blackmore, that was where the similarities ended. At Blackmore, Elaina woke whenever she wanted, went for a ride, and tended her plants in the hothouse for the rest of the day.

At Larkspur, Elaina woke at dawn and spent her days in the estate's overgrown pastures, clearing out overgrown weeds and grass in preparation for new animals. She usually stopped for luncheon in the middle of the day, but sometimes she forgot about eating until the sun started to dip beneath the horizon. There was just so much ground to cover.

At first, the work was exhausting, so much so that Mrs. Harding began to express her concern over Elaina's well-being. "Perhaps you should not work so long or so hard every day," she said while helping her dress for bed one night. "A lady like you was not built for this sort of thing."

Elaina knew Mrs. Harding spoke honestly, but she could not help herself. She still went out every day. She knew Will was busy with the groves each day. They might not finish everything they had to do if she did not contribute. She felt like she *had* to contribute. If Will had married an heiress…

She had to push the thought from her mind. She could not consider that any longer. He had married her. "Can a lady not change?" she asked Mrs. Harding, raising her eyebrows. Mrs. Harding only sighed in response.

Elaina eventually gained a very unladylike tan with calluses on her knuckles and palms. She formed muscles in places she didn't even know could have muscles. It was a painful process, but she felt stronger than ever. She forgot what it was like to rest.

Her old life at Blackmore seemed so leisurely now. She would have loved to spend a day on horseback with her husband, just exploring the estate, but there was no time. She saw him when she woke and at dinner, and that was all.

He also retired much more easily than her, usually giving her one lonely hour to read in between him falling asleep and her falling asleep. She often wished he wasn't so tired so they could make love before they slept. When they'd gone ten nights without sleeping together, Elaina knew their honeymoon was over much too soon.

Why had she expected a honeymoon in the first place? She knew what she was getting herself into. She wanted an estate to care for, and now she had an estate to care for. There was nothing to complain about. Montgomery had warned her, after all. She knew this wasn't going to be easy.

Still, she longed for the days of the house party, when *she* was the only thing that consumed Will. Now he only focused on the estate. Despite the fact that Will claimed he learned not to dwell on his family's lack of faith in him, he seemed to care deeply about making the estate a success. She began to worry about what would happen if he failed.

She hoped he did not one day blame her for his troubles, or wished for a more ladylike wife. More specifically, a more ladylike wife with a much larger dowry. Of course, he'd never admit to it, and they'd live in awkward resentment of each other until the day they died.

But perhaps she was getting ahead of herself.

WILL COULD PAY the men who helped him in the groves very little, especially when he knew no buyers of timber and did not know what to expect in terms of the price timber could fetch. Still, there were plenty of men who wanted to help.

It seemed that Will had developed keen powers of persuasion while he was a captain in the army. There was also the fact that there was little work to be had in those parts in the first place, and any income was better than no income for most families.

Bringing trees down and transporting them to the lumberyard was backbreaking work, even with the help. He did his best to hide his frustrations from Elaina, who remained sunnily optimistic even as she worked all day herself. He wondered if she really felt so optimistic on the inside, though. She had been quiet lately.

Like Elaina, Will was gone from the house from dawn until dusk. After dinner, she would give him his bath in front of the fire in their bedroom, and the one pleasure he had each day was her gentle ministrations with a bar of soap and a sponge every night. He would have longed for more if he weren't so—

"Damned tired."

"What's that?"

Will opened his eyes and lifted his head from the rim of the washbasin. His thoughts seemed to have escaped into the open without him realizing it in time.

"Nothing," he replied. Elaina gave him a warning look, and he shook his head. "I was only thinking I don't think I've ever been so tired in my entire life."

"Even after all those years in the army?" Elaina asked as she rewet her sponge with water.

"Eight years in the army has nothing on eight days as a timber man," he said. "I hope we find a forester soon. I'm not sure how much more I can bear."

She quietly chuckled. "I hope you're not planning on sitting at home and relaxing afterward. I'll find you plenty of work in the fields."

"I'm sure you will," he said, reaching his hand out of the water and grabbing her own wet one, bringing it to his lips and kissing her knuckles, "and I will do it gladly, especially for you. Why do you think I chopped down a tree and lugged it halfway across the estate today?"

"I thought you were doing that for fun," she said. He splashed bathwater at her face in response, and she gasped. "Will!" She threw the sponge at him, hitting him squarely in the nose. "You can wash yourself if you insist on splashing me."

"Luckily for you, I'm all done," he said, standing up in the basin. They were still new enough in their marriage to each other that she couldn't help but look away and slightly blush when she saw him in such a state, so unabashed in his nakedness, even when they had not made love in so long. The sight of her rosy cheeks made him smile, and he swiftly stepped out of the basin, picking her up from where she sat.

"William!" she exclaimed as he carried her to the bed. Thankfully, she was much lighter than a tree. "Put me down!"

"Gladly," he said, depositing her on their bed and crawling over top of her.

"You're getting me all wet," she complained.

He raised one of his brows. "Am I?"

"Oh, you're incorrigible," she said.

"But you wouldn't have me any other way," he murmured, leaning down and kissing her. She squirmed underneath him, using her palms to push him away at his shoulders.

"I smell awful," she whispered. "You must let me bathe first."

He sighed, rolling over so he was beside her instead of over top of her. "If you insist."

She stood up, going back toward the fire and bathtub, grabbing a dry towel from the ground. She took it and threw it at him. "You should dry off, too," she said. "You're getting the bedclothes all wet."

"Yes, ma'am," he said in the same tone a scolded child would use. He couldn't help but grin when she shot him a pointed look in response. He dried himself off, lying back down on the bed when he was finished, not bothering to get dressed. He watched as she undressed herself by the fire, then submerged herself in the basin's soapy water. The picture was so mesmerizing—her nude form, her slicked-back wet hair, the flicker of the fire—that he felt his eyes fluttering with sleep as he watched her.

But by the time she returned to bed, he was fast asleep.

WITHIN A MONTH of first posting the advertisement, Will started conducting interviews for the forester position. He was somewhat embarrassed to meet them in the house's library, what with the bare shelves and missing portraits, and he could only hope his lack of worldly possessions would not eventually deter the right man from taking the position. Will could make no promises in terms of the estate's success as he interviewed potential employees, and as more and more men passed on the opportunity, his father's doubting voice in his mind became louder and louder.

He reminded himself that even if he had secured the hand of a girl with a thirty-thousand-pound dowry to fund Larkspur's improvements, he would have found no comfort with having such a girl at his side. Without Elaina, they'd probably be well behind schedule. Elaina spent most of her days out of doors, clearing overgrown unused fields while he chopped down trees and lugged them to the lumberyard with his hired help from the village.

They made quite the pair, a country squire and his wife with no qualms over physical labor. He was sure the villagers and the few tenants they did have must've thought they were peculiar, for if they were rich, they would have been able to hire laborers to take care of such tasks for them.

But they were not rich. They counted every penny that remained of Will's allowance from his father that year, plus any savings he had from his years in the army, before they made any decisions. The house remained mostly bare for the first four months they were there and would most likely remain bare for at least the next year. Until they could increase the estate's yearly income—from the lumberyard, or the letting of cottages, or an increased harvest every year, or perhaps by an investment in more cattle for meat and dairy —their hands were tied.

Before he found a forester, there were multiple moments when Will considered giving up the whole affair altogether, perhaps rejoining the army and taking Elaina to wherever they decided to station him that time, but he knew that would leave her unhappy and unsatisfied. For her part, she was settled on making Larkspur a success, despite the fact her once-soft lady's hands had become callused and her milky white skin was now suntanned. She would not give up, even when Harding frustrated her and the footmen and maids complained.

There was finally a turning point when Will found Mr. Price, a forester with connections to the coal-mining companies in Northumberland and Durham. His connections would need wood to frame their mines. Price was more than happy to live in the lodge, manage the men in the yard and groves, and take a commission on whatever he sold to the miners. A deal was struck, and Price came to Larkspur by mid-October with his wife. Being similar in age, the Prices became Elaina's and Will's first companions in Larkspur, often joining them for dinner.

Will was happy that Elaina enjoyed Mrs. Price's company.

The woman was his wife's age, as well as kind, well-educated, and funny. Although Elaina admitted to sometimes missing the duchess and her father, she was in frequent correspondence with both of them.

On his part, Will received no further missives from his brother or father. Although Elaina kept asking him about his feelings on such things, he insisted he had none. He could not care less for gaining his brother's or father's approval.

Elaina also maintained correspondence with Lady Clara and Mr. Hunt. Will was happy Elaina found a friend in his brother's future wife, but he did not like that she maintained a correspondence with Hunt. Will never wanted Elaina to respond to Mr. Hunt's missive in the first place, but she insisted, claiming Will was being ridiculous. She said Mr. Hunt had been her friend for a long time, and if he was kind enough to write to her and express there were no hard feelings, he deserved a response.

Will expected their correspondence to stop there, with Elaina's response, but it went on and on, something that bothered him a great deal. She used the excuse that it was not polite to not answer, but he worried she was beginning to regret not marrying him. She worked so hard day in and day out. Perhaps she was beginning to realize it wasn't worth it.

He worried Hunt was trying to woo her back to him, and that he was succeeding. Why else would he write her after she spent the whole house party stringing him along? Any sane man would have been furious. Not Hunt. He insisted on maintaining a "friendship."

The whole thing felt suspicious to Will. He didn't like it. When told Elaina as much, she sighed.

"You know his bank would give us a large line of credit at more than favorable rates if we only asked him," she said. "He is a good friend to have. I will not jeopardize the future of this estate by cutting off communication with him."

He knew she was right, as much as he hated to admit it. There *was* a large possibility they would need a loan if they were to fix all of the outbuildings and pasture fences before winter came.

"We won't need a loan," he said anyway. "We'll have plenty of money after the lumber business takes off."

The lumber business *did* take off, but it still wasn't enough. Will now had two options. He could go to his father and beg him to invest more money into the estate, or he could go to Mr. Hunt and take out a loan. Will decide to wait and ask his father when they returned to Blackmore for Christmas, a decision Elaina deemed risky.

"Even if he says yes, it'll be so late in the season," she said. "You'll risk getting caught in a snowstorm or develop frostbite if you insist on working through the winter."

Will remained stubborn, even when Elaina became angry. He would not give in to her on this one. Not yet, anyway. Still, Elaina insisted on arguing.

"You do not even know the man," she said one night before bed.

"I know he once wanted to marry you," Will replied as he undid the buttons of his shirt. "That is enough for me not to like him."

"So if we find ourselves unable to fund all of the repairs needed to attract enough tenants in the spring, and your father rejects your pleas for help over Christmas, you're saying you will not go to the banker who will most likely give you the most favorable rate on a large loan?"

Will only grunted in response.

She rolled her eyes. "Obstinate man!"

Will watched as she turned over on her side, pulling the bedclothes over her ears and refusing to look at him. When he was finally dressed in his nightclothes, he blew out the remaining candles and joined her, lying on his back as he considered his self-admittedly pointless jealousy.

His wife was probably right. They'd have to go to Hunt or some other banker for a loan if they were to complete the repairs in time for spring, and it'd be madness not to go to Hunt if he would give the best rate. The timber business would only get them so far without some immediate capital, and Larkspur was an expansive estate with much work to be done to be truly successful next year.

He just couldn't bring himself to trust Hunt. He hated the way his wife openly wrote to him as if he was no different from Clara. He hated how he almost lost her forever to him during the house party at Blackmore. Most of all, he hated how he wondered if she'd be happier with him. She could be sitting in her warm London house without a care in the world.

What did Hunt mean by maintaining such a friendly correspondence with Elaina, anyway? He couldn't have been that desperate for their business without some sort of ulterior motive on his mind. Such questions troubled him well into the night as Elaina seemed to sleep peacefully beside him.

Eventually, he rolled over on his side as well, moving beside her so that his hips cradled her bottom. She stirred in her sleep from the movement, sighing softly as he draped one arm over her waist. He nuzzled her neck, taking in the mixture of scents of wintergreen-scented soap and floral perfume.

"Do you really think I'm obstinate?" he murmured in her ear.

"Only sometimes," she mumbled back, eyes still closed with sleep.

"I suppose only sometimes is better than all the time."

He smiled against her neck before leaning back to place

his head on his pillow, falling into a restful sleep, his arm still draped over her body.

WHEN DECEMBER CAME, they were called away from their new estate to Blackmore for the duke and duchess's Christmas party. The lumber business had afforded them the ability to make at least half of the improvements they wanted to the estate, along with small gifts for their family on account of the season, but they would need more funds to make the rest of the improvements happen before spring. Will had resolved to ask his father for the money before going to an actual banker like Hunt, though he recognized the improbability of his father giving him anything after his secret elopement.

The Christmas party at Blackmore was a small affair every year, especially when compared to the summer house party. Only the closest friends and family of the duke and duchess gathered there for the holiday. Will was honestly surprised he and his wife even made the list at all, considering how they departed four months ago. They decided to make their journey there from Larkspur in a day, not wanting to spend any funds on a coaching inn, despite it being an eighteen-hour ride when including rests for the horses. They left early in the morning and arrived late at night with only the butler to greet them at the door, both worn and weary from the long carriage ride.

The butler showed them to Elaina and her father's old apartments. "Mr. Walker took residence in one of the cottages nearby shortly after your departure," he explained. "The duchess thought you would like having your old rooms for the party."

Elaina smiled. "I will very much indeed."

When he left, Elaina found herself wandering through

her old sitting room and bedchamber, reminiscing over what it was like to live there. It felt like almost a lifetime ago.

"Are you still happy you left?" Will asked, watching her from the doorway of her old bedchamber as she looked out into the dark night. "It's been both a long and short four months of matrimony, hasn't it?"

The fireplace was lit, emitting a warm glow from the corner of the room. He, for one, was happy she left, regardless of how she responded. He imagined a life where he went to Larkspur alone, only to return to Blackmore at Christmastime to find her engaged to Hunt. He shuddered at the thought, knowing he would have lost her *and* he would have returned home a failure, for her unwavering devotion to their mission at Larkspur was what kept him motivated over the past four months.

"Of course I'm still happy that I left," she said, smiling as she approached him, the light of the fire dancing across her face. "Are you still happy that you chose me for a wife?"

He furrowed his brow. "After four months, I am confident that I would want no other but you." He gently touched her cheek, pushing back some hair that had fallen out of its pins and winded up in her face. "How could you think otherwise? If anything, I sometimes worry that you would prefer to be with Mr. Hunt!"

She smirked. "I knew you were jealous."

Will frowned. "Yes, I am jealous. I can admit to that much, but what about you? I'm not quite sure you are happy as you say you are."

She bit her lip, as if she was thinking of something to say. Her eyes flickered to the bed at the center of the room. "Did you know I used to imagine what it would be like for you to make love to me in that bed?"

His eyebrows raised, realizing the diversion but not

minding it at all. "Did you?" When she nodded, he grabbed her by the waist, pulling her close to him. "Shall we try it?"

She laughed. "Oh, I'm so tired, but I think we must."

They tumbled into bed, laughing. When they were finished, Elaina turned to Will, frowning. "If I admit whether or not I'm happy, will you admit that you seek your father's and brother's approval?"

Will pursed his lips. "Why would you want me to admit that?"

"So I can tell you that their approval doesn't matter. It's never mattered. All that should matter is your happiness."

"And are you happy?"

She shrugged. "I only miss you sometimes. I think perhaps if you weren't so worried about gaining their approval, you'd spend more time with me when we're at Larkspur."

Frowning, he pressed his lips to her forehead. "I'm sorry you feel that I've ignored you. I'll spend every night and day of this party making it up to you. I promise."

FERGUSON WAS the one who came to wake them the next morning, and Elaina was thrilled to see her old maid.

Meanwhile, Will dressed himself and went down to his father's study. He was there as he always was, seated behind his massive oak desk and smoking his pipe, looking over some papers. When he heard Will in the doorway, he looked up, and his face fell—perhaps not the reaction Will was hoping for after being away for four months.

"William," he said, placing his pipe on his desk and putting the papers in his hand down as well. "You've arrived."

"I have," he replied, shutting the door behind him.

"How is Larkspur?" he asked.

"We've made good progress on repairing the tenant buildings," Will replied, taking a seat across from him. How he admired his father's study now, especially when he knew how bare his own place of work was. Perhaps one day he'd be able to afford his own expensive-looking desk to sit behind. "And I've hired a forester to live at the lodge on the grounds and work the groves and lumberyard for me. We've developed a solid business up north. Timber for the new coal mines is in high demand."

"Have you?" he asked, seemingly surprised at his son's own resourcefulness. Will couldn't help but take offense. He had been a captain in the army for eight years, deployed in both Portugal and Belgium to fight the cursed French. He found himself clenching his fist over his knee in annoyance. He thought of Elaina's accusations that he only wanted their approval. That couldn't be further from the truth. He knew that was something he would never receive.

"I have."

"Hmmm," was all his father said in response. Eventually, the man asked, "Would you like a drink?"

Will figured he needed a bit of liquid courage to get through the rest of the conversation, so he nodded. His father got up from his chair and moved to the room's sideboard, uncorking a half-full bottle of cognac and pouring two glasses of the amber-colored beverage. He moved back to his desk, placing one glass in front of his spot and the other in front of his son's. Will took it quickly, taking an aggressive gulp. The beverage stung his mouth and throat, and he pursed his lips as his father did the same.

"How is the new Lady William finding it all?"

"Elaina has adapted magnificently," Will replied, his voice proud despite the disdain in his father's voice. "There may be less comforts at Larkspur compared to Blackmore, but she is managing the household staff well, and she even helps me with the farms from time to time."

His father half smiled. "I suppose I shouldn't be surprised," he said with a sigh. "She is her father's daughter, after all."

"You seem almost disappointed that we're doing well."

The duke glared at him. "Not at all. I'm happy for you. Why wouldn't I be happy for you?"

Will didn't answer, and they sat in silence for a moment while he considered how to phrase the request he was about to make. He took another drink of alcohol, determined to say his peace. "The truth is, Father," he began, "if we are to complete all the renovations needed to have the place prepared for more tenants in the spring, we really need more funds. We have spent all of my allowance and the interest of my commission. Even when we come into more funds at the start of the new year, I'm afraid it won't be enough."

"I already told you," the duke replied coolly with a shake of the head, "there will be no handouts from me. You chose to marry a girl with nothing to her name. You will live with the consequences."

"But Father—"

"The answer is no, William." His father's voice grew more sharp. "You will procure the money the same way any other upstart gentleman would. You'll take out a loan and pay it off with interest when your estate becomes a success. According to Montgomery, that man Hunt will be more than willing to help you—with favorable terms, too. I'm not sure why, considering you stole his prize right from underneath his nose only four months ago. I know I would not offer you the same."

"I will not sit here and listen to you treat Elaina like an object," Will nearly shouted in response. He took a deep breath. "She was not just a prize to be won, and she is more impressive than you think. I am lucky to have her as my wife, though you think marrying her was a mistake of mine. She has already contributed more to the estate than any rich heiress could have."

"Then why are you asking me for money?"

Will gritted his teeth, staring at his father for a moment. When he realized his father would not budge, he stood up suddenly.

"Fine," he said. If everyone insisted he go to Hunt, then he would go to bloody Hunt. "I will not waste your time any longer. It's clear I'm nothing but a disappointment to you. I beg your pardon for coming to you in the first place."

He bowed slightly, leaving the room without looking back. He went to go find Elaina, who was still in the process of being dressed by Ferguson, the two girls happily chattering away. He forced a smile at them when they greeted him, then paced the bedchamber until they were finished.

"Whatever is the matter?" she asked, furrowing her brow at him when Ferguson finally left.

"I spoke to my father," he replied.

A look of recognition passed over his wife's face. "Ah," she said. "Then he's rejected you."

He nodded. "Yes. He told me to go to Hunt—like everyone else."

Elaina raised a quizzical brow. "Everyone else like me, you mean?" When he did not answer, she sighed. She stood up, moving to take him into her arms. Her comfort almost made him feel better.

"Oh, Will," she said. "It won't be as terrible as you think. I'm sure he would like to be a friend to you as much as he is to me. We will stay over in London on our way home after Christmas and call on him."

"Fine," he replied sullenly, "but you cannot expect me to like any bit of it."

She nodded once. "Very well. You have my permission to absolutely despise the whole affair. Now, shall we find your mother and ask when luncheon will be? Ferguson told me we already missed breakfast, and I am ravenous."

CHAPTER FOURTEEN

Oh, I cannot wait until Christmas when I finally see you again! I must admit I'm quite nervous, as I haven't seen Montgomery in four months. Do you think he will still find me as charming as he did before? I'm terrified that he will no longer pay me any mind now that we are officially engaged. Why would he? It's not like I could back out, not after saying yes. I only hope he craves my company as much as his letters claim.

—an excerpt of a letter from Lady Clara to Elaina at Larkspur Castle, Cambridgeshire

AFTER LUNCHEON, Elaina sought out Montgomery's company, hoping to get a moment alone with him to tell him about Larkspur. Will deserved his brother to know how hard he had worked. He deserved to be appreciated by a member of his family, especially after the duke rejected him so harshly.

She found him at the back of his house, hiding in his study. He wasn't even working, only staring out the window onto the lawn.

"Are you in here hiding?" she asked from the doorway. He jumped a little, turning to face her. He smiled when he saw her.

"Elaina!" he exclaimed, moving across the room to embrace her. "I have missed you. I'm sorry I haven't written. I only—"

"Didn't want to offend your father by being friendly with us?" she interjected. He furrowed his brow. "You do not need to lie to me, Montgomery."

He sighed. "I'm sorry, Elaina. He is very angry. I myself find my anger subsiding, especially after seeing you for the first time in so long. Will you forgive me for not reaching out?"

"*Me* forgive *you*?" Elaina scoffed. She did not need an apology from Montgomery. Her husband needed an apology from Montgomery. "The only person whose forgiveness you're in need of is your brother's. He's toiled away for the past four months building a timber business at Larkspur, and your father has outright rejected him for a loan, despite the fact that I feel he's done a very good job proving himself. We've been at Larkspur, and it hasn't fallen to pieces."

"Yet."

Elaina groaned. "What is it about you Winter men that makes you so stubborn? Why can't you break with your father this once and support your brother?"

"I suppose you're right." Montgomery sighed. "We will fight over his elopement until our last days otherwise."

"That's right, you will. Now why don't you save yourselves two lifetimes of misery by letting bygones be bygones?"

He frowned. "Fine. I will talk to him." He paused for a moment before adding, "You know he's lucky to have you for a wife, right?"

Elaina rolled her eyes. "And I'm lucky to have him as a husband."

WILL WAS STANDING in the library with a glass of brandy before he got dressed for dinner, admiring the filled-out shelves and impressive portraits hanging on the walls. Blackmore Park's library was not quite as large as Larkspur's, but at least it had books. Larkspur's library was not much of a library at all in that case.

"Elaina told me you've created quite the timber business at Larkspur."

Will turned to find his brother standing in the doorway, smiling at him. He took a sip of brandy, studying Montgomery from over the rim of his glass. He decided he hated the way his brother always looked so smug.

"I have," he replied coolly, wondering why his brother had sought him out. If it was to express disappointment over his marrying Elaina again, he did not want to hear it.

Montgomery stepped into the room, coming face-to-face with his brother in front of the warm fire in the hearth. The heat was welcome, it being a cold day in Hampshire. "She said she was lucky to have you as a husband."

Will couldn't help but smile at that. Montgomery smiled back, patting his brother on the arm roughly. "I'm proud of you, Will. Why don't we agree to put the past behind us and support each other from here on out?"

Will hesitated. He knew Elaina must've put his brother up to this. He wouldn't have come to him on his own accord, and that bothered him. Part of Will wanted to fight back, to tell his brother that he didn't care at all about his support. Then he remembered the years before Elaina came to Blackmore, back when his brother was his sole fixation in life. His memory was foggy, but he knew at some level he wanted to be like him. Why shouldn't he finally accept his friendship?

Sighing, Will finally nodded. "Fine," he replied. "We will support each other from here on out."

Montgomery laughed. "Don't sound so glum about it."

"I'm still not entirely sure whether or not you're playing a prank on me."

"I left my pranking days behind at Eton," his brother replied, still laughing. "You are safe—for now." Will's eyes widened, and Montgomery grinned. "Never mind that. Tell me about this timber business of yours. Perhaps I can give you some ideas to make it even more profitable."

Despite her hesitation over attending, Elaina thought the Blackmore Christmas party turned out to be a more than pleasant affair that year. After all, Will was home from war and by her side as her husband instead. What more could she possibly ask for?

Well, she supposed she could have asked for her husband to be less troubled by the work that still needed to be completed at the estate. She knew how much he had hoped for his father to give him—or at least lend him—the money that he needed, and now she was afraid he would spend the whole party wallowing over having to go to Mr. Hunt after all.

Nevertheless, Elaina was happy. The duchess had welcomed them with open arms, and even Montgomery seemed content to let bygones be bygones. Elaina enjoyed watching the two brothers together; she had never seen either one of them so relaxed in the other's presence.

Clara and her father were the latest additions to the Blackmore Christmas party, and Clara was the first to greet Elaina and Will when they entered the drawing room before dinner their first night there. Elaina decided then and there that Clara was a true friend, despite their vastly different social standings and her sometimes draining correspondence.

"Elaina! Will!" she exclaimed upon seeing them, leaving her father to embrace them both. Will seemed uncomfortable with the familiarity, which only made Clara poke fun at him. "Come now, Lord William, we will be brother and sister in another four months. Surely we can embrace without you feeling uneasy."

He shook his head. "Nonsense," he said. "I feel like I've felt your friendship toward us as much as Elaina has, for your letters to her have raised her spirits after many trying days at Larkspur, and that in turn makes me very happy."

She frowned. "Trying days?" she asked, looking at Elaina. "Surely the estate isn't that troubling. You've never mentioned it."

"Will exaggerates," Elaina said, not wanting to upset Clara's more sensible nature. The last thing she wanted was for the girl to worry about her. "There is much work to be done and not much help to be had, but we are making do. I will not deny your letters have been a comfort, though."

Clara smiled. "I'm glad." Bending closer to her, she whispered, "I was beginning to think I was annoying you with all my questions about my future husband."

She turned to look at Montgomery and coyly covered her mouth, giggling. Her awe for her future husband did not seem to have faded over the past four months.

Cousin Julia approached them then, embracing her cousins as Clara had, just as Robbie came to drag Will away from them to stand with the other men. When Will was out of earshot, Julia confessed, "I must say I once dreaded this Christmas party for fear that I would have to see you with Mr. Hunt year in and year out."

Elaina crinkled her brow. "What do you mean?"

Clara laughed once. "Surely you must know about Julia's longstanding infatuation for Mr. Hunt. She spent half of the August party whining to me that you might end up with him instead of her."

"Julia!" Elaina exclaimed. "Why didn't you say anything to me?"

The younger, dark-haired girl shrugged. "I'm afraid you were a bit too preoccupied to notice me at the party in August, considering you were debating whether or not to run away with my cousin."

Elaina grimaced. "Yes, I suppose you're right," she admitted. "Does Mr. Hunt know how you feel about him, though?"

Julia sighed. "I think he knows, he just does not care to address it, for my brother has put it into his head that I'm too young and foolish for him."

"Aren't you, though? Too young, I mean."

Julia shot Elaina a pointed look that said no, she was *not* too young, while Clara giggled to herself. "If Clara can marry my cousin, ten years her senior," Julia drawled, "surely I can marry Mr. Hunt. Now that you're out of the picture, I have no doubt that I can earn his affection by slowly wearing him down with my charms."

"Wear him down?" Elaina echoed incredulously.

"Dreadfully romantic, isn't it?" Clara asked, unable to hold back a much louder laugh.

The duchess cleared her throat from where she was standing from across the room, glaring at the three girls.

"Speaking of romance," Julia said, "you must tell us all about the elopement."

"Oh, all right," Elaina agreed.

She told them all the details she could remember, describing the towns they saw on their long carriage ride to Gretna Green, along with Scotland itself and the legendary blacksmith's shop. They were also full of questions about Larkspur, like when they could visit, and Elaina did her best to spare them the more taxing details of her time there.

Luckily, most of the unused fields had been cleared by mid-November, allowing Elaina some time indoors so her suntan could fade before returning to Blackmore, though her hands had not recovered. Elaina had never been thankful for evening gloves until then. She had no desire for girls like Clara and Julia to see her rough, callused hands, even if they were supposed to be her friends.

The days at Blackmore passed too quickly, though they spent an entire fortnight there. Although Mrs. Harding had been helping her dress, Elaina was happy to have Ferguson back, who she realized was more of a friend than a maid. How Elaina longed to take her back to Larkspur with them.

Other than Ferguson, Elaina finally felt well-fed after months of small meals at Larkspur—they couldn't afford anything too grand—and she spent more time with Will than ever, no longer having to lose him to the lumberyard. She found his mood slowly improved while they were there as well. They rode to see her father at his new cottage every day, and Will had even come to enjoy spending time with his brother and cousin in the evening.

Elaina told herself she would never regret marrying Will, and she didn't, but she started to wish they had gone about it a different way, especially when she realized how much more time they could spend together when they weren't always fretting over Larkspur. Perhaps the duke would have helped them then instead of merely tolerating them, if they'd only been honest with him and begged for his permission to wed. She knew she lacked the large dowry that he wanted for his son, but the duke always seemed to be fond of her. Surely he would have given in eventually.

On their last day in Blackmore, Elaina stood in the library

thinking of these things, admiring the rows of thick hard-cover books and the paintings of Winters past. She wondered if anyone would notice if she took a few of the books for her own and brought them to Larkspur. Elaina and Will had been saving everything for the repairs, leaving very little for themselves. They hadn't even exchanged Christmas gifts that year, and most of the gifts they brought for their family were things Elaina made herself.

Montgomery happened upon her in the library then, coming to stand beside her. "Are you happy to return home today?" he asked.

She sighed, looking at him. "I'm not sure," she said, her voice quiet. "Returning here made me realize how much I miss it. Larkspur isn't so much of a home yet."

He shot her a sheepish look. "I did tell you the place was decrepit, didn't I?"

"You did," she admitted with a sigh, "and I think that's at least the fifth time you've reminded me since we've been here."

He winced. "Sorry about that," he said. "I only thought if I was cruel, I might be able to deter you from doing something foolish."

"But I did it anyway," she said with a laugh. "Oh, Montgomery, I suppose I was so blinded by love that I didn't stop to think just how much work it would be, and believe me, Larkspur has been work and then some. I feel like I might've aged four years in the span of four months."

"If it makes you feel any better," Montgomery said, "Will has told me your company has been invaluable to him."

Elaina smiled. "That's nice of him to say. I try to stay optimistic for his sake—and mine, really—but I will not lie to you. It's difficult at times. I miss my father and Ferguson and the comforts of a *real* home. Sometimes I doubt Larkspur's ability to ever become like Blackmore. It's so vast and empty, and I have no kind-hearted Fergusons in my service."

"You could take her with you," Montgomery offered softly.

Elaina shook her head. "I couldn't. We do not have the money for something as frivolous as a lady's maid. We will stay in London tonight to secure a loan tomorrow."

"A loan?" Montgomery asked incredulously. He furrowed his brow. "Will didn't mention anything about a loan. Is he finally going to Mr. Hunt for help?"

"I think he's ashamed to admit it," she said with a sigh. "Mr. Hunt has been offering to help these past four months, but Will's been too proud to go to him. Now that the duke has made it clear he will not help us, he's finally been left with no other choice. Of course, Will hates the idea of asking him, what with our history. He'd go to another bank with worse rates if I wasn't so insistent."

"I should go with you," Montgomery said suddenly, as if the wheels inside his mind had just begun to turn. "I'll keep the man honest. We've been friends for a long time."

Elaina tilted her head to the side. "You want to help us? After everything that's happened?"

Montgomery nodded once, smiling slightly. "I must admit that Clara's softened me to the idea of helping the two of you. The girl's quite the hopeless romantic."

"I only hope you do not disappoint her," Elaina replied with a laugh.

He frowned. "Oh, I will. There's no doubt about that."

"ABSOLUTELY NOT."

That was Will's response when Elaina and Montgomery came to him and suggested that Montgomery should join them on their trip to London.

"Why not?" Elaina asked. "He only wishes to help. He will help ease any tension between us and Hunt."

Will gave her an unimpressed look. "So you admit that there is tension?"

She nearly groaned. "You know I don't mean it that way."

"This is exactly why I should come," Montgomery muttered.

Eventually, Elaina and Montgomery won the argument, and they all ending up staying at Blackmore Terrace together, the duke's home in Mayfair. The long and narrow brick house was five stories high with large bay windows on every floor and a stone canopy over the front door.

Elaina was pleased when Montgomery had Ferguson come with them, giving her at least one more night with her beloved maid. Elaina had no troubling settling in when they arrived. She knew the house well, having spent multiple Seasons there.

"I think it's best if Montgomery and I go to the bank alone tomorrow," Will said as they settled into bed for the night. From the tentative tone of his voice, Elaina could tell he was nervous to say anything at all.

"Why?" Elaina asked, sitting up in bed.

"Going to the bank to take out a loan to improve his estate should really be the husband's job, don't you think? I will not subject you to such a thing."

Elaina snorted in response. "You will not subject me to such a thing? You had no problem subjecting me to field labor all autumn long."

"I told you that you didn't have to do that," he replied sharply, glaring at her, "but you insisted. You of all people should know there's no stopping you once you insist upon something."

"Then I insist upon seeing Mr. Hunt tomorrow," she declared, crossing her arms and tilting her chin upwards.

Will groaned. "Why? Do you wish to see all that you could have had if you had only just stayed the course instead of eloping with me?"

Her mouth dropped. "Why would you say that?" she asked, clenching her fists at her sides. "Of course not. I only wish to have a stake in our estate that is more than just that of a wife, and that means going with you to take out a loan for the place. We both know I've worked as hard as you to earn a seat at the table."

"Why can't you just stay behind this one time and act like the lady you're supposed to be?"

Elaina gasped. She felt as if the wind had been knocked out of her. His words stung. They stung even harder than the first sunburn she got at Larkspur. She watched Will's face start to droop as he realized what he said. Angry words swirled around in her mind, begging to be said out loud. He hadn't wanted a lady when he married her. He hadn't wanted a lady when the estate had arable farmland that needed clearing and no farmhands to do the tedious task. She swung her feet from under the covers and over the side of the bed.

"Elaina, I'm sorry, I didn't mean—"

"You are just jealous," she murmured, cutting him off. Louder, she added, "Stupidly jealous. I think I'll sleep in the other room tonight. Perhaps while I'm there, you can try and think of an explanation for why your jealousy of Mr. Hunt makes you act like such an ill-mannered idiot."

"Elaina..."

She went through the adjoining door, quickly slamming and locking it behind her. Her eyes immediately fell on the rather imposing canopy bed in front of her. She couldn't remember the last time she slept in such a large bed by herself. Without the fire lit, the room was cold, so she rang the bell and quickly climbed into bed, wrapping the bedclothes around her as she shivered. Tears threatened to spill from her eyes at any moment, but she refused to cry until the footman who had come to light the fire had left.

When he finally left, she lay back and let the tears fall openly. She resolved to cry quietly, so quietly that she could barely even hear herself. She thought of another life, one where she married Hunt and lived in London in a house like Blackmore Terrace. There'd be no drafty windows or endless days of work. She could have ridden her horse through Hyde Park if she wanted fresh air. She once thought she'd be miserable not to live in the country, but now London seemed like a treat compared to Cambridgeshire.

Eventually she fell asleep, and she did not stir again until Ferguson entered the bedchamber the next morning. Elaina slowly rose, wiping her tear-crusted eyes.

"I did not expect to find you in here, my lady," Ferguson said as she drew back to the curtains of the room. "When I heard Lord Montgomery and Lord William were leaving for Mr. Hunt's office, I came to wake you right away. Didn't you want to go with them?"

Elaina only sighed. "No, Ferguson," she replied. "I think I'll be staying here for the rest of the day."

WILL AWOKE FEELING LIKE A CAD. No, he felt worse than a cad, and rightfully so. He felt like a dirty rotten scoundrel for what he said to Elaina the night before, not entirely sure what came over him. Perhaps it was jealousy, but he refused to believe he was jealous of a man who never even had his wife in the first place.

Instead, perhaps it was her behavior at Blackmore. He could hardly explain it, but she somehow seemed… lighter while she was there. He couldn't remember the last time he experienced such a lightness in her, maybe not since their wedding day, when they laughed all the way to the inn from the smithy's shop after she imitated the men's Scottish accents.

But could he really blame her for acting so carefree when there was truly nothing to worry about when they were at Blackmore? They were not in Larkspur with a difficult staff to manage, or a lumberyard to oversee, or tenant buildings that needed desperate repairing.

Perhaps what really set him off was when she confided in Montgomery about their problems, the same man who tried to keep them apart and did not shy away from expressing his disappointment in their marriage. They may have extended the metaphorical olive branch over the holidays, but Montgomery may as well have snapped it in half when he decided to come to London with them. He may have claimed he only wanted to support them due to Clara, but Will couldn't help but think his brother had ulterior motives for joining them in London. He almost thought the man just wanted to get away from Blackmore for some other reason. What it was, he wasn't sure, but he had a sneaking suspicion that Montgomery was hiding something, or maybe someone. His brother went out as soon as they arrived in London the night before, and he seemed groggy when they rose to see Hunt that morning. Will could only assume his brother must've been out late.

Will was groggy himself, unable to rest soundly after Elaina insisted on sleeping in the bedchamber next door to his. They hadn't spent a night apart since they were married. He had considered waking her to tell her to get ready to go to Hunt's as a sort of peace offering, but Montgomery had already agreed that it was best that Elaina didn't attend the meeting.

"I understand she likes to be involved, and that's fine," Montgomery said in the carriage on the ride over to Hunt's that morning, "but there are some things that are better left to the men."

The statement made him uneasy, especially when Elaina had done every manly task possible at Larkspur with no complaints. She was not just his wife. She was his partner, and she should've been there as they asked Hunt for a loan to finish the repairs to the outbuildings. He could have put up with Hunt making eyes at her for one morning. Curse his blasted jealousy! He always knew the emotion was useless, but now it had caused another row between them. She'd only be angrier once she discovered he had left without her.

Hunt's bank was east of Mayfair, just past Covent Garden but before Farringdon Street. Montgomery had already written to him to let him know they were coming that morning, and the man met the two Winter brothers in his office promptly upon their arrival. Montgomery and Will sat across from Hunt, his desk in between them, and Will couldn't help but be reminded of their various interviews with their father, the duke. Hunt's desk was just as imposing, though he smoked no pipe, and he was not nearly as paunchy as the much older duke.

"Lady William did not join you?" Hunt asked as soon as they sat down. Will was sure his entire body involuntarily twitched at the mention of his wife.

"Come now, Hunt," Montgomery quickly interjected. "The office of a banker is no place for a woman."

Another involuntary twitch.

Luckily, they spoke no more about her, and Will offered the reason they came and how much capital he needed outright. There was no point, he decided, to beat around the proverbial bush. Hunt was more than amenable to the request, offering him an incredibly favorable interest rate, or so Montgomery told him later. When the deal was done and the money was distributed, Will thanked the man and got up to leave, but Montgomery stopped him, seemingly content to talk to Hunt a little while longer.

They chatted until Hunt eventually asked if they'd like to join him for dinner at his club later that evening.

"I don't think so," Will said, shaking his head. "Lady William and I must return to Cambridgeshire as soon as possible."

"You must?" Montgomery scoffed. "Surely you can delay your trip another day to spend time with your dear brother." Turning to Hunt, he added, "I'd love to join you at your club, Mr. Hunt, regardless of what my brother says."

"There's actually someone I'd like you to meet that's a regular there, my lord," Hunt said to Will.

"Who's that?" he asked, shooting the other man a confused look.

"You'll see if you join us."

Will sighed. Perhaps Elaina would be happy to see him befriend Hunt. "Very well," he agreed.

WILL FELT Elaina watching him as he got dressed for his evening out that night. He glanced at her. She was already in her nightgown and robe, a lackadaisical expression on her face. He could tell she was not happy that he was going to Mr. Hunt's club instead of leaving for Larkspur.

He moved to stand in front of her, regarding her for a moment as she stared back at him. He bent over to kiss her, but she turned her cheek just in time for his lips to scrape the side of her jaw. He sighed.

"Must you be so cross with me?" he asked. "I am befriending Hunt like you asked."

She only snorted in response. He sighed again.

"Will you be here when I return?" She only shrugged in response. "Very well. I'll see you in a couple of hours or so."

A couple of hours turned into more than a few. Hunt's club, White's, was a popular destination for the men of the ton, and Will was introduced to so many new people that his head was spinning by the end of the night. The one Hunt explicitly wanted Will to meet, though, was Viscount Fitzroy, who Hunt introduced as the son of Earl Gillingham… Elaina's distant cousin. When Hunt told Fitzroy that Will was married to his cousin, a look of recollection passed over the man's face.

"Ah, yes," he said, nodding his head gravely. "I'm afraid we don't talk much about her. I think it still fills my poor father with guilt. He was close to her mother when they were children, yet he still did nothing for the poor girl—your wife, I mean—after her grandfather passed, but she's married to you now, so all's well that ends well, I suppose."

Before Will could say anything, Hunt was telling Fitzroy all about Larkspur, and Fitzroy began to insist on coming to see the place at some point, despite the fact that Will said the house was nowhere near ready for visitors. When Fitzroy finally left, Will turned and glared at Hunt. "What was the meaning of that?" he asked.

"That man will be Lord Gillingham one day," he said. "If your family won't help you in your mission to save Larkspur, perhaps Elaina's will one day."

Will stared at him for a moment. "Why do you insist on helping us?" he finally asked. "Do you still carry some sort of torch for my wife?"

Hunt shook his head. "The truth is, I feel sorry for your wife."

Will's face twisted with anger. "Why—"

"It's not what you think," Hunt said, waving his hand and cutting Will off before he could say something terribly rash. Will swallowed, playing at his necktie while he deigned himself to listen to the man further. "It has nothing to do with her marrying you. My mother was a fine lady, much like Elaina's mother. Her family ostracized her as well when she deigned to marry a banker like my father."

Will was silent. He didn't know that about Hunt.

"In that way," the man continued, "I feel connected to your wife. The only difference is I've never had to worry about abject poverty because of my mother's decision, simply because I am a man. I do not blame her for choosing you, but I do sometimes question your ability to provide for her. Before you say I have no right to care about her, I feel I must point out that we've been friends for almost seven years now, the majority of the time you were off fighting on the Continent."

"Now, listen here—"

"No, no," Hunt said, shaking his head and interrupting him once more. "You finally came for the loan—at least now I know she will not starve to death because of her husband's misplaced aristocratic pride."

"I'm afraid I have no pride left," Will admitted slowly. "I've lugged trees across miles of land, and Elaina works just as hard. She has a very peculiar life with me. I sometimes wonder if she would have been happier with you."

"I don't think that's true," Hunt said softly. "She never struck me as the type of girl who wanted an ordinary life."

Will half smiled. "I suppose you're right." He paused for a moment, debating whether or not to ask his next question. He swallowed. "Why did you want to marry Elaina, anyway?"

Hunt shrugged. "Since Montgomery was getting married, I thought I needed a wife, too. Elaina seemed like a fine candidate. I like your wife… but you should not worry about whether or not I love her. I do not. I'm not sure I'm capable of such an emotion."

"Surely everyone is capable of love," Will said, frowning. "Why don't you think you are?"

"That's a story for another day," Hunt said with a laugh.

Will sighed. "If that's the case, I should be getting home now. It's getting much too late for a married man to be out. Thank you for introducing me to Fitzroy. You're right—perhaps one day he will be a help to us."

Hunt nodded. "I'll see you at Montgomery's wedding, then."

Will nodded once, then left the club for Blackmore Terrace—one might add, without his brother, who disappeared at some point during the evening, mumbling something about an opera singer in Covent Garden. Will supposed this mystery girl was the true reason Montgomery wanted to come to London anyway, and he pitied poor Clara for it.

Considering Hunt's words as he walked home, Will eventually came to find Elaina sleeping in his room. He was grateful to find her in there instead of the other bedchamber. He sat beside her for a moment, admiring the curve of her eyelashes and slightly ajar mouth while she slept. Smoothing her hair, he bent down to kiss her forehead before removing his smoke-scented clothes and curling up beside her.

GRAHAM SAT on Marianne's bed, feeling sick. He had just seen Clara at his parents' Christmas party, and he found her just as charming as ever. Why, then, did he feel the need to run back to London to see his mistress?

Marianne was beautiful to be sure, but the exact opposite of Clara. Petite and plump in all the right places with dark hair and eyes. Normally Graham enjoyed his liaisons with her, but he could not shake the guilty feeling that haunted him that night.

Naked, she crawled across the bed to sit beside him,

nipping at his ear. He jerked his head away. "What's wrong with you?" she asked, pouting at him.

He sighed. "I think we should end this. It's not right. I'm to be married in only four months."

Marianne laughed once. "So? You're a marquess. Don't all fine lords have mistresses?"

He glared at her. "Perhaps I don't wish to be like everyone else. This will be the last night, Marianne." He stood up and began to get dressed. "I'll give you a month to find another arrangement. I'm sure you won't have trouble."

She gaped at him. "Surely you're joking!"

He shook his head. "I'm sorry, Marianne. I'm afraid I'm serious."

Graham gave her one last kiss before he left, knowing this time it would be for good.

CHAPTER FIFTEEN

I'm glad to hear you have arrived safely home to Larkspur and had a successful trip to London. I wish I could have gone as well. Perhaps when Montgomery and I are finally married, we can all travel together. Wouldn't that be grand? After we had such a great time together at the Christmas party, I'm convinced there would be no better traveling party. Wasn't it such a wonderful holiday? Montgomery and Lord William are friends again, and you finally agreed to be my maid of honor. I couldn't have asked for better Christmas gifts!

—an excerpt of a letter from Lady Clara to Elaina at Larkspur Castle, Cambridgeshire

ELAINA AND WILL BEGAN their journey late the next morning, with Will not rising until half past ten after his night of frivolity with Montgomery and Mr. Hunt, much to Elaina's chagrin.

Montgomery seemed worse for wear when they left him in the morning, bags under his eyes. Will said his brother left him and Hunt halfway through the night, and Elaina couldn't help but wonder where he went. Will claimed he knew nothing, even when Montgomery announced he would be leaving London early as well—five days earlier than he had planned.

After a long period of silence in the carriage, Elaina finally asked, "Did you have a nice time last night?"

She kept her voice level despite her growing displeasure with her husband. She was glad to be returning to Larkspur, especially after what she viewed as a disastrous two nights in London, though she hated to part with Ferguson again. They still did not have the appropriate amount of income or savings to warrant a lady's maid, and Elaina insisted on no favors from Montgomery.

"I did," he replied, seeming to deeply consider the words before saying them out loud. "I think perhaps my former opinion of Mr. Hunt was a bit too harsh."

"You do?" Elaina asked, feeling miffed that it took him so long to realize such a thing when she told him all along that he was a good man. Why hadn't he just believed her when she initially told him there was nothing to fear in his character? There was absolutely nothing sinister about Mr. Hunt's intentions; that was not his character. He only wanted to help, and there were certainly no leftover feelings on either end from their brief courtship.

Her husband nodded once. "It should not surprise you that you were right. He only wanted to help. I believe he feels a sense of comradery with you, actually."

She made a little sound of satisfaction. She imagined it was the sound all wives made when their husbands finally admitted they were right.

"Firstly," she said, "of course I was right. Despite what people say about bankers, Hunt doesn't have a bad bone in his body. Secondly, what do you mean he feels a sense of comradery with me? We couldn't be more different."

Will sighed. "Apparently his mother was a gentlewoman

before she married Mr. Hunt's middle-class father, just like yours. He actually told me that after I met a relative of yours."

Elaina froze. Why hadn't he mentioned it earlier? She assumed it was her cousin Fitzroy, for Gillingham was getting too old to spend his evenings at a club like Mr. Hunt's.

"A relative?" she asked. "Which one?"

"Viscount Fitzroy," he replied.

She knew it. Why was she so surprised? Of course Will was bound to run into him at White's, a popular club, and of course Fitzroy would talk to her husband even if he was married to her. Perhaps he didn't even know. Either way, Will was the son of a duke. Although he was second in line, he still demanded a sort of respect amongst the peerage.

"And what did Lord Fitzroy have to say when he discovered that I was your wife?" Elaina finally asked. "Or did you manage to keep that detail from him?"

Will shook his head. "No. We spoke of you, actually."

"Did you?" she asked. Anger was beginning to bubble up inside her. Will knew how she felt about her mother's family. She wondered if Will had forgotten how many of the same parties she and the viscount had attended, only for him to ignore her. What made Will worthy of speaking to instead of her? She nearly shook her head as she reminded herself that she already knew the answer to that. "And what did he have to say for himself?"

"Well," Will replied, "he claimed the reason he avoided you in the past is because his father feels guilt over how his cousin handled the situation with your mother. I guess the current earl would rather no one spoke of your situation in his presence. Apparently he and your mother were close as children, and he feels shame for what happened."

Elaina let out an unladylike snort. "Guilt? Close as children? Shame? Do you honestly believe such tales? I can't believe Hunt dared to even introduce you. What could he mean by doing such a thing?"

Will shrugged. "I think he believes Viscount Fitzroy may be kinder to you when he becomes earl than when his father took the Gillingham title from your grandfather. In his defense, he seemed genuine. He expressed a decided interest in Larkspur and even asked to see it one day."

Elaina could hardly believe her ears. "Yes, well…" The words were suddenly lost inside her throat. She swallowed. "It's funny how conversations between two men in power differ between the ones held between a lowly land steward's daughter and her wealthy cousin the viscount."

"I'm hardly a man in power," Will scoffed.

"You may have all your money tied up in a less-than-profitable estate, but you're still a lord!"

"And you're a lady!"

"Through marriage only!"

"Why are we even fighting right now?" he asked, shaking his head. "I thought Fitzroy to be genuine, as was Hunt's hope to bring us together so that he may become an ally when he becomes the Earl of Gillingham. Is that so hard to believe?"

"Yes!" Elaina exclaimed, unable to contain herself any longer. "His behavior toward me—or should I say lack thereof—since my debut begs to differ!"

Earl Gillingham and Viscount Fitzroy always did their best to avoid her since her come-out. If they did manage to bump into each other at the evening's refreshment table, both of them would suddenly appear nervous before hastily vacating the area. Neither of them ever bid her good evening or asked after her health, even if the Duchess of Blackmore herself was in her company. Elaina could still remember how infuriated their behavior would make the duchess.

"I've upset you," Will murmured, his face apologetic. "I didn't mean to."

She shook her head. "Just like you didn't mean to tell me to act more like a lady two nights ago? I'm beginning to think you've married the wrong woman, and I've married the wrong man. I thought… I thought I'd married someone who actually saw things from my point of view. Now I see that I was wrong."

The words hung between them like anchors dropped from a boat in the middle of the sea. The weight of them never did quite make it to solid ground. Instead, they hung suspended between them, pointless and unnecessary. Elaina regretted saying what she did almost as soon as the words left her mouth, but she could not find her voice long enough to apologize.

She was angry at her husband, and she wasn't quite sure what to do about it. They taught little girls all about love and marriage and children and families, but they never taught them what to do when their husbands disappointed them.

Perhaps she was being a fool. Perhaps Mr. Hunt was right and it would serve Will well—and, in turn, her—to befriend Viscount Fitzroy. Perhaps she shouldn't have been so offended that Fitzroy seemed to pay more mind to the second in line to the Blackmore dukedom than the daughter of his distant cousin with tarnished bloodlines. She thought of saying all that, but she sat in silence instead, watching a shroud of sadness fall over Will's face as she did. He did not bother to defend himself, and that was how she knew she'd truly hurt him.

How she regretted it.

WILL HARDLY SPOKE to his wife over the next fortnight. She made it very clear she was angry with him, and he had no desire to beg for her forgiveness, especially when he was feeling hurt himself.

How could she say that he was the wrong man for her, or she was the wrong woman for him? Larkspur was not perfect, but it was better for them being there over the past five months. What other couple could say they had actually left a place better for living there? They had done everything together, and he was sure no one else could have helped him like she had, and their progress certainly wouldn't have been as rewarding if he had taken some woman's dowry to pay for all the work needed.

But he could not forget her words, and she couldn't seem to forget them either. The one time of day they truly saw each other was dinner, and they ate in silence. He was sure they only shared a bed at night due to there being no others. They slept as far away from each other as possible, with Will going to bed much earlier than Elaina, who was not as active since they returned from Blackmore and London. She took her breakfast in bed every morning, then spent most of the day dictating various tasks to Harding and the staff or reading or writing letters.

She was acting like a lady, and Will wasn't entirely sure if he liked it. He much preferred her with her hair pulled back with a bandeaux in an effort to keep any loose strands out of her eyes while she worked in the fields. He knew it couldn't always be that way, of course. They'd bring on new tenants in the spring if they were lucky, but he had always hoped Elaina would be there to help him when he went on his daily calls. He thought she would have wanted to, as that's what she always did with her father.

Will, meanwhile, rose with the dawn every morning. The loan helped him hire additional laborers and procure supplies for the various improvements that still needed to be made on the outbuildings. He knew the projects would be completed much more quickly if he helped, so he worked every day, even as the outdoors grew colder. Will was predicting a storm any day now—they were certainly due for one—which could put them back weeks if the snowfall was significant and took weeks to melt. He returned home every evening yearning for the fire and the soft touch of his wife. Only one was ever available to him.

Eventually the storm came. He pulled back their bedchamber window's curtain to see white flakes floating in the sky, sticking to the ground beneath—and sticking fast. He quickly got dressed in his warmest clothes and boots, desperate to finish the last of their repairs on one of the barns. As his horse brought him to the work site, he tried not to shiver, reminding himself that he faced much worse tasks in wartime, though perhaps not quite so cold. He was glad to find most of his crew there. Apparently most of them were willing to brave the weather for a shilling.

They worked all morning and afternoon before the last barn was repaired. When he arrived home, Elaina was the pacing the entrance hall. She gasped when she saw him.

"You're soaked to the bone!" she exclaimed, coming toward him to start stripping away layers of wet, foul-smelling wool. "I've been worried sick about you all day. How could you work in a storm like this? Do you have a death wish?"

He tried to smile as he shivered, to reassure her he was fine. In fact, he was more than fine. This was the most attention she'd given him since they went to Blackmore for Christmas. He rather liked it.

Mrs. Harding appeared then, and Elaina told her to go get the fire going in their bedchamber. She brought Will up the stairs, still muttering to herself over how he must've been crazy to do such a thing as work during the snowstorm. He only knew the estate would be better for it, and when spring came, they'd have an outpouring of farmers looking for tenancy.

When they arrived in the bedchamber, Elaina continued stripping him of his clothes, exchanging them for a dry nightshirt and robe. She ordered him into bed as the footmen worked the fire, then pulled him out again and sat him in front of it, wrapping blankets around him as she did. She sat beside him, wrapping her torso around his as she rubbed her hands over his shoulders and upper arms. His shivering ceased, and his teeth stopped chattering long enough for him to say something.

"T-thank you," he murmured.

Elaina only sighed. "Promise me you'll never do that again," she said. "You'll be of no use to the estate if you die, with or without the final barn finished."

"But it's finished," he replied, turning to her. "Now we can rest until spring. Will you rest with me, Lainey?"

She shot him a concerned look. He hadn't called her Lainey since they were children. She reached to feel his forehead with the back of her hand. He was warm. She pulled her hand away and stood up, helping him up with her.

"We ought to get you into bed," she said. "You've had a long day, and you'll need some rest before dinner."

Will nodded, stumbling toward the bed and letting sleep overtake him.

ELAINA WATCHED her husband as he slept. He felt slightly feverish when she touched his forehead, but perhaps it was only the shock of the warm fire against his previously cold-as-ice skin. She sat by his bedside, taking her dinner in their chamber, not bothering to wake him. Eventually she went to bed as well, blowing out the candles and curling up beside him. She watched him breathe for at least a half hour—the gentle rises and falls of his chest underneath the bedclothes —before falling asleep herself.

She woke not much later, stirred by Will's groaning.

"What is the matter?" she asked. When he did not respond, she felt his forehead. There was no question now. He had a fever. She immediately rushed downstairs, waking one of the footmen and sending him in the direction of Dr. Hardy, the closest doctor.

Mrs. Harding stirred with the commotion, helping Elaina take cool towels to the room to drape over Will's forehead, chest, and arms. She paced throughout the bedchamber when she was alone again, waiting for the doctor to arrive. She had never felt more anguished than she did in those two hours of waiting.

When Dr. Hardy arrived, she was surprised by how young he was. As she and Mrs. Harding watched him work, she quietly asked, "Are you sure there isn't another doctor I could call for? He seems so young."

"He is the closest one," Mrs. Harding replied resolutely. Elaina frowned, watching as Dr. Hardy inspected her sick husband.

The doctor eventually diagnosed Will with what he called pleurisy. A dose of laudanum was given to help with the pain in his chest.

"Isn't there anything else you can do?" Elaina asked as she watched Dr. Hardy pack up his medical bag. "Bloodletting, perhaps?"

Dr. Hardy shook his head. "Bloodletting will do more harm than good." When Elaina gave him a look of surprise, he smiled. "How old was your last doctor, Lady William?"

She narrowed her eyes. "Why does that matter?"

"Let's just say I may have more modern ideas about medicine than them," he replied with a slight grin. "You should keep the room cool. He may be shivering, but his fever burns strong, and we must work to break it." He glanced at Mrs. Harding. "Do you have any willow bark? Put that in some tea for his lordship."

"Why willow bark?" Elaina asked.

"It'll help with the fever."

Elaina nodded at Mrs. Harding, who left the room. After watching her go, Elaina turned back to the doctor. "Will he survive?"

He sighed. "It's hard to tell," he said, frowning. "He must fight his fever. If you find him sweating, that is a good sign. His body is winning in that case."

She nodded once. "Thank you, Dr. Hardy."

Elaina did not leave Will's bedside for the entirety of his illness. She helped Mrs. Harding change his bedclothes frequently, which often became damp with his sweat. Mrs. Harding reassured her that was a good sign, despite the fact that Will was still delirious, both from the doses of laudanum and the fever.

Mrs. Harding was Elaina's sole source of support during Will's illness. The older woman sat up with him as much as Elaina did. Her housekeeper told her she should take a break from sitting with him and rest, but Elaina refused.

"I will see him through this." Mrs. Harding watched her with pitying eyes. Elaina sighed. "Will and I fought while we were in London. I will not be able to sleep until I have a chance to make things right between us."

Mrs. Harding nodded once. "I understand."

When Mrs. Harding wasn't in the room, Elaina found herself staring at Will while he slept. She wondered if their last true conversation would be the one they had in the carriage, when she told him they were wrong for each other.

The idea of it was enough to make her cry. She bent over his chest, sobbing, clutching her own chest as heavy gasps came out of her, her body shaking with emotion.

She could not lose him. She could not lose him before she told him she did not mean it.

She realized then that she had never told him she loved him, despite the fact that her love for him had only grown deeper since they married. She thought perhaps she had always loved him, ever since they were children. She just didn't know it at the time.

He may not have been wealthy like Mr. Hunt, or the heir to a great dukedom like Montgomery, but Will had his own merits of character. Any other man in his position may have been content to be a second son and live off his allowance and never take a living. Will joined the army instead, and when he came home, he did not stop fighting. He fought for her, though she was stubborn and refused to admit their connection could not be denied. She probably would have married Mr. Hunt if he hadn't come to her that day in the library!

When spring finally came, Larkspur would be a functioning, profitable estate thanks to their work during the autumn and winter, but what would it matter if Will was not there to share in the success? She dreamed of house parties and bountiful harvests and happy tenants, but what were any of those things without Will at her side? What would even happen to her if Will died? Blackmore would probably sell Larkspur, and she'd be forced to move back to the house and eventually find another husband.

How could any other husband compare to Will, though? Perhaps their passion had faded since their initial elopement. Perhaps he did and said some things that she disagreed with, but she loved him, and she could not lose him. She would not lose him. She lifted her head from his chest, leaning back in her chair at his bedside.

"Oh, Will," she murmured, "please do not leave me. Can't you see there's still so much left to do?"

CHAPTER SIXTEEN

I know you believe Will has betrayed you for being friendly to your cousin, who has treated you so poorly over the years, but I truly don't believe he meant to cause any harm. Perhaps Fitzroy really does mean to make amends once his father dies. As for your aunt, didn't you say she never married? Perhaps she's under Gillingham's thumb as well. Anyway, I do hope you'll forgive him. You can't, after all, stay angry at someone forever.

—an excerpt of a letter from Lady Clara to Elaina at Larkspur Castle, Cambridgeshire

WILL WAS in some sort of fiery hell. His body ached all over, but he thought his chest hurt the most. Every breath he took felt like a punishment, and he almost considered giving up breathing altogether if he wasn't so acutely aware of the presence of his wife.

She would try over and over again to soothe him, placing cool rags on his feverish body and making him drink all sorts of liquid—some cool, others hot, most bitter in taste and difficult to get down—but nothing could diminish the fire raging inside him. He almost longed to be outside again in the cold snowstorm.

How long ago had the snowstorm been, anyway? He half wondered if it had already melted.

He had somehow managed through eight years of war without any serious illnesses or injuries. He was one of the lucky ones, they said. He had witnessed plenty of friends die over the years, but death had never touched him—not until now. It was almost ironic that an estate in Cambridgeshire would be what brought him to his end. He supposed he shouldn't have gone out to finish that last barn in a snowstorm, but he was so desperate to be finished with all the projects, especially when he finally had the funds. He cursed himself for not going to Hunt earlier for the loan, for then all of this might've been avoided altogether. But the man was right. His "misplaced aristocratic pride" was too much to overcome until it was too late.

Inwardly, he was laughing. He wondered if his wife would finally marry Hunt after he died. Rightfully so, he thought. He had only just decided he was a good enough sort of man, and Will knew Hunt could take much better care of Elaina than him with all his money and his fancy, successful bank in London.

While he was sick, his thoughts seemed to drift quickly and slowly all at the same time, his mind following no rhyme or reason. One moment he was thinking of Elaina and Hunt, the next he was thinking of the men from the village who'd labored with him in the godforsaken snow. He wondered if any of the others had fallen ill. Guilt crept into his mind and heart, and in a moment of consciousness, he tugged at his wife's sleeve to his side, making what sound he could to get her attention. She sat up straight, leaning over him so she was closer to him in the bed. His vision was blurry, but when her face came into his line of sight, he wasn't sure if it was his wife or an angel come to take him to heaven.

"What is it, my love?" he thought he heard her say.

He half smiled. She had never told him she loved him. He loved her, though he had never told her either. He wasn't sure *why* he never said it. Maybe because he had never said it to anyone, not even his own parents. Or maybe it was because he thought she had come to regret running away with him. He didn't want to confess his feelings and risk rejection in return.

Truthfully, he thought he may have loved her his entire life, but his feelings became more and more clear the longer they stayed at Larkspur. How he longed to protect her, and provide for her, and make her proud of him. She had always been his motivating factor in life, more than his father, whether he knew it at the time or not.

"The men," he managed to say, though it pained him to even move his lips, "from the village."

She nodded her head as if she understood. "I'll have Mr. Price check in on them."

He wasn't sure how long he was ill. One moment his body was on fire, the next he couldn't seem to stop sweating, and finally, he was better.

When he awoke, he found Elaina sitting beside him, her head tilted back and body slumped with sleep. There was an open book in her hand, one she must've taken from the library at Blackmore, for they had none of their own. He smiled when he saw it. His little thief.

His own stirring must've woken her, for she slowly opened her own eyes to find him staring back at her. It was the most lucid he'd been in days.

"Will?" she asked, her voice soft. She immediately reached out to touch the back of her hand against his forehead. "Your fever's broken. I should call for—"

He reached out to grab her wrist before she could stand up. "Stay," he managed to say, the words somehow dry and sticky in his mouth. He smacked his lips together, and Elaina immediately reached for the pitcher of water on his bedside table, pouring him a glass before he could even ask for it. She brought it to his lips, helping him drink, soothingly pushing back strands of sweat-soaked hair from his forehead.

When he finished drinking, he watched as Elaina put the empty glass back down on the table, then reached out to take her hand, bringing the back of it to his lips.

"My savior," he murmured.

She shook her head. "I hardly did anything, only followed the doctor's instructions to care for you."

"I don't remember much," he replied, "but I seem to recall visions of you hovering over me making me drink various things or changing my bedclothes."

She smiled at him. "I couldn't very well let you sleep in your own sweat and tears."

He smiled back at her. No, she couldn't have. "How long have I been sick?" he asked. "Did you rest at all?"

She furrowed her brow. "At least a fortnight, I think," she finally replied. "At some point, I lost track of time. I was so... I was so..."

He squeezed her hand. "I know."

"I should call for Dr. Hardy now," she said, getting up despite his protests.

When Dr. Hardy came, Will was surprised by how young he was. Was this the man who saved his life?

He declared Will to be out of the woods, but advised on plenty of rest until springtime. A washbasin was brought up by the footmen, and Elaina helped him change out of his sweat-soaked clothes and bathe.

The maids made quick work of the soiled bedclothes in the meantime, replacing them with freshly laundered ones.

He practically felt like a new man when he returned to bed, his wife curled up beside him. He kissed the top of her head. He could have lay there in content silence with her forever.

Eventually she sat up, using her left elbow and forearm to leverage herself. Her hair was tucked behind her ears, and she was staring at him with an intensity he had never seen in those brown eyes of hers before.

"I am… I am sorry that I became so angry when you spoke with Fitzroy," she finally said. "I know you were only trying to help, and how could you have possibly snubbed him in the first place? I was silly for expecting that."

He smiled gently at her. "I *was* trying to help, but I should've told him the hurt that he caused. I should've told him you deserved an apology."

"Perhaps one day I'll receive one in person from him, especially if really does want to reconcile once his father passes."

"Perhaps," he said, sighing. "But who knows when that'll be?"

She shook her head. "I don't care anymore, and I don't wish to dwell on it any longer. I want to sit here and be happy with you now that you're safe."

A moment of silence passed between them. Elaina placed her head on the top of his chest, nestling into the crook of his neck. Her hair tickled his nose.

"There is something I must tell you," she said without looking at him.

"I love you, too," he replied, knowing what she was already thinking. One did not sit at a man's bedside for a fortnight, with no rest of one's own, without loving him.

She grinned the moment he said it, a little laughter bubbling from her lips. "How could you have possibly known that's what I was going to say?"

"I just knew," he said, grinning as well. "I think I've always known you loved me, and that I loved you. The years I was away, you said no one wanted you, but I don't believe that. You may have been poor and of questionable birth, but if you ever really wanted a man… you could have had him. But you didn't. You waited instead, though I offered no promises of my own."

She shook her head. "Every letter you sent me was a promise. I knew you would return, and I knew you would make me yours, though I never thought you'd have to defy your entire family to do so. I was stupid to resist you because of that, or to even consider the idea of marrying someone else at their wishes. I love you, Will Winter. I think I always have. There is some guilt, though." She bit her lip, as if she was considering her next words carefully. "This never would have happened if you married well. You could have had a relaxing winter curled up across a fire with someone like Miss Arnold, but—"

He laughed then. "Do you really think Miss Arnold would have been satisfied living in a dusty old castle?"

She tilted her head back and forth. "Perhaps not," she finally said, "but perhaps another wealthy woman could have."

He shook his head. "When there are too many tenants to interview come spring, you'll be the only one I can trust to make sure I don't make any poor decisions."

"You wish me to help you?" she asked. "You don't wish me to stay away and act a lady instead?"

"Never," he murmured, pulling her closer to him. "I was being foolish when I said that. I blame Montgomery's influence."

She laughed. "Of course you do."

"I'm not sure why you insisted on bringing him along," he murmured, reaching up to bring her face down to his. The last time they had kissed was at Blackmore, which felt like a lifetime ago. Both of their lips were curved into smiles when they finally met, but soon the kiss grew deeper, hungrier. Will's hand drifted from the side of her face to her bottom, pulling her closer to him. She drew back, and he let out a sigh of discontentment as she did. He knew she wanted him as much as he wanted her, for her face was flushed with desire.

"The doctor said you must rest," she said weakly.

"But I do not want to rest."

He grabbed her leg and swung it over his torso. He took her by the waist, forcing her to sit on top of him, positioning her so her own privates were against his. She gasped when she felt him beneath her, already inflamed with desire.

The temptation seemed to be too much for her, and she quickly bent over and planted a series of kisses on his lips and neck. She fumbled with the buttons of his nightshirt, and he inhaled as her deft fingers and mouth explored his now bare torso. She eventually sat back up, reaching around to feel the bulge at his groin. She fondled it through the fabric, and he groaned in response.

Eventually she pushed his nightshirt up and positioned herself over his member, not bothering to remove her drawers and thin white nightgown. Slowly, she lowered herself onto him, and he watched her face as she filled herself to the brim with him, the color rising on her cheeks as she bit her lower lip and closed her eyes. When she began to ride him, she opened her eyes again, taking fistfuls of his shirt as she ground against his body, desperate to hit her peak. He reached out, thumbing her erect nipples through the soft muslin of her gown.

Wanting to see her bare body, he grabbed the hem of her nightgown and pulled it over her head. He held on to her lean waist with both hands as she bent over him, and he gladly took one of her pert breasts into his mouth. Her breathing became more and more haggard, and he could tell she was close to achieving her release. He flicked his tongue around her pale pink areola and grabbed onto her bottom, kneading the flesh there and bending his knees, using his feet to leverage himself further and further inside of her.

When her dam broke, so did his, unable to resist her intimate muscles' gentle squeezing and releasing of his cock. When the waves of her pleasure ceased, she seemed content to just lay on top of him, her soft chest against his firm one. He wrapped his arms around her, kissing her cheek and playing with the strands of brown curls splayed against her bare back. Eventually she got up, going to the fire and washbasin for a warm towel to clean him and herself. She was quick to fall asleep when she rejoined him in bed, nestling her head in the crook of his neck.

He kissed the top of her head, finally content to rest as well.

THE REST of the winter seemed to crawl by, especially with Elaina insisting he must rest for the majority of it. It was another fortnight before she allowed him to take his meals downstairs, and a whole month before she let him call on the men he hired to help him make repairs to the last of the outbuildings that needed them. He was happy to find them in good health and eager for more work, for he'd have plenty of it when new tenant farmers were found. Elaina was the one who put the advertisements in the papers.

While they waited for responses, they went to visit the Prices. Elaina seemed happy to see Mrs. Price, who she hadn't visited with since before Christmas, and Will was eager to hear the latest on the Larkspur lumber business. Construction on new coal mines had come to a halt up north, but Mr. Price had plenty of prospective buyers lined up for when spring finally came, so the man seemed hopeful enough for the estate's continued success. Will was pleased with the news, for he did not plan to stay indebted to Hunt for long.

At the end of the visit, Mrs. Price announced that she was expecting, and Elaina insisted on having a celebratory dinner later that week now that the weather was warming up and it was easier to travel.

"With the Prices expecting, I can't help but wonder when we'll welcome a little Winter of our own," he mused out loud as they rode home later that day.

"I confess I was wondering the same thing," she replied after a moment of consideration, her voice soft. "One would think I would have fallen pregnant by now. I hope… I hope nothing's wrong with me."

Will turned to her, eyes filled with concern. "Of course there's nothing wrong with you!" he exclaimed. "How could you think such a thing?"

She half smiled. "Perhaps it's a blessing in disguise," she said. He tilted his head, looking at her for further explanation. She sighed. "We don't want to worry about another mouth to feed right now, do we? I much rather wait until the estate is in order and the loan is paid off."

He brought his horse to a halt, and she did the same a little ways ahead of him, turning to look at him. "What is it?" she asked.

He sighed. "I want you to know if you had told me you were pregnant three months ago, or if you tell me tomorrow or three years from now, I will be excited and eager to welcome the babe into the world whether we were as poor as paupers or as rich as my father. A babe from you could never be a bad thing. Do you understand?"

Hesitating, she slowly nodded.

"Good," he said, urging his horse forward again with a

click of the tongue. "I suppose I'll just have to try harder if I want to produce a playmate for the upcoming addition to the Price family."

She shot him a pointed look, but she couldn't help but laugh after a moment. "But if I were with child, I couldn't race you home," she said, "and what a shame it would be not to beat you in a race every time we went out."

Her horse moved quickly, racing down the lane to the Larkspur stables. Despite Will's best efforts to chase after her, Elaina still won, much like she always did and most likely always would.

When they finally arrived back at the house, Mrs. Harding presented them a stack of letters, which Elaina excitedly declared must've been responses from potential tenants. She took them to the library, with Will following her closely.

With no furniture, they sat on the floor as Elaina read each of them out loud. Gathering the now open pieces of parchment up, she wrote out responses at Will's desk with him hovering over her shoulder. He took the responses from her when she was done, eager to post them himself rather than wait for Harding's daily trip for post the next day.

Interviews were held, and by the time they went to London for Montgomery and Clara's wedding, all of the new tenants had moved into their cottages. New cattle were brought in—shorthorns and sheep—along with plenty of chickens and new equipment for the farmers to use to tend the fields. The village became more prosperous with the added jobs, and soon enough, Will's monthly income had nearly tripled, and it would only go up when Price was able to transport more lumber up north.

"I believe the next time I go to London, it'll be to pay off my loan to Hunt," Will declared as the carriage rolled through their busy estate on its way to the city.

"Let us hope so," Elaina replied, a hopeful smile on her face.

Montgomery and Clara were to be married at St. George's Church the next morning, and when they arrived at Blackmore Terrace late that afternoon, the duchess immediately came rushing to greet them. Will and Elaina raised their eyebrows at each other, both agreeing this was very unlike his mother.

"Thank goodness you are here," she said, using one hand to hold on to Elaina's wrist and the other to clutch at her chest. "She's refusing to marry him. Clara is refusing to marry him."

CHAPTER SEVENTEEN

We have arrived in London a fortnight before the Winters, and although I'm eager to become married, I'm looking forward to attending the first balls and parties of the Season. I find myself wondering what it would have been like if I came here a single woman. Would I have found someone to marry quickly? Would Montgomery and I have met anyway and still married? I suppose there's no use asking such questions.

—an excerpt of a letter from Lady Clara to Elaina at Larkspur Castle, Cambridgeshire

As soon as the words left the duchess's mouth, Elaina turned to her husband, looking at him in complete and utter shock. Judging by his own twisted brow and confused expression, she assumed he was just as surprised as her by his mother's strange declaration.

"What do you mean she's refusing to marry him?" Elaina asked, turning back to the duchess. The poor woman looked dreadfully pale, as if she might faint any moment.

"I mean exactly what I've said!" the duchess exclaimed, sounding exasperated. "The girl won't marry him!"

Without removing her pelisse, Elaina took her mother-in-law by the arm, leading her down the corridor to the nearest drawing room with Will close on their tails. She found a chair for the woman to set herself down in, leaving her there as she handed her effects to one of the footmen—bonnet, pelisse, gloves. She sat across from the duchess then, Will taking a spot behind her, still standing. The duchess began to shake her head, her eyes starting to water, seemingly on the verge of tears.

"First an elopement, next a canceled wedding," she said with a tone of disbelief. She shook her head. "The family cannot take another scandal! She *must* marry him."

"Has she told you why she wishes to cancel the wedding?" Elaina asked, feeling a pang of guilt for being part of the duchess's list of scandals. Still, she found it rather hard to believe that Clara wouldn't go through with the wedding. Her last few letters from the girl had been of the pleasant sort, filled with nothing but excitement over her upcoming nuptials.

The duchess shook her head. "She won't speak to me."

"Have you spoken to Montgomery?" Will asked softly. Elaina looked back at him, then back at the duchess.

"He won't speak to me either!" the duchess exclaimed. The loud sobs started to escape her lips then, her chest heaving with emotion. Will offered his mother a handkerchief, and Elaina stood up as the older woman dabbed her eyes and nose.

"Where is he?" Elaina asked.

"Up-upstairs," the duchess replied between sobs. "In the study."

Elaina nodded, but Will stopped her before she could go. "Wait," he said. "I should go speak to him."

She shook her head. "No. I must find out what he's done for myself if there's any hope at salvaging this wedding."

"How do you know he'll admit to any wrongdoing?" he murmured, stepping away from his mother so he was closer to his wife. She faltered in her step, knowing Montgomery had always been guarded with his emotions, even though they'd spent a total of six Seasons in London together. Looking at her husband, she had the feeling he knew something she didn't.

"Is there something you're not telling me?"

He sighed. "When we came here after Christmas, I think Montgomery only decided to join us so he could visit his mistress."

Elaina's mouth fell open. "His mistress?" she asked, her voice rising. Her husband shushed her, and she looked back at the duchess, who was still weeping in her armchair. In a softer voice, she asked, "What do you mean *his mistress?*"

"He mentioned something about an opera singer in Covent Garden."

Elaina closed her eyes tightly and opened them again, fighting back a sudden urge to scream. "Of all the clichés in all the world," she muttered to herself. To Will, she asked, "Why didn't you tell me this before?"

"You weren't speaking to me for a long time before I got sick."

Elaina sighed. "Fair," she said simply. Shaking her head, she added, "Never mind all that, then. I must go talk to him and convince him to go to Clara. I still think I can fix this."

Will nodded, and she turned on her heel, reentering the corridor and marching up the stairs to the third floor. Montgomery's study was in the back of the house, and she hastily knocked on his door when she came upon it, hearing a groan coming from the other end.

"I told you, Mother," he said in a sulky-sounding voice, "I'm not in the mood to speak."

"I am not your mother," Elaina said back, jostling the doorknob to find it locked. "Open this door at once, Montgomery."

Another groan. "Montgomery," she warned, her voice low.

She heard movement on the other side of the door, then the click of the lock and the door opening. She pushed inside and closed the door behind her, finding Montgomery nursing a glass of what must've been brandy. The pair of them stared at each other for a moment before Elaina shook her head.

"Why are you acting like such a petulant child?" she asked, walking toward him and snatching the glass out of his hand. "You've always been spoiled rotten by your parents, but I've never seen you like this."

He glared at her, snatching the glass back and taking a large gulp of the amber-colored liquid sloshing around in his glass. He peered down at her with a menacing gaze. "What gives you the right to speak to me that way?"

"Whether you like it or not, I am your sister now, and Clara is my friend, and no woman takes kindly to brothers hurting their friends," she said.

He laughed once. "If she doesn't want to marry me, she's a fool," he spat. "Her father could have stuck her with much worse."

"Much worse than a selfish man who continues to entertain a mistress in the days leading up to his wedding?"

Montgomery shook his head. "I gave that woman up four months ago!"

"If that's the case, then how did she discover your affair?"

He sighed. "Her cursed father brought her to London ahead of the wedding and a jealous debutante shared a rumor she heard about me and a certain opera singer. Clara came to me and demanded that I dispute it. I could not, and I would not apologize. I will not apologize for doing what all men do. Naturally, she reacted poorly."

"Oh, Montgomery," she murmured, sitting in one of the chairs in front of his desk. She shook her head. "How could you?

"How could I?" he asked angrily. He went to his desk to pour himself another glass of brandy. "I am a marquess. Why should I be forced to give up my mistress just because I marry?"

"Because Clara deserves better than that."

He stared at her. After a moment, he sighed, looking down and pushing his hair back with his hand. "She does, doesn't she? That's why I'll honor her request. That's why I'll—"

"Oh, don't be so melodramatic, Montgomery." Elaina sighed. "You say the affair was finished four months ago. Do you mean it?"

He nodded, still looking down. "I ended it after I came to London with you and Will after Christmas. I felt so rotten afterward, feeling as though I betrayed her." Looking back up at Elaina, he added, "She's a sweet girl, you know. Clara, I mean."

"I know," Elaina said with a slight smile.

"I only wish she wasn't so upset."

"You can hardly blame her for being upset, Montgomery," Elaina replied in a low voice, shaking her head at his stupidity. "The whole ton will be laughing at her on her wedding day."

"Why should they? She'll be a marchioness—and a duchess after that. They'll never compare to her."

"It's not about that, Montgomery," Elaina said, shaking her head again. "Surely you can't blame her for wanting the man she's about to marry to want her and not someone else. She's an eighteen-year-old girl about to be forced into something she hasn't chosen."

"And what of me?" he asked, placing his two hands on his chest. "Am I not being forced into something I haven't chosen?"

"Well, yes, but surely you can see how easy to love Clara is," she replied. "You could at least *try* to have some measure of affection for her by not having an affair right under her nose."

"I *do* try," he said, shaking his head, "but I met my mistress long before I met her. You, of all people, should know how difficult it is to cut ties with someone you have history with, even when you know there is a much more suitable match in the works. I will not apologize for it."

Elaina stiffened. The allusions in his words did not surpass her. "I thought you said you didn't love this mistress of yours."

"I didn't," he said. "What is love, anyway? I'm sure I do not know it. I've no urge to throw her in a carriage and take her to Scotland against my entire family's wishes, if that's what you mean."

"Then why is it so hard for you to apologize for your past behaviors instead of defending yourself for your mistakes?" Elaina asked with an exasperated sigh.

"Even if I do apologize, will it really guarantee that she will marry me tomorrow? I will not grovel at her feet for nothing."

"No one is asking you to grovel," Elaina replied with a roll of the eyes. "I'm afraid there are no guarantees in matters of the heart, Montgomery. Either you risk your pride for Clara or lose her forever, I'm afraid. Your mother has already described this as a scandal worse than my elopement. I would advise risking your pride if you wish to maintain your parents' favor."

He sighed, finishing his last bit of brandy before slamming the glass down on the desk. "Fine. I will go to her."

"I will join you," Elaina replied. He started to protest, but she silenced him with a raised hand. "She may not agree to see you without my encouragement."

After he reluctantly agreed to her joining him, they left Blackmore Terrace straightaway, leaving Will to look after the duchess, who was still beside herself in tears by the time they exited the study. Will watched them go with a hint of trepidation, to which Elaina kissed him on the cheek and smiled reassuringly at him.

"Do not worry, my love," she replied. "I will have this patched up in no time."

WILL PACED the front drawing room of Blackmore Terrace, looking out the window every so often to look for Elaina returning to the house. His mother had ceased crying and now seemed to be watching him closely from where she sat in one of the room's armchairs.

"You're just like her," he thought he heard her murmur.

He looked at his mother with a confused gaze. "What was that?"

"You're just like her," the duchess said more loudly this time. He stopped pacing. "If she did not receive a letter from you in the post for over a month, she would take to pacing all day long, sending one of the footmen to check the post day and night until something arrived."

Will didn't say anything.

"She always accused me of not fretting over you enough."

"Can you blame her?" Will asked, taking a seat in the chair

across from her. "I received very few letters from you or Father."

"It wasn't for lack of caring." The duchess sighed. "I only didn't know what to say. I feared losing you but didn't know what to say. I was afraid you might find me insincere."

She paused for a moment. "Your father always paid so much more attention to your brother, so I suppose I did, too. I often wondered why, since he was once a second son himself. Perhaps he only wanted you to receive the same sort of treatment he did."

Will was silent as he looked down at the floor. If he looked at her, he might end up brushing his angry feelings aside, and for some reason, he didn't want to do that today.

"You must know that I'm proud of you."

He level his gaze on her almost immediately. "How could I? You've never said so."

"But I am," she said with a resolute nod. "You were an army captain, and I'm sure you're doing a fine job with Larkspur. Why do you think I spent so much time showing you off to the single daughters of my friends at the house party?"

He smiled. Perhaps she was right. Perhaps his mother had always been proud of him, even without saying so. He always assumed he was an embarrassment, ever since he struggled and left Eton. Ever since he was nothing like Montgomery. Perhaps all that had been in his head.

"You know, I secretly always wanted you to marry Elaina."

He raised an eyebrow. "Really?"

"Of course," she replied with a nod. "I could have sat her next to Hunt that first night, but I didn't. Do you really think I didn't know what I was doing? You have me to thank for your marriage."

Will laughed loudly. "Whatever you say, Mother."

· · ·

THE DUKE OF EDGERTON'S London home was not far from Blackmore Terrace in Mayfair, so Elaina and Montgomery decided to walk, it being rather warm and dry for a day in April. Montgomery attempted to make small talk as they walked.

"How is Larkspur?" he asked.

"Much improved," she replied. "All of the tenant cottages have been let for the growing season. Additional livestock and machinery have been bought and delivered. The lumber business continues to grow." With a wink, she added, "Soon enough, Larkspur will be just as successful as my once precious Blackmore."

He laughed once. "I have no doubt it will be. I also doubt that Will would have been able to do it without you. Father should really be thanking you, if you ask me."

She shook her head. "I think you underestimate Will's ability to inspire and lead the men who work for him. He was a soldier, after all. Not just a soldier, a captain. He is far from the shy and timid child you remember him as."

"Maybe," he replied, tilting his head back and forth as he considered her words. "I often wonder what Will has done to improve you, though."

She stopped for a moment, staring at him. "It's not a man's job to improve a woman, nor is it a woman's job to improve a man. I like to think Will and I complement each other. That is why we work so well together. One without the other… well, that'd be a recipe for disaster."

They continued moving then, and after a while, Montgomery asked, "Do you think Clara and I complement each other?"

"I'm not sure," she replied. "You do on a superficial level, I suppose. You're both tall, fair, and handsome."

"You think I'm handsome?"

She returned his grin with a pointed look. "If you really

want your marriage to be a success, you need to learn how to give and care—and not just about yourself. You cannot turn out like your father or all you'll end up caring about is the estate and your title and who your offspring marry."

"I get the feeling you resent my father."

Elaina shook her head. "I did not always resent him. I don't even think resent is the right word. I've only disappointed him. He deserted his son, and I cannot forgive him for that. Did you know that Will almost died this winter?"

"What?" Montgomery asked, sounding shocked. "Why didn't you write and tell anyone?"

"I was too busy caring for him to write," she replied. "The doctor called it pleurisy. It came on after he spent all day working on one of the outbuildings in a snowstorm. Foolish, I know—I could have killed him myself for such stupidity—but I can't help but wonder if it ever would have happened if your father had only just supported us. Of course, he was so reluctant to go to Hunt, and that's his own fault, but he was positive his father would change his mind and help us… but he never did."

Montgomery sighed, seeming to consider her words but saying nothing. They walked the rest of the way in silence. Edgerton House looked similar to Blackmore Terrace, except its front wasn't as narrow and it was three stories instead of five. They were greeted by a butler upon knocking, and he took them to the drawing room. When he came down next, he unsurprisingly told them Clara would see Elaina in her private sitting room. Montgomery shot Elaina a nervous look, but she only shook her head, urging him to be calm.

She climbed the stairs to the second floor with the butler. She was announced as she entered, finding Clara sitting by herself in the middle of the small but well-appointed room. A small fire was burning in the fireplace at the corner of the room, and the furniture all matched the room's green wallpaper. Clara herself was wearing green muslin. Her face was not nearly as luminous as when she saw Elaina at Christmas, but she still stood up and rushed to greet her friend with an embrace.

"I'm so glad you're here," she murmured in her ear as they hugged. She pulled back then, leaving her hands on Elaina's shoulders. "But why have you brought Montgomery with you? Surely your family has told you that I have no desire to see him, let alone marry him."

They walked to the collection of settees and chairs at the center of the room, taking seats across from each other. "Yes, well," she said, "I'm here to convince you to marry him anyway."

"Surely you must know that I cannot," Clara replied, looking shocked that Elaina would even suggest it. "I cannot marry a man I do not love, and after what I've discovered, I certainly do not love Montgomery."

Tea had been brought in before she arrived, and Elaina gestured to the pot on the table in between them. "May I?" she asked.

Clara nodded, and Elaina took to pouring herself a cup, adding in generous helpings of milk and sugar, two things that had long been in short supply at Larkspur. She took a sip of tea and considered the frustrated-looking Clara over the top of her cup.

"You were ready to marry Montgomery before this happened," Elaina said. "Did that mean you once loved him, and now you don't?"

"I-I..." Clara stuttered, stopping for a moment to consider her words. "I don't think I ever loved him. I think I was infatuated with him, but now that the truth has come out, how can I go through with it? He will never love me. He loves someone else."

Elaina shook her head. "Montgomery is like most men,"

she replied. "He took a mistress out of boredom, but I've spoken to him. Clara, he gave her up four months ago out of care for you. He wants to give your marriage a real shot, and he's here to apologize."

Clara pursed her lips. "I gave him a chance before to apologize, and he did not. He *would* not."

Elaina sighed. "I'm afraid you have a very stubborn fiancé, Clara. I cannot guarantee your marriage will be perfect as a result. My marriage is not perfect, yet you consider our elopement to be one of the most romantic tales you've ever heard—but not everything in a relationship is romance, Clara. Marriage is difficult work. Do you want to know what I believe?"

Clara nodded.

"If anyone has a shot at taming Montgomery," Elaina said slowly, "it's you—or at least I think it's you. You're strong and you're spirited. You won't let a man like Montgomery get away with anything you don't like. You threatened to call off an entire wedding to a marquess the day before the date, for God's sake."

Clara smothered a giggle with her bare hand. Elaina smiled kindly at her. "Would you like me to send him up?" she asked.

Clara nodded, and Elaina stood up, going back downstairs to find Montgomery still in the front drawing room. "She will see you now," she said. "She's on the second floor. It's the first open door you see when you get there."

Montgomery started to leave, but she grabbed him by the arm. "Montgomery," she said softly, "do not make me regret convincing that girl to give you a second chance."

He nodded, despite hesitating briefly. Elaina could only sigh as she watched him go, hoping he had it in him to love someone other than himself.

· · ·

GRAHAM'S HEART had started to pound the moment he entered the drawing room. Clara sat by herself, sipping a cup of tea. She looked up when she heard him, smiling. Not the same bright, happy smile he was used to seeing. This one was much more reserved, almost polite but unfeeling in nature.

"Graham," she said, putting her cup of tea down. "Have a seat."

She had this authoritative way about her that late afternoon that he didn't quite recognize. He was used to Clara being pleasant toward him. Now she was treating him like a child. He had to force himself to do what she asked as a result.

"Elaina told me I should marry you," she said after he had sat. "Do you agree with her?"

Graham swallowed. If he cared about Clara's sake and Clara's sake alone, he might've said no. Clara *shouldn't* marry him, he was sure of it. If she had done the things he had done… well, he wouldn't have forgiven her. Why should she forgive him?

But still, he couldn't quite imagine himself marrying anyone else but her. His betrothed had been a part of his life since he was ten, whether she knew it or not. He had always kept a certain distance from women, never wanting to fall in love, for he knew he would give up love for duty, and Clara was his duty.

But what if he could love Clara as well? What if duty and love could overlap? That idea was what made him leave his mistress in the first place.

"I came here to apologize to you, not tell you what to do," he finally replied. Clara looked taken aback. "I've come to say I'm sorry for the lack of judgment I displayed, and I hope you will forgive me for my indiscretion."

He thought he saw her lip quiver. "What if you do it again?"

"I would not if we were married." Graham watched as she turned away from him. He procured a handkerchief from his pocket, getting up from his seat and kneeling before her. She turned her head to look at him. Her eyes were rimmed with tears. He handed her the handkerchief. She took it.

"Clara, you do not have to marry me if you don't want to," he said, looking up at her. He reached for her free hand, the one that wasn't dabbing moisture from her eyes. "If you decide that you cannot forgive me, we can end this however you like. I can leave you, or you can leave me—whatever you think is more favorable for your reputation. I will never utter a bad word about you. Your father may force you to leave London and come back next year for your first true Season, but if we were ever to cross paths at a party, I hope we can treat each other with kindness."

She stared down at him, and he wondered what she was thinking. Losing her would be a blow to his relationship with his father. He knew it. He wondered if *she* knew it.

Whatever she was thinking, she started to nod slowly. "I will marry you," she said softly, holding the handkerchief to her chin. He smiled at her, bringing her hand to his lips.

"And do you forgive me?" he asked, staring at her with earnest.

She hesitated. It did not escape his notice that she hesitated. But when she started to slowly nod again, he couldn't help but stand up, bringing her with him so he could hold her in his arms.

WILL WAS thankful when Elaina finally returned, especially when she told the duchess the wedding would go on the next day as planned.

"Thank heavens!" the duchess exclaimed, standing up and throwing her arms around her daughter-in-law, kissing her cheeks. "I should've known you'd make the finest Winter girl! Oh, my sweet daughter!"

Will almost laughed as he watched his mother smother his wife. When she left to go tell his father and Montgomery had returned to his study, they stood together at the drawing room's bay window, looking out onto the busy London street. It was just beginning to get dark.

"Did you hear that?" he asked softly, pulling his wife into an embrace. "She should've known you'd make the finest Winter girl."

Elaina laughed softly. "I once thought receiving your family's approval to become your wife was all I ever wanted," she said, looking up at him. "But we still managed to build something without that approval, didn't we? I suppose we never really needed it in the first place."

"Perhaps not," he said with a slight smile, pushing a strand of brown hair behind her ear as he looked down at her. "For what it's worth, I always knew you'd make the finest Winter girl."

"Even when compared to the daughter of a duke?" she asked.

He nodded once. "Even when compared to the daughter of a duke," he repeated, bending down to kiss her softly on the lips. When they broke apart, the duchess had reentered the drawing room.

"Your father would like to see you, Will," she said. Smiling at Elaina and pressing a kiss to her knuckles before he left, he made his way to his father's study on the second floor. The door was open, so he entered right away, shutting it behind him.

"Will," his father said. Surprisingly, he was not smoking his pipe, or drinking a glass of brandy, or poring over any papers. He merely sat at his desk and smiled at his son. He waved to one of the armchairs across from him. "Sit down."

Will did as he was told, and his father continued. "Your mother tells me that your wife has just saved the day."

"It would appear she has," Will said.

"And Larkspur?" he asked.

"All of the cottages have been leased, the timber business continues to do well, and we recently made an investment in more livestock and new machinery for the tenants."

"Then it would appear that you've made the estate a success without my help or that of a rich wife."

"So it would appear," Will said, nodding once.

The two men sat there for a moment, silently regarding each other. "I'm proud of you, son," he said. "And I was wrong about Lady William. No one could be a more perfect wife for you."

Something about his father's words felt hollow to him. He thought perhaps he should let it go, smile and nod and thank his father for his recognition, but he could not do it.

"Were you not proud of me before for having a successful career in the army?"

The duke furrowed his brow. "The army? Plenty of men have success in the army. Not many men have successful estates, though."

A wave of disappointment crashed over Will. He had joined the army to make a name for himself, to prove something to his family… had it not worked? Only Elaina and his mother had seemed impressed.

Why, though, was he so keen on impressing people? Most of all, why was he so keen on impressing his father? After toiling over the estate during the entire fall and part of winter, receiving his father's approval had been the least exciting part.

Now he had tenants and a timber business. He had the promise of true success. Those things were what drove and excited him now. Along with his wife, who may have never been his if he had listened to his father.

Will stood up suddenly. His father shot him a confused look. "Why don't you stay and have a drink with me?"

"Maybe after dinner," he replied, attempting a smile. When he left the room, he found Elaina hovering outside.

"How was it?" she asked quietly when the door had been shut behind him. He only shrugged.

"He said he was proud of me."

Elaina smiled. "Rightfully so!"

She looked so happy that he decided not to let her in on his little secret, that he had left his desire to please in his father's study. He was his own man now, and his father had no more power over him.

WILL WAS SUMMONED to his brother's room early the next morning. His brother's valet was tying his cravat when he arrived. Montgomery's face lit up when he saw his brother in the doorway.

"You came," he said happily.

"Why wouldn't I?" Will replied, giving his brother a perplexed look. "Your room is just down the hall from mine."

"I only wished to share a small toast with my only brother before my wedding." With his cravat tied, Montgomery's valet was dismissed, and he moved to the sideboard in his room to procure two glasses and a bottle of brandy. He poured a drink for himself and then his brother.

After handing Will his beverage, he raised his own glass and said, "To my wedding!"

They both drank, and Will wondered why his brother was being so peculiarly friendly with him. Why hadn't he called his father if he wanted a celebratory drink?

They stood for a moment in awkward silence, staring at

each other as they took additional sips of brandy. Montgomery sighed. "I wish I could have eloped."

Will furrowed his brow. "Why?"

"There's something much more romantic about secretly running away with your lover than marrying the girl your father chose for you at ten in front of what feels like all of London."

Will frowned. "I would have liked to have had a real wedding with Elaina. Maybe not in London, but back in Blackmore."

Montgomery laughed once. "Believe me, you don't want that sort of attention."

Another silence fell over the room. As Will regarded his brother, something dawned on him. "Do you ever wonder if we've ever disliked each other because we want what the other has but cannot have ourselves? You wish to have a quiet, secretive wedding in Scotland, while I longed to have my family accept my choice in bride like they do yours."

Montgomery smiled slightly. "Perhaps."

Will went on, thinking of other examples. "I resented how much Father adored you, but you resented the amount of freedom I had. I wished I was the marquess, while you wished you had no responsibilities, like me."

"You make a fair point." Montgomery brought his brandy to his lips again, a look of consternation on his face.

"Why do you like me now, then?"

Montgomery shrugged. "It was something Elaina said when we were all in Blackmore last. She said I should save you and me from having two miserable lives by letting bygones be bygones."

Will smiled. "That sounds like something Elaina would say."

"Besides, didn't we already agree to support each other?

That's why I came with you to London when you met with Hunt."

Will didn't bother mentioning that he believed his brother only came so he could see his mistress while they were there. Instead, he continued to smile. "Let us drink to our newfound friendship, then."

"Hear, hear!"

MONTGOMERY AND CLARA were married at St. George's in Mayfair. Elaina had never attended such a crowded wedding at the church in Hanover Square, and she was nervous to take her spot beside Clara as her maid of honor. Will was his brother's only attendant as well, and this was the first time either had been seen out in society together since their elopement.

Elaina only caught a few people staring at them and whispering when they gathered at Blackmore Terrace for the wedding breakfast. Perhaps the friendliest face they saw was Mr. Hunt.

"Lord and Lady William," he said, approaching them and smiling.

"Mr. Hunt!" Elaina exclaimed. "It's so nice to see you."

She half wondered if she shouldn't have said it for her Will's sake, but when she glanced at him, he didn't seem at all perturbed by her proclamation.

"How is Larkspur?" Mr. Hunt asked.

"Successful, thanks to you," Will replied.

Mr. Hunt bowed his head slightly, smiling. "Will you be in London long?"

"A few days, perhaps."

"May I call on you tomorrow, then?"

Elaina nodded. "Of course!"

"Mr. Hunt!"

Elaina peered over the man's shoulder to see Cousin Julia approaching him. She couldn't help but smile, remembering her conversation with Julia at the Christmas party.

"Miss Winter."

Knowing that Julia was probably looking for a dance, Elaina asked, "Has anyone asked you to dance yet, Julia?"

"I'm afraid not, cousin," she said with a slight frown while looking up at Mr. Hunt through her eyelashes.

"May I have this next one, then?" Mr. Hunt asked, offering his arm.

"I'd be delighted!"

As they watched them walk away, Will bent down and whispered in Elaina's ear. "What was that about?"

She laughed, explaining what Julia had told him at the Christmas party. Will was inclined to agree with his cousin Robbie. Julia *was* much too young and foolish for a man like Mr. Hunt.

The duke and duchess approached them next, expressing their thanks to Elaina once more for saving the day and helping the family avoid another scandal, as ironic as it was that Elaina was the cause of the first one. The duke went so far as to tell her he was proud to have her as his daughter-in-law, despite the ill-advised elopement.

When Elaina and Will danced together later on, she asked, "Do you think he meant it?"

Will shot her a puzzled look. "Do I think who meant what?"

"Your father," she replied. "Do you think he meant it when he said he was proud to have me as his daughter-in-law?"

He smirked. "Well, when I gave him my report on Larkspur yesterday, he told me he was wrong about you, and no one could be a more perfect wife for me. No doubt he pins the entire success of the estate on you, seeing as how brilliant your father has been in the management of Blackmore."

Elaina frowned. "I wish you and your brother would stop saying those sorts of things," she said. "You are every bit a part of Larkspur's success as I am. You know that, right?"

He nodded. "Of course," he said. "I've come to take everything my father says with a grain of salt, and my brother and I have agreed to let bygones be bygones."

Elaina raised her eyebrows. "Have you?"

He nodded. "Oh, yes. I believe I have you to thank for that."

She flushed. "I only encouraged him to spend time with you over Christmas. Perhaps he's finally realized what I've known all along."

"What's that?"

"Why, only that you're so worthy of love, of course!"

She smiled up at him as they twirled around the dance floor, wishing she could live in that moment of time, dancing forever.

CHAPTER EIGHTEEN

We have arrived safely in Paris! My, what a thing it is to travel by boat! Even Montgomery seemed rather taken with it. The roads to Paris were good, and it was a very easy trip there from where we landed in Calais. I wish I had nothing but good news, but I find looking at my husband difficult sometimes. I still think of his mistress, and I wonder whether or not he is comparing me to her in everything I do? Oh, Elaina... is that so very wrong of me?

—an excerpt of a letter from Lady Clara to Elaina at Blackmore Terrace, London

As promised, Hunt called the next day on Will and Elaina at Blackmore Terrace. Elaina had been excited to receive him, especially now that he and her husband got along.

Elaina was excited, that is, until she saw who he brought with him: her cousin, Viscount Fitzroy. Except, apparently Viscount Fitzroy was no longer Viscount Fitzroy. He was Earl Gillingham, his father dead some two weeks ago.

She looked at the new Gillingham and Mr. Hunt, who

were sitting across from her and Will on opposite settees in the front drawing room of Blackmore Terrace. She was sure her face looked pinched, as she was trying so hard to remain expressionless even though she wanted to stand up and yell at Mr. Hunt.

"I am sorry we have not been able to do this sooner," the new Gillingham said as Elaina poured them tea from the tray that one of the servants had just brought up.

"Are you?" she asked. She handed a cup to Gillingham, then Mr. Hunt, then her husband. Will looked terrified, as if he knew his wife was on the precipice of snapping at someone, with Mr. Hunt being the most likely victim.

Hunt should've known better. He had been there to see her be snubbed by her cousins over and over again at London parties. He should've recognized the pain they had caused her.

She reminded herself that perhaps she was being too stubborn. Reconciliation between her and Gillingham would help her standing in society, as well as the standing of her future children. She didn't care so much for her standing now that Larkspur could be her permanent escape, but she did care about her hypothetical children.

"Yes," her cousin replied. He was blushing underneath his freckles. Her cousin was tall and pale with red hair. She gazed at him tentatively, waiting for him to say more. He swallowed. "You see, my father was a very stubborn man. He wanted to honor the old earl's wishes by never recognizing you and your mother. I maintain that I think it pained him to do so—he and your mother were close in childhood, and I remember him being upset in spite of himself when she passed—but nevertheless, he maintained a tight hold over the actions of your aunt and I."

"He prevented my aunt from answering letters?"

Gillingham laughed, almost nervously. "I know it sounds ridiculous, but yes. Your aunt never married. When her father died, she depended on my father's kindness to survive, but she has longed to meet you for as long as I can remember. She often asked me to describe you to her whenever I saw her. I told her she should come to London one Season and see you for herself, but she couldn't bear the idea of seeing you and then being forced to ignore you."

Elaina frowned. She supposed she knew what it was like to live on another person's kindness. She remembered how afraid she was to elope with Will against his parents' wishes when she had depended on their kindness for so long.

"I'm sure this must be something of a shock for you, seeing me here after I've ignored you for so long, but I really do wish to make things right."

Elaina nodded once. Unsure of what to say, she only softly uttered, "I understand."

The rest of the tea was awkward and uncomfortable. Mr. Hunt and Will getting along turned out to be the least of her worries. Gillingham left first, telling Elaina and Will that they were welcome to visit Lyman House, the family's homestead, whenever they wished, and he would be there for the rest of the month.

Elaina watched as he went, and when she was sure he was out of earshot, she turned to Hunt, her gaze angry. "Why would you bring him here, Mr. Hunt? You know how I feel about him."

Mr. Hunt nodded once. "I know, Lady William, but I thought you had the right to know your cousin had died and there was a new earl."

"You could have told me yourself!" she exclaimed. "You could have given me some time to warm up to the idea of seeing him and being friendly!"

"There's no need to yell at him, Elaina," Will interjected. "Mr. Hunt was only trying to help."

Her cheeks started to flame. These men! Why did they think she needed their help anyway? She was nearly six-and-twenty now. She no longer needed her mother's family's approval.

She stood up suddenly. She looked down at Mr. Hunt, who appeared unbothered by Elaina's unladylike outburst. "Good day, sir."

Elaina remained in a daze for the rest of their stay in London, unable to listen whenever her husband tried to reason with her. He was patient in his pleas, and she found herself wondering why it was so hard to forgive her mother's family.

Her father had come to London for the wedding as well, and she was looking for him on their last night in town. If anyone would know what to do, it would be her father. She found him in the library reading a book, his spectacles far down his nose. She smiled at the familiar sight, which almost made her long for Blackmore again.

He looked up from the book and smiled at her. "Hello, my dear. Why aren't you with the others?"

Elaina shrugged, taking a seat by her father. "I wanted to see what you were doing. This will be my last night to see you for who knows how long."

She snuggled close to her father, resting her head on his chest. He seemed surprised by her sudden need for closeness. She hadn't needed her father's comfort like that since before finishing school. "You seem upset, Elaina. Is this about the new Earl Gillingham coming to see you?"

She nodded against his chest. "Yes," she replied, leaning back and looking at her father in the eye. "How can I possibly forgive him without offending Mama's memory? Her family caused her so much pain."

Mr. Walker sighed. "Your grandfather caused your mother so much pain. The new Earl Gillingham was just a baby like you were."

"What about my aunt? Apparently she wishes to see me as well. She was alive when it all happened."

"I'm afraid it's much more complicated than that," her father said solemnly.

Elaina rolled her eyes. "You sound like the new earl now."

"If your aunt had married, I have no doubt that she would have visited your mother. She would have visited *you*. Unfortunately, her father—and later her cousin—did not allow it. When your mother was alive, she bore her sister no ill will. She understood the position she was in. She would have wanted you to understand as well."

Elaina was silent. Perhaps she was being too unforgiving, and that was doing her mother's memory a disservice. She barely remembered her mother, but she did remember her being kind. She would have wanted Elaina to make amends with her family.

Elaina sighed. "I suppose I'm off to Essex, then."

WILL and Elaina decided to head straight from London to Lyman House in Essex. They sent word the day before, so Elaina only hoped her cousin wasn't too shocked when they arrived. After her coldness when he called on her in London, she wouldn't blame him if he was a bit surprised seeing her so soon.

The house was one of the largest that Elaina had ever seen, practically palatial in size and possibly bigger than both Larkspur and Blackmore combined. Clad with gray stone, the house had two entrances, one at each end. The carriage stopped at the first.

When she stepped out, Elaina couldn't help but look up and feel a little awestruck at the fact that her mother had grown up in such a place. There were at least three floors of living space at Lyman House, with multiple towers extending even further into the sky.

The house's butler greeted them upon their arrival, bringing them through a large salon with plasterwork ceilings, into an almost equally large drawing room. She caught herself staring upwards once more. She had never seen such ornate ceilings in her life. She looked back at Will, who smiled assuredly at her as they were announced.

Gillingham stood upon seeing Elaina and her husband. Memories of him and his late father ignoring her at parties flitted through her mind, but she felt determined to push those memories out of her head for good. She would not let those past slights spoil whatever relationship her and her cousin might try to have now.

There was woman with familiar-looking dark hair and eyes standing with Gillingham as well. She smiled tentatively at Elaina, and Elaina knew her to be her Aunt Elizabeth.

"Lord and Lady William, this is my cousin, Lady Elizabeth," Gillingham said, gesturing to the older woman standing beside him. "Lady Elizabeth is your—"

"My aunt, yes," Elaina said, her voice practically a whisper. Seeing her aunt conjured up long-forgotten memories of her mother. Lady Elizabeth looked like how her mother would have; perhaps that was what had shaken her.

"My dear," she said, coming to Elaina and embracing her. "How good it is to meet you."

Elaina froze under her embrace, unsure of what to do.

"When Andrew told me about your interview in London, I was sure you wouldn't come," she said. "I couldn't blame you, of course. I would have been angry, too."

Elaina smiled slightly. "Well, I'm here," she said with a shrug, "and I'm quite determined to not be angry anymore."

"Come, let us sit, and I shall ring for tea," Gillingham said.

The group sat, while Elaina remained unable to do anything but smile politely as her aunt gazed so... well, almost lovingly at her.

"I was sorry to hear of the passing of your cousin," Will said to Elizabeth. Elaina glanced at her husband thankfully, happy to let him lead the conversation for now.

Elizabeth only shrugged. "I'm afraid I'm not. I'm only lucky that Andrew turned out more like his mother than his father."

The tea tray was brought up by one of the footmen. Elizabeth busied herself with serving everyone a cup as Elaina watched. Gillingham asked Will a question about Larkspur, starting their own conversation while Elaina struggled to find something to say to her aunt.

"You look so much like her," Elizabeth said, handing Elaina a cup of tea.

Elaina raised her eyebrows as she took a sip. "Do I?"

Elizabeth nodded. She then turned to face Will, teacup in hand, listening intently to one of his stories about Larkspur. Her aunt seemed to enjoy them, smiling and laughing at all of Will's jokes.

"How did the two of you come to fall in love?" she asked. Elaina was a bit surprised by such a forward question, and it must've shown on her face. Her aunt smiled but didn't retract the question.

"Well, we grew up together," Elaina said, finding herself willing to take the lead on the conversation now that she was finding herself much more comfortable. There was something about her aunt's presence that put her into eventual ease. "I guess it all started as children. When my mother died, Will's mother brought me to be raised in the Blackmore nursery. We were the best of friends as children and wrote each other all through Will's time at Eton and in the army."

"Did you fight against Napoleon, Lord William?" Elizabeth asked, looking impressed.

Will nodded. "I married Elaina when I returned from Brussels."

"I'm surprised I didn't see a marriage announcement in the paper, seeing as how you're a war hero. Your parents must be proud."

"We actually eloped." Elaina glanced at Will, looking for any trace of embarrassment. There was none. "My parents didn't want us to marry, seeing as how Elaina did not have much of a dowry."

Gillingham and Elizabeth shared a glance, and Elaina wondered if they felt guilty for not coming to her aid sooner. She knew that they couldn't have, though, and there was no use dwelling on that.

"But we are married now," Elaina said, reaching over to grab Will's hand. She squeezed it. "That's all that matters."

ELAINA AND WILL RETIRED to a bedchamber much grander than their own that night. Dinner was an enjoyable affair, especially when she stopped worrying so much about the past. Gillingham and Lady Elizabeth were fine conversationalists, and she found her aunt shared similar passions for horseback riding and gardening.

"Are you enjoying your visit so far?" Will asked as he helped Elaina get undressed.

"Yes," she said. Then, after crinkling her nose, "No. I don't know."

She heard her husband's soft laughter from behind her.

She turned and looked at him. "And what, exactly, is preventing you from enjoying yourself completely?" he asked.

"I can't help but wonder what my mother would think of all of this," she said, letting out a frustrated sigh as she stepped out of her evening dress. She'd almost felt embarrassed to wear it tonight in such a grand house.

She had realized all of her clothes were becoming outdated when she went to London for Montgomery and Clara's wedding, but she could not bring herself to spend any money on new dresses while she was there. After living so frugally for so long, one started to take pause before buying any sort of frivolous thing even after the time for frugality had passed.

"What do you mean?" Will asked.

When she turned around, he was starting to get out of his own clothes to switch into his nightshirt. "Her cousin, Gillingham's father, deserted her. Her own *sister*, Lady Elizabeth, deserted her. Were they so afraid of the earl that they could not think for themselves and love her anyway, regardless of who she decided to marry? My father says I should forgive them, but..."

Will sighed, sitting down on the bed. "There's no rush to forgive them, Elaina. You don't have to forgive them at all if you don't want to."

After changing into her nightgown and taking down her hair, she sat with him. "I keep thinking of what my father said to me, though. He said my mother would have wanted me to forgive them—and I believe him!"

"Can't you see, darling?" he asked, reaching out to her to push a strand of hair behind her ear. "Your father wants you to be happy. Will having your mother's family in your life make you happy?"

"Well, yes, I think so. I've always wanted them in my life."

"Then why don't you let them in your life?"

"Well, my mother—"

"Your mother would have been just like your father," Will said. He kissed her forehead before gazing at her seriously. "She would have wanted you to be happy."

She bit her lip. "Do you think so?"

"I do," he replied, nodding.

He kissed her full on the mouth then, pulling her back onto the bed with him, keeping her there until she was thoroughly distracted from thoughts of her mother's family.

ELAINA AND ELIZABETH spent the next morning walking through the gardens at the back of the house, which were just as expansive and impressive as the rest of Lyman House. They must've gone on for at least a mile, filled with fountains and colorful flowers and man-made streams and ponds, at the very end of which was a Roman folly.

The two women had much in common, which made conversation easy, but the betrayal of her mother by her aunt still weighed heavily on her.

"May I ask you something, aunt?" she finally asked as they approached the folly. They sat down together on the steps, looking out onto the garden they'd just traversed and the house behind that.

"What is it, my dear?"

Elaina sighed. "I'm having trouble reconciling myself with the fact that I don't know how my mother would feel with me being here, sitting with you. With the way her family turned their noses up at her—at *me*—when she decided to marry my father, I can't imagine she would want me to forgive too easily. It must've pained her very much."

"I was only seventeen when your mother ran away with your father," Elizabeth began to explain. "I was at finishing school when it happened, and when I returned home and your mother wasn't there, I was forbidden from asking any questions about her. My father was very irate."

"Was your father—my grandfather—a cruel man?"

"I had never known him to be cruel until your mother ran away," she said, shaking her head. "I think your mother's decision to elope felt like a betrayal."

"But why wouldn't he just approve the match between my mother and father?"

"He was sure Eleanor wouldn't be happy to live in some cottage as the wife of a land steward. He thought it was a phase."

"But it wasn't!"

Elizabeth nodded. "No, it wasn't." She paused for a moment before continuing. "I like to think my mother would have talked some sense into him about the whole thing, but she had passed some years before. It took a Season in London and listening to the gossip to figure out what truly happened, and when I finally found out where your mother was, I tried to write her, but a servant told my father, and my letter was stolen."

She sighed. "The plan was I would marry someone who wouldn't mind having a sister-in-law who was a land steward's wife. I would be allowed the freedom to visit when I was out from underneath my father's thumb. Unfortunately, your mother died before I found anyone. I couldn't even attend the funeral."

Her aunt paused, taking a haggard breath, on the verge of tears. Elaina placed her hand on her aunt's back, comforting her.

"When my father finally died," she continued, "I wanted to visit, but the new earl forbid it. I couldn't believe it. I thought he would *want* to see his cousin. They were close, but he was afraid of dishonoring the old earl's memory."

"What a strange thing to be afraid of," Elaina murmured, furrowing her brow.

"My father always wanted a son, you see. He hated the idea of leaving everything to his nephew. I think my cousin was trying to prove something to my father, even after his death."

"But what about you? You had nothing to do with that."

"I think he was mad at me for never marrying," she said. "You see, there came a time in my life when I realized I wasn't made for men, and men weren't made for me. My cousin agreed to take care of me after my father died, which is more than many cousins would do for a woman in my position, but—"

"You had to live with his rules," Elaina murmured. Frowning, she added, "I'm sorry, aunt."

She shook her head. "No matter, my dear. I am only glad the new Gillingham agreed it was time to let the past rest and make you a part of the family again."

"I hope you know you are always welcome at Larkspur," she said. "Will and I don't have much right now, but one day I think we will."

Elizabeth smiled, placing her hand over her niece's. "I have no doubt you will."

On their last day at Lyman House, Gillingham asked to see both Elaina and Will in the smaller of the house's two libraries. They sat across from each other—Gillingham by himself and Elaina with Will—on two separate settees. Elaina looked around the room, admiring all the books sitting in the bookcases that had been built into the walls.

"There is something I would like to discuss with you that I discovered while going through my father's accounts with the family's solicitor," he began, leaning back in his seat, crossing his leg, and folding his hands over his stomach. "As I'm sure you know, Lady William—"

"Please, cousin, you must call me Elaina."

Gillingham smiled. "Very well, then. As I'm sure you know, Elaina, your father was never given your mother's dowry when they were married. You may have wondered what happened to that money." He paused for a moment, and Elaina leaned forward in her chair. "The answer is nothing. Your grandfather did nothing with it, as did my own father. The sum of Lady Eleanor's dowry, as well as Lady Elizabeth's, remains intact, tied up in some investments and a dower house on the grounds. I've spoken to Lady Elizabeth, and we both agreed it would be best to sign over those investments to you. I will keep the dower house should I ever marry and have any daughters of my own."

Elaina stared at him, unable to speak—or even think, really. Will cleared his throat. "How much exactly are those investments worth?"

"Thirty thousand pounds."

Elaina inhaled sharply. "I cannot accept such a thing."

"Elaina—"

"You will accept, cousin," Gillingham said, interrupting Will. "It's the least I can do after my family has done nothing for you these past six-and-twenty years."

She turned to Will, who looked as if ready to shout with excitement. "I cannot."

Will turned to Gillingham. "Will you leave us for a moment, Gillingham?"

The earl nodded, standing up and leaving the room. Will looked at Elaina. "Elaina, he will transfer the investments to me if you do not take them."

She paused a moment, then simply said, "I forbid it."

"But *why*?" he asked, exasperated.

Elaina shook her head. "I have no good reason," she

finally said after a moment. "I only do not feel worth such good fortune."

"Oh, Elaina," he said, his voice bursting with emotions, tears in his eyes as he pulled her into an embrace. "You deserve all the good fortune in the world. You went to Scotland with me, lived in my decrepit castle, cleared acres upon acres of old farmland, dealt with my jealousy, nursed me back to health, and saved Montgomery from a terrible scandal." He paused for a moment, laughing, almost shaking her. "What more do I have to say to get you to understand that you deserve thirty thousand pounds?"

She laughed once. "I'm not sure. We would be able to pay back Mr. Hunt, wouldn't we?"

Will nodded. "And then some."

"All right," she said. "I'll accept it."

Her husband got up to leave, then came running back to the settee, leaning down to kiss her. "I love you."

She smiled up at him. "I love you, too."

ELAINA SAID her goodbyes to her cousin and aunt later that afternoon in the driveway of Lyman House.

"You'll come visit Larkspur soon, won't you?" she asked.

They both nodded, and Elaina smiled at them, positive now that her mother would have been happy she came. Her cousin was generous, and her aunt was more than loving. Both were more than deserving of Elaina's affection.

Will helped her up into their carriage. When they began rolling down the drive back to Larkspur, he looked at his wife and smiled. She was watching the house fade into the distance from the window.

"Are you happy, my darling?" he asked.

"Quite," she replied, turning to him and smiling peacefully. "I have the most handsome husband in the world, a beautiful estate in Larkspur, and now two families that love me—Gillingham and Blackmore. What more could a girl hope to have?"

In the case of Lady William Winter, it would seem not much else.

EPILOGUE

Your announcement over Christmas has given Graham some ideas... ideas of having more children. Now, we are all excited for another Winter grandchild, and I do not begrudge you your happy marriage or your second baby in less than two years... but could you at least try and think of me next time? You're probably laughing at me while reading this, perhaps even telling Will how ridiculous I am, but I must insist upon you warning me before you announce it to the entire family next time. Before you write anything back to me, know this: I adore little Oliver. Do not mistake my lack of desire to have more children for lack of love for the one I have. I only worry he and whatever little ones follow him will take after their father.

—an excerpt of a letter from Lady Clara to Elaina at Larkspur Castle, Cambridgeshire, written in January 1818

Cambridgeshire, England
June 1818

ELAINA DECIDED that morning she was a fool for not canceling—or at least postponing—that year's house party. Heavily pregnant with her second child, she barely fit into the dress that Ferguson had selected for her that day, and the warm weather made for a miserable existence. She yearned for the babe to just come already, though she supposed he— or she—must've been too comfortable to budge.

Elaina was convinced this child was a boy, for she felt twice the size of when she was pregnant with Caroline. At only eighteen months old, her daughter wasn't quite sure what to make of her mother's increasing size. Looking at herself in the mirror after Ferguson left her that morning, Elaina wasn't quite sure what to make of it either, turning to study her profile and running her hand over her stomach.

Surely the babe would come any day now, yet she was supposed to host a four-day-long social gathering!

This would be Larkspur's second house party, the first one being last year. After Gillingham transferred the invest- ment accounts pertaining to Elaina's mother dowry to the Winters, Elaina and Will were able to start making progress on the actual house, taking a trip to London to buy furniture and paintings to fill their once bare rooms. Walking through Larkspur now, it was hard to believe the estate was ever on the brink of ruin.

They were able to hire more help as well, bringing in more footmen and maids, and even sending for Ferguson at Blackmore, though Will still insisted he didn't need a valet. They were even able to hire a nanny when little Caroline came along two Januarys ago, though Elaina insisted on being a more hands-on mother than perhaps some of her peers. She went to the nursery first thing every morning, bringing Caroline with her to play in the drawing room while she had her breakfast.

Her daughter reminded her so much of Will with her fair

hair and blue eyes. If Elaina had not birthed her herself, she may have doubted taking any part in the little girl's creation. Little Caroline smiled upon seeing her mother enter the nursery.

"Mama!" she exclaimed, toddling over to her mother, holding one of her dolls as she went.

"Good morning, my dear," Elaina said, scooping the little girl up and putting her on her hip. "Did she sleep well, nanny?"

"Through the night," the woman replied.

Elaina gasped, looking at her daughter with a delighted expression. "What a good girl! Shall we go down to breakfast now?"

Caroline giggled, then excitedly nodded. She didn't speak much—yet—but she knew a few small words, like mama, papa, nanny, horse, cow… As long as the weather was fine, Caroline would often accompany Elaina whenever she went to visit the tenants with Will, delighting in riding there with her father. Elaina enjoyed watching them together, loving her husband even more now that he was a father.

Will was already sitting in the drawing room with his newspaper, scraps of his breakfast on the plate in front of him, when Elaina and Caroline went downstairs. Caroline greeted her father with the same enthusiasm as her mother. Will folded his newspaper, taking the little girl into his lap, while Elaina took a deep breath and rested a hand on her back. She wasn't sure how much longer she could remain in her state *and* carry Caroline down the stairs.

"Good morning, dear," Elaina said, placing a kiss on her husband's cheek and sitting down beside him.

"How are you feeling?" Will asked.

"Like I'm about to explode," Elaina muttered. "I don't know why we decided to go through with the house party this year. I'm going to be dreadful company."

He chuckled. "I thought you liked hosting our friends and family."

"Perhaps not while eight and half months pregnant," she said, shooting him a pointed look.

"Who is coming this year?" he asked. "The usual suspects?"

"The usual suspects."

Living in the country, their acquaintances were limited, especially when they made infrequent visits to the city. Their guest list was small, reserved for close friends and family, nothing like the duchess's fête in August. No, Elaina was happy to let her mother-in-law hold the grandest country soiree every year, limiting their guest list to twelve people: Will's parents, the duke and duchess of Blackmore; his brother Lord Montgomery and Montgomery's wife, Clara; his cousins, Robert and Julia; Elaina's father, Mr. Walker; her cousin, Earl Gillingham, as well as her aunt, Lady Elizabeth; their banker, Mr. Hunt; and finally, the Prices.

"When will they arrive?" Will asked, waving Caroline's doll in front of his daughter's face.

"Sometime this afternoon, I suspect," she replied. "I plan on having luncheon laid out in the hall for when they arrive."

"Price and I might be late," he said. "We are showing a potential business partner the lumberyard today."

"Well, try not to be *too* late," Elaina warned. "I've been working on these dinner menus with Mrs. Harding for weeks."

"I wouldn't dare miss dinner," he replied, lifting Caroline off his lap and putting her on her own two feet on the floor. He stood up and bent over to kiss his wife on the cheek. "I am off for the day. Good luck with our guests."

Elaina sighed. "I wish I could join you."

He chuckled. "The new babe will be here any day now,

and you'll be back to riding your horse in no time. Isn't that right, Caroline?"

Will made a face at Caroline, causing the little girl to giggle and shout, "Horse! Horse! Horse!"

Elaina watched them, smiling.

As PREDICTED, the guests started arriving at Larkspur mid-afternoon, and all the while, Elaina had grown increasingly uncomfortable. At some point in the morning, shortly after Will left and she was playing with Caroline in the drawing room, she felt a sharp pain in her lower abdomen. She winced, slowly taking Caroline back up to the nursery so she could lay down.

The contractions continued all morning, mostly mild ones, until the guests started to arrive for the party. She forced herself to get up and go downstairs and greet them. Earl Gillingham and her aunt arrived first. Lady Elizabeth had visited Elaina and Will in Larkspur often since they reconciled, and the woman could immediately tell something was wrong with her niece.

As Gillingham went to sample the assortment of finger sandwiches, cold meats, cakes, and fruits that had been placed out in the hall, Elizabeth pulled her niece aside.

"Are you all right?" she asked. "You look unwell."

Wincing, Elaina clutched her swollen stomach. "The baby's coming." Shaking her head, she added, "I knew having this party was a bad idea."

"I will send for the doctor," she said. "I'll send for Will, too. You should go upstairs and get some rest. I will play hostess for the afternoon."

Elaina shook her head. "Don't send for Will. He had an important meeting today. He'll be back before the baby comes."

Her aunt nodded, and Elaina quickly apologized to her cousin before leaving the room. As she climbed the stairs, she had an intense contraction, causing her to come to her knees, and she wondered if she'd be able to make it to her bedchamber at all. Taking a deep breath once it passed, she stood, and eventually she managed to make it all the way to her room, climbing onto her bed and lying on top of the covers, closing her eyes and doing her best to steady her breathing as the contractions became more and more frequent.

The doctor arrived within an hour, pulling out the same medical instruments he used when she gave birth to Caroline.

"Is everyone settled?" Elaina asked as Elizabeth bent over with a towel to wipe a bead of sweat from her brow. She winced. Another contraction.

"Yes, and Lady Montgomery has been a great help in making sure everyone is comfortable," her aunt replied, helping her take a sip of water while she did.

"Have Will and Mr. Price returned from the lumberyard yet?"

Elizabeth shook her head. "Not yet," she said. She glanced out the window, where the sun was starting to set. "I'm sure they'll be back soon. It's almost dinnertime."

WILL RETURNED HOME with Mr. Price that day to a full drawing room, though one person seemed to be missing: his wife. Looking around for her, his cousin Julia rushed to him as soon as their eyes met from across the room.

"Oh, thank goodness you're finally back," she said, placing a hand on her cousin's shoulder. "Elaina's gone into labor."

Will's heart dropped. "Why didn't anyone send for me?"

"She insisted we not. She said your meeting was too important."

He shook his head. "Nothing is more important than my wife." He turned to Mr. Price and nodded once. "Excuse me."

He climbed the stairs two at a time, taking long strides to the bedchamber. When he arrived, Elaina's aunt was by her side. She stood up upon seeing Will. Dr. Hardy was there as well, standing at the side of the room and laying out various medical instruments that Will thought looked more like torture devices. Childbirth was a nerve-wracking thing, and it had never escaped Will's recollection that Elaina's mother had died while giving birth to her second child, losing the babe along with her.

"Will," Elaina said, reaching for her husband from where she lay.

He went to her, taking her aunt's old seat and taking her hands into his. "Why didn't you send for me?" he asked.

"Oh, I knew you'd be home in time," she said. "Besides, Dr. Hardy here will surely kick you out at any moment now." She winced. "I think it's almost time."

"I'm afraid it is, my lord," the doctor said from where he stood at the side of the room.

Will nodded, pushing his wife's damp hair away from her face and planting a kiss on her forehead. She smiled. "I'll be waiting on the other side of the door," he said.

She shook her head. "Go enjoy your dinner. Please. I've worked on those menus for so long. I must have an honest opinion on how it was later."

WILL DID NOT ENJOY his dinner. He could barely touch it, in fact, for his stomach was too busy being twisted up into nervous knots to digest food. Robbie tempted him with a glass of brandy after dinner to calm his nerves, but Will would not have it.

"Not until I know I have a healthy child," he said. *And a healthy wife*, he thought.

The entire party waited with him until late into the night, when the doctor finally came down. Elaina had given birth to a healthy baby boy. Mother and son were resting upstairs. A wave of emotion—relief, happiness, awe—came over Will. He had a son.

"She is asking for you, my lord," the doctor said.

Will looked back at his family and friends who had gathered in the drawing room. They all smiled at him, urging him to go on. When he arrived in their bedchamber, Elaina was sitting up in bed, holding the new baby in her arms.

"Hello," he breathed, closing the door behind him.

"Hello." She smiled at him, and he grinned back. "Would you like to meet him?"

He nodded, coming around the opposite end of the bed from where she lay, slipping off his shoes and climbing on top of the covers, sliding his body next to hers. He looked down at his son, admiring his tufts of dark hair on the top of his head. His eyes were closed, but he almost recognized the babe, as if he had met him already once before. He looked back up at Elaina.

"He looks like you," he said.

She laughed once. "It's only fair since Caroline looks so much like you."

He nodded, smiling. "True. May I hold him?"

"Of course!" She handed the swaddled babe to him, and his son fidgeted in his arms, making strange little croaks of displeasure until he was comfortable in his father's arms.

"Have you thought of what we shall name him?" Will asked.

"I think I like the name Peter," she said, nuzzling close to him so that her cheek was resting on his shoulder as she gazed down at their baby boy.

"Peter," he repeated, testing the name, seeing how it felt in his mouth. He turned to her, smiling. She smiled back. "I like it."

The three of them sat together in bed, with Will and Elaina snuggling close while he cradled the infant in his arms. He watched his son with wide-eyed wonder, then turned his gaze on Elaina, feeling amazed at the woman his childhood friend had become.

"I didn't think it was possible," he whispered, shaking his head, "to love you more than I did almost three years ago when I begged you to run away with me. But I do. The more I come to know you, Elaina Winter—as my wife, as the mistress of my estate, as the mother to my children—the more I come to love you. I didn't think it was possible."

"And him? Do you love him?"

He smiled, looking down at the baby nestled in his arms. "Yes. I may even love him more than you. Caroline, too."

She laughed at that, and little Peter squirmed in Will's arms. "Regardless of who you love more, please never stop, Will. I don't know what we'd do without you."

"Don't worry, my darling," he said, pressing a kiss to her forehead. "I have no intention of ever stopping. Not in a million years."

ACKNOWLEDGMENTS

When I set out to write this novel at the beginning of 2020, I did not expect the year to turn out as it did. This project was a light for me during some very dark days, and I have a multitude of very talented, insightful, and creative people to thank for helping me prepare it for publication, especially my wonderful editor, Melinda Utendorf, and my cover designer, Agata Broncel. I'd also be remiss not to mention Jennifer from Romance Rehab, who read a very early version of this story and motivated me to keep moving forward with it.

On a more personal note, I'd like to thank my parents, for instilling a love of reading and writing in me from an early age; my boyfriend, Chris, for giving up nights and weekends where we could've relaxed together, but I chose to write instead; and my friends Michelle, Carla, Georgia, and Corinne, who have been my writing cheerleaders throughout various stages of my life, including this one.

Most of all, I'd like to thank you, the reader, for taking a chance and purchasing a book from a new author you've never heard of before. I hope I didn't disappoint you.

ABOUT THE AUTHOR

Becky Michaels is a historical romance author and self-proclaimed Anglophile. After graduating from Boston University with a degree in English, she reluctantly decided to get a day job but never stopped writing—or dreaming. *THE LAND STEWARD'S DAUGHTER*, a Regency romance set in 1815 England, is her debut novel. Despite the cold winters and high rent, she still lives in the Boston area with her boyfriend and cat.